EXECUTIVE DECISION

A FORBIDDEN BILLIONAIRE ROMANCE

LAKESHORE EMPIRE
BOOK 1

MAUDE WINTERS

There shouldn't be billionaires.

But if there must be billionaires, let them be kings who know how to treat a lady.

AUTHOR'S NOTE

Executive Decision is the first in the Lakeshore Empire billionaire family saga series. These books feature forbidden love, age gaps, and a lot of spice.

Note: The book takes place over an eleven-year time span, with the majority of the book set in present day. There is a time jump to six years after Cal and Daphne meet and then again to present day. I promise you will appreciate this relevant backstory and I won't leave young hanging about the time jumps, reader!

Executive Decision is set in Chicago—not far from where I grew up—and I am so excited to share it with you all. Below, I will post content expectations. Worried about even a hint of a spoiler? Don't read on.

Content Expectations

- Foul language, dirty talk, and spicy situations
  - Mentions of partner physical abuse (off the page) and emotional abuse (on the page)

- Mentions of secondary infertility
- Loss of a parent to cancer

PART I

BEGINNINGS

1. ACQUISITIONS

Eleven years before...

Daphne

There was business, and then there was *family* business. Sometimes, being a Delphine was too much. My family reached institution status over a decade ago, but I stood in the shadow of this legacy—new to corporate law and hungry for more responsibility since leaving Oxford. I sat surrounded by stacks of bankers' boxes related to a British acquisition. I'd agreed to spearhead the work but wondered if I'd flown too close to the sun—something I had not seen in days.

"I'm going out!" My brother closed his laptop and stood.

"Davey, we have tons more to read through. These financials are a disaster!" I protested.

Davey was the oldest, but not the most reliable. Only a few years my senior, he got by on charm. While he could be great at finessing deals, he didn't want to do the work that kept them going. Mergers and acquisitions were my bread and butter, but he was the charismatic force I needed on the front end. I wasn't the charming one. I wasn't much for schmoozing.

"You got this, kid!" Davey left the conference room.

As the elevator doors closed, I screamed in sheer frustration. "Motherfucker!"

I miscalculated, thinking I was alone in our tower on Chicago's mag mile. Footsteps approached. My father's protege and favorite confidant—Cal Markham, stood in the doorway.

"Are you alright?" Cal asked.

"I'm fine. I thought I was alone." I did not need others involved in this process.

Cal leaned on the doorframe: one eyebrow raised. "It doesn't sound alright."

Cal was handsome as hell, charming, and annoyingly good at everything. As Chief Marketing Officer, he always tried to show his worth—much to Davey's chagrin. I usually let their territorial spats play out, secretly enjoying it.

"You can tell me, Daphne. I am glad to help if I can."

"It's nothing you can help with," I said. "It's just... David Jr... He leaves me to pick up all the pieces. I need him to step up and handle the face-to-face aspects of this."

"But he refuses to educate himself?" Cal snickered. "Welcome to dealing with Davey."

I rolled my eyes. "You have no idea."

"No. I do. Your dad does, too. You should ask him for advice or get him to come down on Davey for doing none of the work. You're drowning—"

I set my jaw. "I'm not drowning, Cal."

"I don't mean it as a negative, but leaders ask for help."

So, you can look like a winner and edge in even more?

"I will just work harder."

"It is eight on a Friday night, and you're here. The city

awaits you. For once, take a page out of Davey's book. Say fuck it and go out."

"That will not win this fight. You don't get it." I shook my head.

"I do. I've been you. My greatest regret is *not* living a little. Besides, I'm glad to help where I can."

"Yet, you are Dad's favorite person," I murmured.

"I'm not," Cal chuckled. "You are, Daphne. Live a little."

His tone felt genuine. He didn't argue. He wasn't reacting to my prickly, exhausted energy. How the hell was he always so *calm*?

I groaned. "Can I ask you a question then?"

"Sure," Cal agreed.

"What would you do to engage them on integrations? Are you getting a feel for it working through branding? I know I haven't even made it to that part with you, but… what is your read?"

Cal approached and sat across from me. "It's a mess. If I were you, I'd start by telling your dad the CFO is a joke. You'll confirm what everyone knows but hasn't said yet."

"Is that not cruel?"

"Nah. It's business."

I snickered. "Wow. I am… surprised."

"By what?"

"You don't seem like the ruthless type, Cal."

Is it a trap?

I rolled a pen between my fingers, thinking through my next move. He stared through me in a way that made me fidget. His brown eyes searched me.

"I got where I am because I was honest. Be the ruthless one. Prove your worth by using your brain, Daphne. That is what David expects."

"You make me sound like a tough bitch," I said, annoyed.

He chuckled. "I would never call you a bitch. I *would* call you demanding and tough."

That's precisely how men call women a bitch in the boardroom without saying it! I bit my pen, frustrated.

Cal softened. "It's a compliment. I wouldn't give you advice and insight if I didn't view you as a peer, Daphne."

I couldn't meet his gaze or trust his words.

"You don't get a say in that. I don't report to you," I said.

"Well, if my opinion matters at all, I'd like you to stay."

He couldn't possibly know what the stakes were or how my internal battle over staying in Chicago dominated my life.

"I tell you what," Cal continued. "As a goodwill gesture and because your brother is on my last fucking nerve, I'm grabbing food from the Lebanese place. I'll pick up some for you, too. We can then sort through more of this mess."

"You don't have to—"

"If we are both going to be hermits on a Friday night, we should eat well, Daphne."

I remained cautious of his motivations, but was a sucker for a kebab. "Get me that kofta thing. And thanks."

"Anytime. We're a team, Daphne. We need to get this across the finish line."

* * *

Cal

"Yeah, fuck them all," Daphne snickered. "God, this is a mess. If I was in charge, I'd have all their heads. Sack them! Is that terrible?"

I watched Daphne Delphine scroll endlessly through emails. She bit her pen, wholly focused on keywords. How she knew what to look for, I didn't know. She organized chaos and dove headfirst into any assignment. While people assumed he groomed Davey for greatness, I knew David prized Daphne above all even if she lacked her brother's confidence.

I chuckled. "No. I'd do the same. Tell your dad everything. Lay out the case. You gotta find the risks—to find where the bodies are buried, right?"

She adorably cocked her head. "I never thought about it like that, but yes."

"Then do your job. You will be rewarded for your honesty."

She removed her glasses and took down her ponytail, fanning an impressive head of wavy blonde hair. I tried not to ever think of my female coworkers as attractive—it was rude, and I was above shitting where I ate. However, Daphne was objectively pretty.

She exhaled, then flipped her hair back and replaced her glasses.

"So, this fucking guy. Look at this!" Daphne beckoned me to her side.

I read over her shoulder as she drank beer. She found gold in a bad admission from the CFO about contracts he signed but didn't review—legal catnip.

"If we got audited right now, we'd be fucked," Daphne said.

"I had no idea."

"You're not a lawyer. I know you are *creative* and good at that, but we still have to have the foundations there so we don't get fucked."

Did she just call me out? I should have taken offense to a twenty-something nepobaby reading me. Instead, I stared into her green eyes and read her. Her lighthearted chuckle morphed into a serious intensity I'd missed before.

"What? Can't you handle a bit of criticism?" Daphne quipped, playing it off as a joke.

"I'm a big boy," I said. "I can handle it."

She bit her lip, which sent me over the edge. In the past few hours, I watched her flip her ponytail nervously, sift through papers like a naughty librarian, and now, give me hell. I shouldn't want her. I was a little drunk and a lot drawn to this slightly chaotic version of my boss's daughter.

"You and Davey are both grown men but sometimes fight like kids!" Daphne doubled down.

"I pay no mind to that."

"Uh-huh."

"Are you doubting me, Daphne?" I raised my eyebrows.

A playful smirk curled around her lips. I wanted to kiss it off her face. Too distracted, I said nothing as she reached across me to grab another file, brushing against me. Her perfume and the feeling of her long, soft hair brushing against my arm triggered something.

I leaned in to kiss her. As our lips met, she kissed me back. I reveled in how her lips felt pressed against mine and how sweet she smelled. I shouldn't do this. It was a disaster in the making, but as she kissed me back, I felt like I'd just let out a breath I didn't know I was holding.

She pushed me away and stood as if waking from a nightmare.

Daphne rambled, "Shit. I don't know what I did... I don't... I'm..."

"Sorry. Sorry. I don't know why I did that." I backed away. "I felt like we were having a moment and all that. I guess I wasn't and— "

"It's okay," Daphne lied. "It's... fine."

But she wasn't fine.

"I am sorry if I gave you some signal, Cal. I feel so stupid.

I have a boyfriend. And… it's a little complicated, but… I would never cheat on him."

"I'm gonna go," I said. "It's nothing you did. I feel terrible. It's inappropriate, and I am so sorry. Please forgive me."

I felt like I was pleading for my job.

"It's okay. We're both a little drunk," Daphne said. "I am not upset. We both got our wires crossed. I appreciate your help, but we should take a step back."

And a cold shower.

"You're right," I said.

"I'm not going to say anything to anyone," Daphne said. "Just relax. You didn't mean to offend me. I'm… it's okay."

She relaxed. It was an honest mistake. I should have held back. I stepped on the elevator worrying I opened Pandora's box.

2. THE BOARD

Daphne

I STOOD BEFORE THE MIRROR, MOPPING TEARS. MY FATHER'S secretary, an older woman who'd been with Delphine Holdings forever, looked on sympathetically while washing her hands. She debated asking what happened but knew better. On the other side of that door, a presentation awaited—one that could redefine my future.

I should not cry in a bathroom while a man—again—stole my moment.

She turned to leave, but stopped. "Daphne, if you need something, sweetheart, you can always ask. Are you okay?"

I shrugged, dropping my gaze to the tile floor.

"Because it's okay to confide in people. Sweetie, I watched you grow up. It's okay to come to me if something is going on."

"I'm fine," I lied.

I wasn't. I'd just gotten off a plane after having a breakup conversation with a man who claimed to love me but asked too much.

"Well, alright." She left.

I powdered my face. *You've got this, Daphne.*

I tucked my compact into my desk, grabbed my laptop, and headed to the conference room. I threw aside the ultimatum I'd left behind in London. I sat near my brother in back.

"Time to nap." He snickered.

I rolled my eyes, "It isn't *that* bad. You need to focus on strategy. That's all this is."

"Robertson will go on and on again about audits and I cannot even."

I snickered. Our Chief Compliance Officer wasn't much of a fun time. I had biweekly meetings in his side of the house with legal. Even for me, it was anything but thrilling.

"It's like Aunt Kara at thanksgiving describing her trips to Europe," Davey groaned, pretending to sleep.

"Slides, too. She's not gone there."

"Yet. Don't speak it into existence, Daph."

Davey wasn't much for feels—despite being sensitive. He was a people pleaser with a fragile ego. However, he knew me well. Knowing something happened in London, he clowned to distract me.

"You're going to kill it with the presentation," Davey added.

"Try not to fall asleep. Okay?" I joked.

I caught Cal's eye. He entered the conference room, nervously ignoring me. I rarely saw him since we were here alone. He sat with the other C-suite guys.

I nervously shifted in my chair as Dad entered with the president and board. They chatted with Cal. He nodded at Davey and I, but didn't make a big fuss. I struggled sometimes with his dichotomy of big boss and doting dad. I didn't want to be overly familiar, but sometimes I wanted a hug. Today was one of those times.

With a full conference room, the meeting began. When it

was my turn, my father's assistant nodded at me and queued my slides.

"David Jr., are you presenting this?" Our president asked my brother.

"No, Daphne took this one," Davey answered. "She just got back from London. She has been providing the white glove service."

"Oh, alright."

Finally, I got some credit for busting my ass while he slept with half of the girls in River North! He was the first man who gave me that in the past twenty-four hours.

"Thanks," I said. "So, as Davey explained, I literally just returned to O'Hare two hours ago. Apologies if the slides aren't super pretty. I did them on the plane."

"They're fine, Daphne," Dad assured.

I took a deep breath. *Don't undermine yourself, woman!*

I updated them on financials, and liabilities before addressing compliance concerns.

The president cut me off. "We have no consolidated branding. Why is that?"

I stared, deer-in-headlights, at Cal, who should have spoken. He was radio silent.

"We don't have it yet," I said.

"And why is that, Miss Delphine?"

This wasn't even this prick's domain, but here we were. I looked to Cal to chime in. Instead, he stared at the wall. I set my jaw, annoyed.

"Cal do you have an update?"

Cal, looked up. "Uh… we weren't contacted—"

I crossed my arms. "I sent you three emails with read receipts. If your team is too busy, it's understandable, but I haven't received a response."

He flushed red. "Well, it's not as if we've had adequate time to prepare much, you know?"

Don't bullshit me, Cal!

"When did you receive the request?" Dad asked, concerned.

"A week ago. We haven't made headway—"

"It was ten days ago," I answered. "I was working late on financials and contracts and told you we needed branding assistance. I sent a follow-up on Monday morning. No response."

"We were flooded—"

Dad cleared his throat, cutting his protege off. "Cal, I need to see movement on this. When Daphne sends an email about an urgent issue, please do not delay."

"I wasn't, David. We wanted to return with actual information."

"Well, at least say you've seen her request."

"Apologies. I thought Sarah responded," Cal said. "She didn't reach out about any clarifications?"

I didn't believe him.

"No," I answered. "No response."

"Well, maybe she assumed it could wait until we could meet with you, David?" He looked to Dad for guidance.

"You're both adults. I delegated all the work on this matter to Daphne and David. Is that not clear?"

"It's clear. Yes," Cal said. "But couldn't you have come to me, Daphne?"

"She was in London," Davey scoffed.

He wanted to let loose on Cal. I dreamed of accountability, but not wiping the floor with Cal.

"You're right," Cal backed off, knowing when to call it.

"In the next week, I want a branding kit plan on Daphne's desk," Dad said. "Can you two work on that?"

"Yes," Cal and I said in unison.

With no more time, I sat. Cal stole the rest of my presentation by derailing things with his own lack of preparation.

"He thinks the sun shines out of his ass," Davey whispered as I returned to my seat. "I've got your back."

* * *

Cal

I wanted to punch a wall—the wall Daphne nailed me to—but couldn't blame her. I didn't do my job to the best of my abilities. Now, David wanted to speak to me in his office. I planned to take my lumps and move on, but I'd not cross Daphne again. I obviously angered her. Was this blackmail?"

I left my office, ready for a bruising and passed Daphne in the hall. She stood at the espresso machine. Her gaze averted mine, turning immediately to the shot pouring out of the expensive machine. I debated passing, then stopped.

"Do we have an issue?" I remained calm.

"I don't need this right now." Daphne shook her head, deflated.

"I'm not coming for you."

"Right," she said sarcastically.

I softened my face. "I'm not upset with you."

"You have a funny way of showing it, Cal. I don't need your grief today. I was out of fucks before crossing the Atlantic. Don't try me. You dropped the ball, I gave you two chances to make an excuse, you didn't, then you blamed me. Don't come for me unless you want to watch my father and brother tear you from limb to limb."

You'd probably get off on that.

"Your dad is about to dress me down. You're right. I fucked up but... I just didn't know. I'm sorry. I wasn't trying to deflect."

She didn't buy it. "Well, it won't be bad. The sun shines

out of your ass. And no, I haven't said anything. So, don't continue to take it out on me."

I grabbed her hand without thinking. "Daph, I am not out to get you. You were right to call me out, okay?"

Daphne's big green eyes finally met mine. For a moment, I saw the sweet side of her. She returned to all business, pulling her hand away.

"I… I just want us to get along," I said.

"Well, we are fine if you do your job and don't try to infantilize me. Next time, try not to derail my presentation."

"Got it." I let it go.

She didn't care about the kiss, just that I stole her moment.

Daphne said flatly, "Your tie is a mess. Fix it."

I adjusted it in the espresso machine's reflection, quipping, "To the gallows!"

Marching to her father's office, I should have felt lighter. Daphne didn't give a fuck about the kiss—the best-case scenario. Sadly, I wished for her to take it out on me rather than take the high road.

"Cal," David's face lit up as I came in for my punishment, to my surprise. "I have good news."

"Oh," I shut the door.

"Is everything okay?" He read my expression.

"Sure," I said.

"Oh, you thought I was dragging you to the woodshed?" David chuckled. "I feel like Daphne did that better than I could. I assume you will—"

"I've already told my team it's top priority, David."

"Great, great. Don't let her scare you. She's Danna's daughter. She doesn't give anyone a pass."

Lady Danna, David's wife was a perfectionist and no doormat.

"It's a good quality," I said. "She holds her own. She was right."

"Good. Then I don't have any reason to think you two aren't going to make this bit work?"

"No, sir. We just discussed it. We're fine."

"Great. Then, let's talk about a new project. This doesn't leave these four walls," David brimmed.

"Oh?" I sat before his desk.

"I have an opportunity to buy a property and start up a venture. I cannot manage it all. It's too much to add to my portfolio without a steward."

My heart leapt. I hoped like hell he was saying what I thought he was.

"I'd like you to manage it."

My face erupted into a wide smile. Reading it, David chuckled, "Yeah, yeah. I knew you'd be excited. It's not done yet. We won't count our chickens."

"Of course not. How can I help?"

"When I tie it all up, I'll bring you in. Until then, keep your head down and focus on helping Daphne with the merger."

"Will do," I agreed. "Thank you, David."

"Now, let's get into the specifics of it," David continued. "You are going to love this mixed retail plan. It's a boutique feel. The branding needs to be *perfect*."

David regaled me with the details for my hopeful new project. I stared out the window at the city and thought about what *could* be. Any concerns about Daphne faded as I mentally wrote my next chapter.

3. THE LAYOVER

Daphne

WHILE PREPARING FOR TAKEOFF IN MY FATHER'S CORPORATE jet, I couldn't shake my feelings of inadequacy. This week, I traded the beautiful skyline of Chicago and my office facing Michigan Avenue for quiet in a tropical paradise. While my official reason for this pleasure trip was my cousin's wedding, I needed a vacation and a sign that I was on the right track.

I spied other executive jets at O'Hare through the window, waiting for their owners to arrive. Where were *they* headed? What were we waiting for? At this rate, I'd miss my connection to Hawaii. *We needed to get to LA. Why weren't we already in the air?*

"Excuse me," I asked the passing flight attendant. "Can you tell me what the holdup is? Is there something wrong?"

"We're waiting for one more, Miss Delphine," she replied. "We will leave very soon."

It wasn't uncommon for someone else to hitch a ride on the company plane, but it was unusual when the entire family was already far from the mainland. Who else remained? A man's head popped into the cabin, and I put it together.

Cal Markham arrived, dressed casually in jeans. *Fuck!*

"Daphne, how are you?" Cal asked. "Sorry. Traffic was a nightmare."

"I'm fine," I said, curt.

After our previous run-in, I wasn't big on small talk. With his marketing plans, I could finish my job. I didn't need to think about how it felt to kiss him or how I wanted to give into a base urge. While I wanted to shake it off, Cal's slight stubble and warm smile didn't help.

The flight attendant dimmed the cabin lights as Cal settled.

"Why did you get stuck here? I thought everyone went ahead."

"Acquisitions hell," I answered. "I agreed to stay back and wrap it up."

"You poor thing," Cal said, as if I was a child. "You drew the short straw."

"Yes, boo-hoo me."

Did he infantilize me even now? I was grown enough for him to kiss me, wasn't I? His face twisted awkwardly. A pang of guilt shot through me.

"Sorry," I sighed. "I just... I'm angry because Davey is already drunk off his ass and I feel like I got the thankless job."

"You did. I get it," Cal agreed, settling in and leaving me alone.

I worked through takeoff, only turning off my computer at cruising altitude. By then, Cal was asleep. I pitied him. He was a social chameleon, but he'd never be one of us. Long weekends skiing in Switzerland or a three-day-summits in Shanghai primed me to never make such a mistake. Why was *he* my father's most trusted person? What made Cal so remarkable?

In LA, we travelled together from the private terminal back to slumming it in commercial. Cal took my luggage without asking if I wanted him to, which annoyed me.

"So, you're in the bridal party?" Cal hoisted the garment bag holding my bridesmaid's dress over his broad shoulders.

"Yes," I answered. "Sarah is my closest cousin. And you are, too?"

He flashed a boyish grin. "I'm Erik's best man, so yes."

I fought the urge to roll my eyes. *It was always about the competition!*

"I don't need you to carry my dress," I said.

"My mother would have my ass for not helping you, Daphne."

I rolled my eyes.

"Would you like me to be rude and walk off, leaving you in the dust, Daphne?"

"No," I answered. "I didn't ask you to be *rude.*"

"Well, you don't have your boyfriend—what is his name? Chase, Casey, Carlton? Where is he?"

I pulled the handle on my suitcase so hard it clicked loud as a gunshot.

"Chandler Walker," I answered, wanting to chuck Cal across the room. "And he's not here because he's not my boyfriend."

"What? Since when?"

A week ago, when he dumped me for telling him I didn't want to get married and pop out babies within the next two years.

I set my jaw. "Is it really fair to ask such a personal question, Cal?"

"I'm sorry to hear that. You're right. It was... inappropriate."

"Given your past, I'd mind myself," I reminded him.

"Point taken. I swear I didn't mean anything by it." Cal sounded pained.

We walked in silence towards the gate. While I wanted to strangle him, Cal projected genuine remorse. It wasn't his fault Chandler broke my heart or that he feared my retribution.

"I'm sorry. I'm being a bitch," I sighed. "Look, it's fresh. It's messy. And I don't want to hear more about it because my mother has already said too much."

"I'm sorry. Breakups are hard. And couple that with a wedding… I'm sure it's worse for a girl than for a guy."

"It's not great."

"I'd like to say the whole 'you'll die alone' thing gets better, but in my late thirties, I'm still hearing the same song and dance, Daph. I can also say you're far too young to worry about any of that. Ignore the haters. At your age, I was wild."

"Tell my mother that," I said. "She loves Chandler. She would be glad for us to get back together. The trouble is, we're just in different places. Like you said, I'm young. I have no desire to settle down and have children. He wants them."

I felt stupid. Why was I telling Cal all my secrets? Had I not learned my lesson the last time we tried to partner on something? We did not socialize outside of work or family parties. We were *not* friends, but he was so damn easy to talk to! And unlike everyone else in the inner circle at Delphine Holdings, his outsider status gave him a unique vantage point.

"Well, you're about to be in paradise—for a few days with no consequences. Chin up, Daphne."

I smiled. "Yeah, you're probably right."

* * *

Cal

We arrived at our gate to find our flight delayed.

"Well, we didn't have to rush," Daphne groaned.

"Yeah. Shit. That sucks." I said it like I meant it, but didn't.

Ever since I boarded the plane, Daphne gave me attitude. I went from worried I'd be fired to hopeful. Since I got under her skin, I knew she was still thinking about the kiss. So what if she nursed a breakup while stranded in the airport with me for a few more hours? I could work with that.

"Come on." I waved. "There's a lounge. We can eat a little and drink."

"I need a fucking drink," Daphne admitted, reluctantly following. "Take me there."

I laughed until she called out sharply, "Wait!"

I turned to see her scowling.

"Can we please slow the fuck down, damn it?" She held out her hands. "I don't want to walk with you. Give me my bag."

She balled her tiny hands in fists.

I chuckled, finding her protests adorable. "Daphne, don't be ridiculous. I was giving you shit. I'm just trying to help. I promise no speed walking."

She dug herself deeper into the airport flooring. "You're straight up laughing at me."

"I was… you're adorable when you swear. I never expect it. I laughed because it amused me."

She let out a low growl of frustration. "Fine, if you will walk at my pace."

"Scouts honor."

She walked my way. "Why was there a delay? You are loving this, aren't you?"

I restrained myself from mocking her grievances,

"Daphne, you really do love to argue. Come on. I'll get you fed and watered. Are you hangry?"

"Yes, I'm famished." She groaned. "And I've not slept."

"Why not?"

"I want to reset my clock. It's a strategy everyone should adhere to."

"I trust you have a system, but a nap won't hurt you."

"I am sleeping on the flight there."

"Ah," I said.

"I'm grumpy. I know. You are going to hate me by the end of this."

"Nah. I've travelled with your parents enough, Daphne. You couldn't possibly rival your mother's level of eccentricity. Also, don't forget who the women in *my* life are."

She giggled. "Fair."

"I shouldn't laugh."

Entering the lounge, Daphne flashed her frequent flyer elite status, and I didn't bother. I got in free either way.

We approached the crowded buffet area.

I asked, "Drinks first?"

"Yes."

Daphne dealt with a crush of taller businessmen. Her tiny frame went largely unseen. With my hand on her lower back, I guided her, breaking yet *another* rule. She didn't bristle or react. Everything inside me wanted clarity on what she thought. I couldn't read her.

We sat at the bar. She ordered whiskey, and I stuck to a martini.

"Yet, you did it. Why are men like that?" Daphne asked, head propped on arm, elbow on the bar top.

"I don't know. It was the moment and what I felt at the time."

"So, now the moment has passed, and you're over it?" She swirled her drink seductively.

"I am neither over it nor smarter," I admitted, my eyes never leaving hers.

Daphne fought her reaction, but the blush on her cheeks gave her away.

"You say that to me stone-cold sober?"

"I didn't say it was *smart*."

"Is it opportunism?"

"Nah. Maybe? But… you still come back to it. Why?" I implied she wasn't over it, hoping to hear just that.

She snickered. "I'm going to get food."

Nothing. She left, torturing me. Did she get off on being opaque about *everything,* or was this just a good poker face? It drove me crazy, but that was what she wanted. I didn't like giving her all the power, but it solidified that I wasn't taking advantage of her like I'd initially feared.

I watched her cross the lounge, hips swaying.

"She's hot," the bartender said. "You two… together?"

I sipped my drink. "She's the daughter of a *very* powerful man. Trust me, you do *not* want to fly that close to the sun, dude."

"By the end of the day, I predict you're going to end up either fucking or scratching each other's eyes out—daddy issues or not."

"She doesn't have daddy issues," I snickered. "I do. Her dad is my boss."

"Oh, man… you are so fucked."

Indeed.

Daphne returned, setting a plate down. She took a sip of her drink, turned back to me, and said, "What do you want me to say?"

"The truth. You just argue with me, Daphne. I never know what is going on."

"Because I'm a mess. But what does it matter, Cal?" She put her hand on mine. "It wasn't nothing, okay? I'm not a fucking robot, but if I threw myself at you, it'd only make it worse. For you, I mean."

I couldn't resist, freeing my hand to run it down her back —resting it too low on her ass. I leaned over, whispering, "I already told you I'm stupid, Daph. I want what I shouldn't have—a woman who continues to put me in my place."

She whispered back, "You like the abuse, Cal."

I swirled my hand. "No, I suspect *you* do."

Mouth gaping, she gazed back at me and shook her head. She said nothing, but she thought about it. She wanted to do more. I let it percolate.

4. TROUBLE IN PARADISE

Daphne

"Daphne, your hair! It's too wild!" Mum called across our hotel suite's living room.

I ignored her.

"Daphne, I am *speaking* to you."

I spun, tossing my hair over my shoulder. My mother's stick-straight, impossibly shiny chestnut locks were perfect. She loathed my wavy blonde strands. Sea air only made my hair more defiant.

I crossed my arms. "My hair is *fine*. I am not supposed to over style it. I was told it must be somewhat dirty tomorrow so the stylists can put it up."

Mum pulled a face. "That will not do. Put it up. You are so pretty when you are composed."

"Uh-huh."

"You are a great beauty, Daphne. I wish you would see that," Mum softened.

Wanting out, I gave up arguing. I needed to breathe, and the longer I stayed, the more the walls closed in. I strode back to the double room I shared with my three sisters. I had my own room when this weekend began, but it was handed off to my older brother like a great big prize when it emerged my boyfriend dumped me, and I was alone.

My seventeen-year-old sister Delanie, known as "Lanie," to us, sat in bed with her laptop while Dora, my sweet eleven-year-old sister lay on her belly reading. She was the surprise. My middle sister, Dahlia, watched TV. At not-yet-twenty-one, she wasn't old enough to attend the drinks reception our aunt and uncle hosted for the soon-to-be-newlyweds.

I passed my sisters into the bathroom to pin up my hair.

Mum crowded into the doorway, annoyance pulling her brows into an angry line. "I think I can see a panty line in that dress."

"Fine, I'll change them," I said, beyond frustrated. "I am putting my hair up. I will change my panties. Can I please, please just have space?"

"Fine," she sighed, exasperated.

I slammed the door behind her, then braced my hands on the marble vanity. I let out a guttural groan at myself in the mirror. I didn't see a VPL. I debated not changing my panties before I decided to throw a big middle finger at my mother. I pulled off my sensible underwear, popping them in the trash. If she didn't like panty lines, well, she'd get no panties at *all*.

I continued to pile my hair on my head when there was another knock.

"I'm changing my panties and doing my hair!" I shouted.

"Daph, it's me, sweetie." It was my father.

"What?" I asked, mortified. "I thought you were Mum. What do you need, Daddy?"

"I just wanted to tell you we got the completed contract back and to say thank you."

I opened the door.

"You did a great job, sweetheart. I am so proud of you for

running this from start to close. I couldn't have done the same at your age."

"Thanks, Daddy," I said.

He smiled broadly. "What is wrong?"

"Mum is driving her fucking nuts!" Lanie called.

"Don't say fuck," I corrected.

"You did," Lanie batted back.

I rolled my eyes, "You're a child."

"Barely."

Dad ignored it, focusing on my achievement. "Ignore Mum, okay? She's all stressed and you know how she is. Go out, live a little. Get a drink before all of this begins."

"It starts in like twenty minutes, Dad."

"Not now. There were issues with the seating arrangement, and Anita went ballistic," Dad said. "Go, be free. I'll keep you Mum-free all night if it gives you both a breather."

I hugged and kissed his cheek. "Thank you."

5. GOOD TROUBLE

Cal

I FOUND THE RESORT'S MAIN BAR EMPTY. I'D MADE IT TO THIS little bit of Hawaii without much fuss. It was a long trip, but worth it to stand up in a wedding for two dear friends, Sarah and Erik. Engaged for two years, they booked the entirety of the latest and greatest resort for a wedding that might make the history books. The dead bar confused me.

I sidled up and popped down.

"You in the wedding, sir?" The bartender asked.

"Yes. Where is everyone?"

"There was an incident with the arrival dinner floorplan. The bride's mother lost it. They've pushed it back ninety minutes."

"Damn," I chuckled, "All dressed up and nowhere to go."

"Good time to have a drink, sir. What can I get you?"

"What is good?"

"A Mai Tai usually does the trick around here." He winked.

"Sure, of course. Let's start there."

I pulled out my phone and scrolled through my emails.

One came from the boss man just a couple of minutes before. David Delphine never stopped working.

The bartender fixed my cocktail. I scrolled more before typing a response to next year's spring campaign proposals. Consumed with business and sipping my drink, I barely noticed the woman who'd arrived.

"Just anything. Anything with liquor."

I spied Daphne wearing a swishy cocktail dress, her wavy blonde hair pinned atop her head. I tried not to stare because it would give me away. I hadn't learned my lesson. I enjoyed her slightly grumpy look with a flare to her nostrils and sense of expediency.

"Are you alright, Daphne?" I asked.

She turned as if not noticing she was alone. "Cal, hi. Uh, it's a long story."

"Well, don't be a stranger. Come, sit. I don't bite."

Daphne obliged, sitting on the stool by me. She flung her clutch onto the counter and groaned.

The bartender raised one eyebrow. "Should I make the lady a Mai Tai?"

"Yes, please," I answered. "Put that on my tab."

"You don't—"

"You obviously need a drink, Daphne," I said.

She sighed. "If you ever see me again, Cal, remind me not to fly to Hawaii."

I raised my eyebrows. "I thought we had fun?"

"It isn't you," she assured. "My mother swears I am a grave disappointment."

"That, huh?"

"As predicted."

We watched the waves. Rather, I watched Daphne watch the waves. She was content to take it all in—in contrast to her older brother, who never shut up or said anything wise.

The bartender sat a drink before Daphne.

She smiled. "Thank you."

Daphne took a long swig and smiled. "That's brilliant, thanks. I'm alone in paradise."

"Keep them coming, please," I said, delighted. "As long as it pleases the lady."

"It does. I am giving up trying to control the future. This week, I have a get out of jail free card."

Her fiery look suggested my hopes for a wedding rebound hookup could grow legs. She was less inhibited, a little brazen, and single.

"So, did you know they pushed the party back?" I asked.

"Dad told me," Daphne answered. "After he announced they signed the paperwork."

"Amazing," I said. "You did great, Daph."

"If only Mum understood," Daphne said. "Instead of a 'congrats, well done!' I get commentary about my hair."

"What about your hair?" I asked.

"I am not allowed to let it be down. Like me, it's too wild today."

"I like wild," I said, unable to miss the opportunity.

Daphne tucked a strand of hair behind her ear, now aware I was flirting.

"Anyone devaluating you because of your hair is stupid."

She shook her head. "Says the man whose mother made her fortune on cosmetics."

I chuckled. "Damn, Daph, slow down. If you're going to hand me my ass, at least buy me dinner first."

She bit her lip, thinking what to say. I hung on her every word, just waiting to see if she'd take the bait. A guest we didn't know entered and changed the conversation.

"Oh, shit!" She slapped her hand on the barter.

"What?"

"We didn't say cheers, Cal!"

"You're fun, Daph, like this, I mean. I am enjoying this version of you."

"Well, I may have had some whiskey upstairs." Daphne said.

Fuck. Staring at her little heart-shaped face in anticipation pained me. I found the strong urge to haul her upstairs and do terrible things. Only the worries about the fallout from another miscalculation restrained me. Apart from that, I was dumb, wanting to use a precious gift of time plus opportunity to worship every inch of my boss's daughter.

I wrapped my arm around the back of her chair and whispered, "I may have had a bit with lunch. We're in paradise. Why not?"

She shook her head, doubting me. "Are you not worried about all of this? The risk—"

I leaned in and whispered, "Daph, the stakes are even higher than before, but we're here alone right now. We get a chance to live it up, right?"

She flustered, playing with her hair. "Maybe you can live it up down here, but I am in Bridal Hell."

"I think we both get a pass, Daphne."

Daphne continued to deflect. "Sarah's mom went totally apeshit about the seating charts for the rehearsal dinner. I'm all caught up there, and there are too many people. So, even if I want to enjoy a moment looking at the ocean, I cannot."

It was a gift! I had one last comeback and it was my strongest yet.

"I have a great room, though. You're welcome to crash there anytime."

Daphne torturously sipped her drink.

She grinned mischievously. "Maybe I'll let you show me around after I finish this drink?"

"What's paradise if not the best place to misbehave?"

Her cheeks flushed, but she squeezed my knee, confirming *something* was about to happen.

I had never wanted Daphne to drink something faster in my life. She slammed it like a good soldier and set the tumbler down definitively. The bartender quietly slid the check my way before I asked.

Check signed, I followed her obediently to the elevator, then picked the button to my tenth-floor room. I'd booked a suite with a sea view, massive shower, and great big bed I hoped was about to get some action. She followed me to my room, still silent, and walked in the room ahead of me. I marveled at how good her ass looked in this dress.

"So, where's the tour?" Daphne asked. "Are you going to show me?"

"I promised the lady a tour and a tour she will get," I chuckled. "This is the entry. That's the bathroom. And that's the bed."

"You want to build an empire with a boutique real estate portfolio and that's the pitch you give me, Cal?"

She had her father's way of making something critical seem humorous.

"How did you—"

"Remember, Dad talks about you all the time—in a way that annoys the shit out of my brothers—so I have heard about what your *actual* dreams are, Cal Markham. And I gotta hand it to you, you're going to really anger your mom when you make that work for you."

Her gaze lingered too long. Then, she turned on a dime and strode out to the balcony. The urge to unravel her overcame me. I shouldn't want this.

I said, "Maybe, maybe not. But I'm a grown man and make my own choices. I avoided a real tour for two reasons. One, the view sells it better than I could. Two, we both know that's not what we're here for, princess."

Daphne turned. "Cal, what are you on about? You'll never get anywhere with me."

"Then why are we standing here?" I asked.

"Why would you even bother?"

"Because I find your lack of togetherness delightful, and I'd be dumb to turn you down."

Daphne approached slowly. "If my father finds out you fucked me, you know you're toast, right?"

Standing before me now, I smiled down at her. I pulled her chin towards mine. "Then, it's good both of us can keep a secret, right?"

* * *

Daphne

Cal's deep brown eyes burned into mine. Gorgeous and with a jaw that could cut glass, I couldn't look away. Slowly, Cal bent down, softly and slowly pressing his lips to mine. Palms sweaty and heart racing, I kissed him back. He ran his hands through my hair, kissing me deeper, but I bit his lip and pulled back.

"You want me? Then, do more."

The words rolled out, but I was clueless as to where they came from. I'd only done this with Chandler and never spoke like that to him.

Cal's eyes widened.

"I… uh… just…" I stammered, suddenly embarrassed by my own demands.

Unphased, Cal kissed my neck and gripped my ass. He pulled me closer until his erection ground against my midsection.

"How should I have you, Daphne?"

Cal ran his hand to my front and down to my thigh,

slowly pulling my dress up so he could explore the part of me wet and ready for whatever I should run from.

"You're not wearing panties, Daphne," Cal said.

"I had few ways to protest. This was one I could agree to," I said. "Makes your job easier?"

"It's not about easy or hard, Daphne. It's about getting you off and having you scream my name."

His hot breath hung on my lips while his fingers tickled around my upper thighs, missing my pussy by only a hair. He tortured me. I wanted it, but not out here. It was too dangerous.

Lips brushing his, I said, "Not here It's too risky."

"Tell me where you want me, princess," Cal growled. "I'll let you take full advantage of me."

Fuck!

"I… I don't usually do this," I said.

"To be honest, Daphne, I never do this either. I'm not much for a one-night stand," Cal admitted, pulling me back into the room.

It surprised me. "Why me?"

"I shouldn't want you, Daph. I should run, but you in this dress coming apart like this, I cannot resist you. What can I do for you?"

"I… I dunno."

"You don't know what to ask for?" Cal slowly rolled his thumb along my jaw.

"I never… just bark orders."

"Now's your chance. I want to give you anything you want." As Cal kissed me again, his deference sent shivers down my spine.

"I want to be on top," I said. "Take your pants off."

I couldn't get off in missionary—at least I never had.

"Alright, princess."

Cal kicked his shoes off, then stripped down to his boxers. I couldn't look away.

I grinned, realizing the power I held. "Get naked."

"Will you do the same, Daphne?"

"No," I said. "Getting back into this dress will be a nightmare. Take me like this, or leave me."

He complied, standing naked before me. I couldn't help but enjoy this. Cal was mine to command. I was in charge of this fit man with a particularly impressive cock.

"Get in bed, Cal."

"Yes, ma'am," he chuckled.

Chucking my heels across the room, I climbed into bed. By this point, Cal was rolling a condom over his very swollen cock. He approached, falling into bed next to me. I bent down to kiss him—controlling every aspect of the moment. This time, he kissed me back, hard—strong, longing, and like he could devour me. As I pulled away, the hunger in Cal's eyes sent a shiver down my spine.

Silently, I climbed astride his strong body and lowered myself onto his hard, long cock. As he filled every inch of me, I let out a loud moan and dug my nails into his abs.

"You like that, princess?"

"Uh-huh. It feels so good," I said.

"You're very wet, Daphne. I did all that? With nothing but a kiss."

"You have a dirty mouth," I said. "No one gets to talk like that to me."

"And yet… I did. And you liked it."

I craved, feeling high as I ground my pelvis against his. I bit my lip as I panted. I felt flushed—not just from the booze. Cal gripped my ass tight, watching me come alive. He bathed in the vision of me unravelling, looking superior. He knew he was good. He didn't have to ask if I was close. Instead, he took charge, plowing into me from below and picking me up like a toy—bobbing me until I completely lost myself.

"Scream my name, princess."

"Oh, fuck, Cal!" I screamed. "God, don't stop!"

He didn't. Harder and harder, our bodies met until I came in the most wonderful way. I saw stars. My eyes rolled into my head. I lost my mind, squealing and gripping onto his hips for support. When I came back to the surface, I looked down to see a crooked, satisfied grin on Cal's face. I didn't want to let on that he'd just given me one of the best orgasms in my life.

"Was it good?" Cal asked.

"It was…" I panted, "so good."

"You want more?"

I nodded, unable to speak. I continued to grind against him, but suddenly wanted him to take me from behind. I knew he'd be rough with me—something I didn't even know I liked until now—if I asked him.

"Fuck me from behind, Cal."

Cal slapped my ass hard. "As you wish, Daphne. You give the orders."

He wanted to please me. He wanted whatever I wanted.

"Face the mirror," Cal repositioned my hips as I bent before him. "I want to watch you cum again. You're so beautiful when you lose yourself."

I was nervous for a moment, but I strangely trusted him. We faced the mirror attached to the wardrobe Cal left ajar. He'd hung his tux and left it open, thankfully. I watched him press his cock gently inside me—all from this new angle— and settle his hands on my hips before plowing into me.

"Your pussy feels so good, Daphne. It's so tight."

"It's so wet. You just sent me to another planet, Cal," I moaned. "Do it again."

I loved watching him watch me in the mirror. Gazing at

his strong, bare chest as he pumped thrilled me. I admired the pleasure I gave him at that moment. He got to own me— all to please me. While it *felt* good, the sight of us in this base, desperate way brought me over the edge. I threw my head back, screaming again as I pulsed around his cock.

"Oh, Cal, fuck!" I cried.

"Cum for me, princess," Cal growled, digging his hands in my hips.

As he sped up, slamming into me harder, I thought my breasts might hit my chin. Yet, I didn't care. I was so spent and my needs so well met, I could only wait for him to reach the end. I wanted to watch him cum, too. He did so a moment later, staring at me in the mirror. He slammed into me, holding on for stability. For a quiet moment, I appreciated where I'd brought him. His nostrils flared and his chest flushed. Cal slowly pulled my hips back as he sat behind me, sliding out slowly, savoring me.

He gave my ass a hard swat. "You are no lady, Miss Delphine, but I'd have it no other way."

6. JUST REHEARSING

Cal

"WHAT DO YOU WANT, DAPHNE?"

I awaited directions, while perched over Daphne's midsection. As her chest heaved, I suffered. We played all day —being good, having an after-lunch hookup. Now I waited for whatever she wanted. I hung on her every word all day— trying not to obsess over her. It was difficult to ignore my feelings.

"Just take me," Daphne gasped.

I could have easily pinned her to the bed and slid inside. I knew she was wet and desperate. I'd fingered her in the elevator on the way back to my room—a bad, yet irresistible idea. Instead, I wanted to hear her come alive while delaying my own gratification. Daphne may have been neglected by her ex, but I wasn't about to ignore her needs callously.

I kissed down her stomach before she sat up quickly.

I looked up at her.

"No," Daphne said. "I don't... I don't want that."

I'd yet to meet a woman opposed to cunnilingus—at least

not since high school. I thought about suggesting she might like it if she knew what it *could* feel like. I assumed the ex was just lazy in the sack and phoned it in. Given the concern on her face, I acquiesced.

"Oh… okay."

"Do you want to get me off?" Daphne asked.

"Yes," I answered.

"I want to be on top, Cal."

Again?

"You really like it up there," I chuckled, falling by the wayside.

"I get off up there. And you feel *so* good," Daphne climbed astride me.

No complaints were lodged as she enveloped my cock in her tight, wet pussy. Her face flushed as she dug her nails into my chest.

"You don't get off in other positions?" I asked.

"You get me off from behind," Daphne said.

That implied no one else had.

"You deserve better than you've had, Daphne."

"Oh, don't you think *you're* perfect?" Daphne giggled.

"I think I am giving you more than others have."

She didn't deny it, just picked up speed while grinding against me. I loved the way she tightened and focused on her own orgasm. She wasn't selfish—not that I'd mind as I always benefitted from her inhibitions. No, she was just one to savor a good climax. This time, Daphne braced back against me, hands on my upper thighs as she was about to cum.

"Oh, Cal, fuck!" Daphne gasped, digging her nails into my legs as she arched her back and leaned back. She was a vision —the version of her I'd never thought I'd see and couldn't imagine. I couldn't. She'd been nothing but the boss's serious, dedicated daughter.

"Take your bra off," I pleaded. "I want to see all of you."

"No," Daphne replied. "You cannot make demands, Cal."

Was it a power dynamic? A game?

"Can I at least ask you to play with my balls while you're back there? Or better yet, have you flip around?" I playfully spanked her. "Turn... around."

She cocked her head

"It could feel good, and I'd enjoy your ass. If you're not going to mind my request, it's what you deserve."

Nervous, but curious, Daphne turned around, lowering herself back onto me. She did abide by my rules as I pumped her on my cock. She only managed to stroke my balls for a few moments before I brought her back to orgasm again. It struck me as curious that a woman who struggled not at all to cum—and cum gloriously when she did—was neglected by prior partners.

I held her tight against me and came, listening to her and feeling her brace against my thighs. She was suspended like a rag doll before picking herself up on unsteady thighs and rolling sideways. I found her still panting, flushed and satisfied by the time I returned from tossing the condom.

"Are you pleased?" I chuckled.

Daphne smiled coyly. "I... I'm good, thank you. Was I?"

"You're amazing," I pulled her towards me. "But what's with the bra. Why?"

She shrugged. "It's... a thing. I don't... I don't know."

I didn't press. That wasn't what this was about. I'd made her vulnerable enough, I suspected. She was like a half-read novel. I'd only reached the set up for the plot, but never quite got the ending. There was much more to Daphne Delphine than her competitive streak or her perfectionism. She had her demons but knew what she wanted.

"I enjoy this version of you," I said. "Enough that I'm

going to be sad to head back and pretend it didn't happen, Daph."

She peeked up, grinning in a way that melted me. "You will get over it, I'm sure."

"We'll see," I deflected.

I wasn't sure I would.

7. A SURPRISE GUEST

Daphne

After an early afternoon taster with Cal, I revisited his room for a nightcap. I lost myself and got away long enough before my mother demanded that I return to my room to discuss tomorrow's hair and makeup protocol. I didn't want to leave, longing for him to please me in the morning. I knew I overstayed already and gave him a long goodbye kiss before disappearing.

"Where were you?" Mother demanded.

"Having drinks by myself," I lied.

"Why?"

"I am lonely and bored," I shrugged. "Sorry if I'm not taking the best care of myself here in paradise."

"Go to bed. Just rest." She waved dismissively.

I went to my room, landing in one of the two occupied queen beds. There were four of us—Dahlia was the middle sister in every way. She was old enough not to ask where I'd been. Instead, she snuggled next to me. Lanie and Dora didn't stir. I longed for them to stay precious—far from the eyes of gossip blogs and newspapers. I envied the freedom just to *be*.

"You smell like cologne and whiskey," Dahlia giggled.

"Mum is having a meltdown."

"Ignore her. She wants this to be *your* wedding. Just enjoy yourself. Let Sarah have her moment. We'll make the day magical for her tomorrow."

Dahlia saw the good in every day.

I wrapped my arm around her waist and nodded. "It's true."

We fell asleep, our breath synced. I slept in peace—satisfied.

* * *

I woke to Mum banging on the door, demanding my presence in the suite's living room. I pulled on a robe and emerged looking a mess. Chandler Walker sat in the living room. I stood speechless, unsure if I was in the middle of a nightmare—or was it a dream?

"Daphne, you have a visitor," Mum said brightly.

"I can see," I crossed my arms. "An uninvited one."

"Daphne, darling, my name was on the invitation."

"And you rejected the invite," I said.

"Daphne, he came across the world to be with you," Mum intervened.

In her eyes, if I did anything but say yes to Chandler, I'd live a life of regret. He came to grovel. The right thing to do was to accept him back into my life, right? She knew better. I had a wild weekend with a man I couldn't have. Here was the man who wanted me—even if he had to lose me to know that.

"Daphne, I love you and made a mess of things. Your parents were kind enough to arrange my trip so I could be here with you today. I regret everything and want to have you in my life. I love you."

I did love him. Yesterday didn't change that I'd been heartbroken since I returned to the US for the wedding. I wanted to give him a chance—but not like this. I needed to wash Cal Markham off me before we could even converse.

"I am glad to talk," I said. "I will give you a chance to explain, but I'm a mess after dancing last night. Please give me a while to shower. Let's meet for tea downstairs before I do my hair and makeup. I don't have a lot of time, Chandler."

"Whatever works for you, my love. I promise."

He sounded remorseful. I had to give this one more chance, even if it made things awkward with one of the groomsmen. I washed quickly. I knew I wasn't supposed to wash my hair and do makeup, orders from the glam squad. In a rush, I brushed out my wild, wavy hair, sprayed it with dry shampoo that would cover the smell of Cal, and put it up in a high ponytail. Sufficiently scrubbed and bare-faced, I met Chandler downstairs.

"I hope you don't mind that I ordered for you," Chandler said.

I smiled, taking in the waffle and cappuccino. "No. don't mind at all. Thank you. You always remember my order."

"Love, I want to apologize for all the pain I caused you. I never should have put that pressure on you. I know you were changing jobs, and… you were torn between two worlds. I don't want to limit you, but I cannot leave the UK. I need to run for office next year. I know Labour will call an election by—"

"I don't want to take your political career away," I said. "But, Chandler, that's not all I want. I am excelling back in Chicago. I have this big new world—and brilliant opportunities."

He shrugged. "Those don't only exist in Chicago."

"No, but right now, they do. You feel like home. I missed that so much this whole time, but I don't have job prospects like this in London."

"What if you did?" Chandler raised an eyebrow.

"But I don't. I was stuck in a junior position at the firm."

"And you wouldn't be."

I lowered my utensils and dabbed the corners of my mouth, confused.

"Come home, my love. I want this to work. I know you want to have a career and a life. That's all we've wanted—for three years—to build a life together."

He appreciated my ambition on paper and loved me deeply, but he never understood how much I longed to write my story out from underneath the family name.

I stared past him, spotting Cal around the corner. He didn't see me. Caught between two worlds, I panicked, pulling my hands back.

It was all a dream. I tried to shake it off. But as Chandler kept talking, it festered. Cal's eyes met mine for only a second as he passed, then he ducked out of sight. He knew Chandler was here. I couldn't let him think I used him.

"Oof, I need to use the ladies," I lied. "Give me a second."

"Of course, darling," Chandler said patiently. "Are you alright?"

"Yep. My schedule is just all over the place."

I raced to find Cal, hoping for what, I didn't know. I just couldn't leave it here. It was off.

Cal

I went down to the veranda's cafe to play gopher for the groom. I had a spring in my step thinking about seeing

Daphne. I ordered coffee at the bar to be sent to the room and took my time back to the elevators. Then, I spotted Daphne. She was busy talking to a tall guy about my age. My stomach sank and I saw her hold his hands across the table. I never met Daphne's ex before. And right about now, I wasn't sure he *was* her ex.

She looked at me, then turned away out of embarrassment. I didn't dare stop to chat. I made a beeline for the elevators. I needed to leave before I lost all of my pride.

The elevator doors opened and I prepared to take anything—up or down—but was stopped by David himself.

"Cal! How are you? I feel like I said barely two words to you last night," he said.

That was because I ran off before the party got started to crawl into bed with your daughter.

I scratched my head, "Yeah. Wild time."

"Where are you headed?"

"I am the coffee guy. I had to put in orders for everyone."

"Great. Well, I was hoping to give you good news this morning, but—"

He looked down at his phone. "That might be it. I will find you later. Fingers crossed!"

As if suffering whiplash, I went from low to high.

David patted my shoulder. "I'm going to take this."

He left, answering the phone. And just as I thought the universe might have a plan for me, Daphne rushed from the other side of the hall in a panic.

"I swear it's not what you think and—"

Panicked that any words to leave her pretty little mouth would put my prospects in danger, I pulled her onto the next open elevator and mashed the door close button.

"I cannot talk about this right now, Daphne," I said.

"Cal, my parents flew him in. Chandler—"

"Daphne," I said with a stern voice, "you should go back to him. If he came all this way—"

"It's the same story every time, Cal." Her voice wavered with emotion and she grabbed my arm.

I pulled away, unwilling to admit my true feelings. "You and I aren't anything."

"Cal, there is something there. I know it is stupid and—"

"It is a vacation fling. It was fucking idiotic, okay? I got caught up in you. You're beautiful and fun and—"

"You care about me, Cal. You enjoy this. Please don't say—"

"Daphne, that is a respectable man who loves you," I said. "And what we have? It's the thrill of the chase. I want you because I shouldn't have you. It was fun. That's all it was."

She reached for me again, tears welling in green eyes, "Don't cheapen this."

"Daphne, it was nothing. And if you ever cared about me, you'll let me get off this god damn elevator in one piece."

"Cal, there is a way—"

"There is no way, Daphne! You're David's daughter and we're about to go into business together. You're gorgeous and you… you're smart. Don't let any man tell you otherwise, but this isn't real. This was just a bit of fun. I cannot let it jeopardize my career. Run back to your boyfriend."

The doors opened and I stepped off, leaving her behind in tears. I was an ass, but I couldn't let a vacation hookup end it all. It was either Daphne or my career and I didn't love her. I made the best choice for both of us. She'd marry well. I'd grow a business. We'd both be happier like this.

8. A DEAL

Daphne

I DIPPED INTO THE BATHROOM, SETTING A TWO-MINUTE TIMER —the time allotted for a good cry. When the timer sounded, I left the stall and wiped my tears. I tried to cover up how badly all of this affected me—how Cal's words hurt.

I didn't believe him, but couldn't ask him to put his career at risk over what? What even *was* this? *It was all a dream.* I tried to shake it off as I once more took my seat across from Chandler, my loving boyfriend.

"You alright?"

I wasn't. I was confused and bothered by everything that just happened.

"Did you hear me?" Chandler asked, brow furrowed.

"I think so," I lied.

"Daphne, I just want to get to the next part—why I'm here, you live under your father's shadow. Here you will always just be a Delphine. In London, you could run your *own* empire. We could build our own dynasty." Chandler's face lit up.

I turned back to what I had left. "And right now, I'm building a career."

"But you could do that in London. James has a position open. We're talking partner track, acquisitions out the nose, and it's yours if you want it, Daphne."

I couldn't breathe. It sounded perfect. I held my breath for the attached "but".

"You could do great things, Daphne. And you will." Chandler squeezed my hands. "Come home."

"I… I want to be my own person. I love you. I don't want to throw away three years of happiness, but I need to be myself," I said. "Your ultimatum… it felt unfair."

"I realize it was." He took my hands again. "And for that, I am sorry. What you said you wanted was a chance to build a career. You *can* and *will* do that. Here, you will always have to chase your brother and fix his messes. In the UK, you can just be the attorney you want to be."

"I want to say yes. I want to be that woman," I said. "But I don't want to have babies right away. I cannot stomach that idea. That's what I'm worried about."

"I thought you wanted children, Daphne?"

"I do," I said. "I want nothing more than to be a mother someday. I also want to have a career settled by that point. Can you give me a few more years to build something?"

"Fine," Chandler said. "Let's table the children issue until when?"

"Thirty," I said. "Give me a few years, alright?"

"I can handle that. Is that all you wanted? Because I'm fine with everything, my love. I want you back in my life. I need you. You make everything so wonderful. The house is too quiet without you. I miss this every morning—just us."

He reached for my hand across the table and squeezed. This time, I didn't pull back.

Relationships are hard, Daphne. This could be everything you ever wanted. Don't turn your back!

I put thoughts of Cal aside and focused on Chandler's sweet face. This was the man who hand-picked me and saw my capabilities at a young age. He always found ways to bring me along. I had to trust it was true.

I smiled. "Me, too, baby."

* * *

Cal

I stood at the bar watching Daphne dance with Chandler. She gazed at him, occasionally laughing at a joke or two. I avoided her all day. Watching them together hurt, even if I denied I cared. I waited for David's word. I told myself it would all be worth it. But as they danced, totally invested in one another, jealousy cut like a knife.

"You're here!" I turned as David approached.

"Yeah, I'm here."

"I never thought I'd catch you. I suspected you'd run off with that redhead."

"Jane?" I asked of Sarah's college friend. "Nah. She's not my type. She's funny, but... I'm pretty focused on work right now."

David patted my shoulder, "All work and no play—"

"I know, I know."

"Look, I've got good news—finally—since it's all tied up."

"Oh?"

"That Lincoln Park project will get approval—mixed retail and residential. Are you in?"

"Fuck yes," I chuckled.

"Great! Let's say you'll start with the retail concept. I trust your plans to target a younger demographic with a smaller footprint, but let's liven the brand up while we go. What do you say, Cal?"

"Partners?" I asked.

"I trust you. You are my right hand. But I cannot keep you forever in this role, Cal. You've earned something new. It's time for you to grow, Markham. I thought this was what you wanted?"

I smiled. "I do. Very much, David. Thank you."

He patted me on the back. "Then we're in business?"

I extended my hand. "We've got a deal."

"To new beginnings!" David raised his glass.

I clinked it. "To new beginnings."

"It's going to be a whirlwind," David said. "Daphne and Chandler are back together. I suspect we'll be doing this all again in a year."

"She's going back to London?"

"Yeah," David said. "I'm going to miss her. I won't lie and say I'm not gutted, but… she's got a big opportunity over there. Chandler did some work to make sure she had a chance to thrive and they reconciled. I never thought he'd stay away long. Her mother is so relieved."

"Oh, good for them. Daphne will be an asset to anyone," I said. "The year will fly by, I guess."

"Be thankful Danna will be distracted with planning Daphne's dream wedding so we can get this thing off the ground without her complaining about the extra hours."

I'd done the right thing. We'd both get what we'd wanted. Daphne would have the society wedding of her dreams—the one she'd always deserved—and a big job abroad. I'd have a company to run. In the end, our wild time didn't matter. It was a nice distraction.

9. THE GOOD WIFE

Six years later...

Daphne

"Daphne, why aren't you dressed?" Chandler laughed. "Darling, we're pressed for time."

"I know," I reeled from the realization as he pulled on his watch.

"Well, as much as I'd love to throw you on the bed like that and have my way with you, I don't think it would be advisable given what I assume you just spent on your hair."

I self-consciously pulled on a silk robe and stared at myself in my wardrobe cabinet mirror, covering the long-line bra and high-waisted underwear required under my evening gown. I met his gaze as he adjusted his tie. He looked ready for a party as I should have been, but I'd been staring at myself for the past twenty minutes wondering how to say what I needed to. And I wasn't sure how he'd react. His smile faded. I pulled my robe closer and spun to face him.

"So, don't freak out. I know with leadership elections… it's not the best time—"

"Daphne, we're really running late—"

I took his hands in mine. "I know. And I know you said no surprises, no changes, no nothing, but, Chandler, I'm… I did something and…"

My voice faded as I stared at him.

Just do it, Daphne!

"I forgot one of my small bags at home," I said. "In London, I mean. And it wasn't a problem until… now. It has some important things."

"What is so important you forgot it?" Chandler groaned.

"Well, my diamond studs and—"

"Daphne, you really cannot keep your head attached, can you?"

He threw his hands around, wildly.

"Well, that's not what I'm most concerned about, Chandler. It also had my pills in it. So, without them… if you want to… well, we are in a bit of a pickle."

"Are you saying what I think you are?"

I tread softly. "I'm saying if you want to have sex, you're either buying some condoms on the way to the party or we're just diving right in."

He threw his hands up and I winced.

"Daphne, I am not about to hit you," Chandler chuckled. "I know I said no changes, but it's wonderful news! Yes. I want that. Why were you so worried?"

"Because I thought you'd…"

I didn't finish the statement. Focusing on past squabbles and Chandler's tumultuous temper around elections wasn't helpful. This was progress. He beamed. I'd finally made him *so* happy. He kissed me the way he had when we first got together—sweetly, deferentially. I felt loved up for the first time in weeks.

Mum knocked. "Daphne, we are leaving. Are you dressed?"

"Just wrapping up, Lady Danna," Chandler answered. "I distracted her a bit."

"Fine," Mum's footsteps disappeared down the hall.

"This is the best news, Daphne. The *best* news."

"I'm scared," I fought tears. "I don't know what will happen or if I will ever be ready."

He cupped my face, rubbing my cheeks with his thumbs lovingly. "You will be a wonderful mother. And then you can quit your job for a bit and focus on that. Won't that be a relief?"

I dropped my gaze and cleared my throat. "Yeah. Of course. Uh… I need to get in that dress before Mum burns the house down."

Chandler took the dress from the wardrobe and carefully pulled the hanger. "Your mother is like a drill sergeant."

"I know," I sighed. "Some things never change."

* * *

Cal

"Kristy, I have to go. This is a critical—"

"You have to go or you just don't want David's rich friends to be offended?" My girlfriend, Kristy, demanded.

I shook my head and leaned on the doorframe of my condo's bathroom, trying not to lose my cool. She was beautiful, but I'd somehow set her off. I had the *worst* timing.

"Kristy, baby, you know that I am showing up because it's Dora's sweet sixteen. It's a big deal. Everyone is going."

She threw down her toothpaste on the vanity in annoyance and began applying her makeup aggressively. "Don't look at me like that!"

"What?"

"With puppy dog eyes!" She waved a makeup brush at me before bending over to apply something to her brows, inching closer to the mirror. "It's a black-tie event for a teenager."

"Kristy, David is your boss—"

"Yes, well, I'm just the help. *You* are the one he wants there."

"Kristy, I do not have time to fight about this—"

"Just admit it. Ever since Eric Stevenson came up to you and suggested you should run for mayor; you've been lining up endorsements. Cal Markham has once more moved his own goalpost."

"Kristy, we don't—"

"We don't what? Cal, I've stood in the background watching you win awards and make money and accomplish *all* your dreams."

Ever since I confided in her about our local kingmaker's interest in running me as a reform candidate, she never let it go. Kristy didn't understand that none of this was set in stone.

"And that means so much to me, baby. God, you're my rock!" I said. "I am not going to do anything to—"

"I want to build my own business, live a life I am proud of, and answer to no one, Cal. I do not want to be a politician's wife. You know just how much I hate stuffy society parties. I'm not doing this for the company. I'm doing it for you. I'm all a part of your strategy."

I balled my fists and turned.

"It was my turn, Cal!" Kristy called. "It was supposed to be *my* turn."

I spun. "Kristy, I promised you that when the building was done—"

"No. You won't, though. You won't stop. If you're mayor, I'm not building a business."

"It's years from now, Kristy. I know you want me to take a backseat, but can't we both—"

"You loathe the idea of me flitting between here and New York. I will need to do that for two years. If you're running for mayor, what would the press think? It's better if we end it. It's better if you just find the perfect political wife who will smile, nod, and just do what you need her to do. We're not getting married. I'm not settling for the shadows. And I'm not a mayor's wife."

I adjusted my tie. "Can we rehash this at another time?"

Kristy turned from the mirror. "Fine. But this isn't a place I'm willing to negotiate. Let's table it."

I checked my watch. "We're running so late, Kristy."

"Go ahead. Schmooze and apologize to David that I'm late. Make up an excuse."

"He will not care if you're late," I said.

Knowing a bit of space might be good for us, I climbed into my waiting car and left for the Palmer House Hilton. The entire place swarmed with grown-ups dressed in their finery and teens turned out like movie stars. Lady Danna had outdone herself by transforming the historic hotel's ballroom into some sort of fairy castle six months *after* her daughter's birthday. It was a showpiece, so the date had to avoid society weddings, holidays, and all the usual charity events. This date meant the most people could attend and gaze at her handiwork.

I entered, greeted by David himself.

"Cal, how are you?" He shook my hand and patted my arm.

"I'm doing just fine. Kristy apologizes. She's running late."

"Oh, that's too bad. She's going to miss the harpsichordist."

I furrowed my brow, confused.

"I have no idea why we needed one. Dora Elizabeth was rather… insistent. Well, I sense this was about a power struggle she fought with her mother over a preference for classical or baroque music."

Much like Kristy's point about the black-tie event for teens, Daphne's sister's preferences didn't have to make sense. Little about the Delphine's did to an outsider. And try as I may, I remained the man looking in.

"Come in, get a drink. Enjoy some food. Dinner will be served in twenty minutes," David said. "I'll find you in a bit. I was going to run something by you."

I patted his shoulder. "Sounds good, man. See you in a bit."

I approached the bar, sidling up to a short woman in a long gold dress. I turned to look at her only to discover who it was.

"Daphne, hi," I said, surprised. "You made it?"

She turned, giving a timid smile. "Yeah. I mean, if I didn't make it, I think Mum would have disowned me."

I chuckled and ordered a drink while she hung around. Daphne was cheerful, but reserved. The gown clung to her in all the right places. I hated myself for noticing it, but it was hard to ignore her. She was still a smoke show.

As if sensing my stare lingered too long, she blurted, "My husband came, too, of course. He's taking a few days off—a miracle, really."

She nodded in Chandler's direction.

"Ah, sure" I took my drink from the bartender and stepped back. "Kristy is on her way. She had a makeup snafu."

"Cool, cool." Daphne nervously looked off in the distance.

I turned where she looked and saw Chandler approach. While the man always smiled, it appeared fake. I wondered if anything about him was ever genuine. Daphne bristled as he wrapped his arm around her waist possessively. I didn't like this man and sensed something was off. Of course, Daphne would never *admit* it.

"Hello. You're… Cal?" Chandler asked.

"Yes," I said. "David's business partner. And you're Daphne's mysterious husband?"

The prick chuckled nervously. "Mysterious? No!"

"You never visit with her." I sipped my drink.

"Well, I'm a busy man. And she is, too—for now. Maybe in the next year she'll have a reason to slow down?" He winked at his wife. She flushed red even in the low light. "I need another drink, darling. And since you didn't offer—"

"You were busy chatting with Aunt Anita. I—" Before Daphne finished, he was gone.

She sighed, annoyed. "Sorry."

"Are you about to change jobs?" I asked.

"No," Daphne looked down at the ground. "We're trying… for a baby. And… he thinks once I get pregnant, I will want to stay home."

I cocked my head. "Is that what you want, Daphne?"

"I don't know. But… he's going to be busy in parliament. It makes sense for me to be home to support him and our children. It's not forever."

"Okay, okay. I made it!"

Kristy derailed my questioning, appearing in the red dress I loved most. I kissed her cheek quickly.

"Kristy, you look gorgeous," Daphne suddenly changed the subject.

"Thanks. Apologies for the delay. I got out of the gym late and it all sort of fell apart. How are you? You look good."

"I'm—"

Chandler grabbed Daphne's hand, cutting her words short. "Darling, your mother wants to introduce me to someone. Come along."

Kristy watched them leave in horror. Chandler didn't even bother to apologize as he hauled Daphne away like a mother would a wayward toddler.

"He's such a dick," Kristy said.

"He really is."

"I keep hoping she leaves him, babe."

"That's not nice," I whispered. "They've been married five years. They're good."

"Uh-huh." Kristy held a hand out, signaling I should give her part of my drink.

I handed it to her as she sipped authoritatively. The woman wasn't subtle. Her eyes never left Daphne and Chandler.

"I honestly don't know why she puts up with it." I shook my head. "She's the one with the power and influence."

"She's the good wife—the good little wife of a politician. She was bred and raised by Lady Danna to do her job. Just wait. She'll pop out a kid soon and we might never see her again."

"Kristy!"

It wasn't that I denied she was right. It was that I didn't want it to be true. Daphne was wasted on a middling position at a law firm. I saw Kristy's point about me moving the goalpost, but didn't know how to make it right. I didn't wish to see her turn into an introverted, subservient woman like this iteration of Daphne. I also didn't want her to leave me.

10. LAST GOODBYES

Present day...

Cal

"YOU CAME!" DAVID DELPHINE'S VOICE RANG OUT CHEERFULLY through his study.

The family's palatial home on North Astor Street was the sort of building you couldn't buy. Your family owned it, and then *you* owned it. Generations of Delphines lived here, but the sense of the place always remained. A huge billiards table sat in the room. I passed it to where David sat by the fireplace. He invited me to sit opposite.

"I did, yes," I said.

"Well, you're headed into the runoff strong, right?" David asked.

I shrugged. "I have hope."

Two days ago, I emerged as the top performer in Chicago's mayoral election. With forty-six percent of the vote, I had a substantial lead over the next favored candidate, Harper Morris, with just a quarter of the vote. As with *anything* in Chicago politics, the field was flooded with Democrats—twelve this time. I'd face the other opponents in the top-four runoff election in two months.

"You'll be fine, man. You'll be fine," David said.

"It's a foregone conclusion, I think. Unless I seriously fuck up, I'll get through. Did you call to congratulate me?" I chuckled. "You've been AWOL, man. How was Michigan?"

David and Danna spent the past two months at the family's vineyard, farm, and estate in Southwest Michigan. It was odd to see them not return in the new year, but David swore it was to give his oldest son space to run the company on his own.

"It was a good time," David answered. "Quiet. Davey managed the flames."

"If this is business, David, I must turn you down. I think I will have to give it all up soon."

"Nonsense! Nah. It's not that. You're going to be mayor, man. That's enough. And, either way, I'm not the man to propose twice."

I chuckled. Two years ago, we'd stood in my now-Penthouse in a brand-new building we'd thrown up in River North and he'd offered me the CEO chair. I finally told him my plans to run for mayor—plans that didn't include that promotion. Even now, every time I saw him, I worried I'd made the wrong choice.

David's voice lowered, the joke and smile leaving his face. "Although, I suppose I proposed three times."

Daphne turned him down. She was his first choice, then me. While he'd always laughed it off—saying she'd have children soon and it didn't make sense for her to leave the UK—I knew her stay abroad wore on him. Until now, he'd never admitted his disappointment so openly.

"Are you sure you're okay?" I asked. "Did something happen with Daphne?"

"No," David quickly replied. "She's... fine."

David notably did not mention her husband. I sensed it was a bad sign, but did not pry. I'd not seen my friend like this since he lost both his parents. Even though we shared a lot, he rarely spoke of personal challenges. He gloated about the kids, complained about Danna, and did anything to avoid vulnerability.

I joked, trying to lift the mood. "So, are you here to lobby me before I'm even mayor-elect?"

"Nah. This is more of a social visit. I didn't need anything in particular," David said. "Speaking of which, help yourself to whatever."

I wasn't used to David offering me open-range on his bar cart. The Delphines were terrific hosts, but the man was anal-retentive. Everything had a place. One did not touch anything on David's desk unless they were his beloved children. He had patience for them alone. Surprised, I poured some Macallan into a crystal glass emblazoned with the Delphine dolphin crest found throughout the house. Their motif dated back to the ornate tile work in the bathrooms first built in the late 1800s.

"Thanks," I sat. "So, what is the social call?"

"I'm unsure how to say it, so I'll just say it. I'm dying, Cal."

I nearly spat out my first sip of booze. "What?"

"I'm dying. I have pancreatic cancer. I was diagnosed in September. Because it made me miserable, I kicked chemo in December, and now they've given me a couple of months. I'm alright. I guess I am, anyhow. Every day, I hurt a little more. It's why we stayed out in Michigan for so long. I wanted to spend time with the kids. I suppose the joke is on me since they're all so busy."

How had I missed this?

In the low light, I'd overlooked his gaunt face and shakier hands. He still had the same high-energy smile of yore, but something about him was worn down. I couldn't imagine what he felt. It was a gut punch. The world was a better place with him in it. And now—even still relatively young—we'd lose him. I fought the emotions that bubbled, remaining strong.

"I'm sorry, David. I am so, so sorry. I didn't realize I'd been so busy with the election that I'd—"

"Don't blame yourself, Cal."

"You've been sick half a year, and I didn't even—"

"Cal, I didn't want you to know. Despite Danna wanting me to run out and tell everyone, I didn't. I'm a proud man. The last thing I wanted was for my friends and kids to fuss over me. Don't remember me like that, okay?"

I fought tears and nodded. While I understood the impulse, I regretted not spending time with the man who had become one of my closest friends.

"Don't do it," David warned. "I don't need you getting all choked up."

I pulled myself together. "Fine. I won't. What can I do to help? Anything?"

"Other than listen to me bitch about it? Nah."

"Well, I'm here now, David."

"I know," David said. "And I appreciate that. I missed you while I was out there. You realize you're always welcome, right?"

"I know."

"When I go, things will be a mess. And I feel bad saying any of this since you're about to be the busiest man in town, but… can you watch over them? I know it's silly. Davey could learn from you. He's still so green. I wish Daphne would move back, but her husband barely lets her see us. He's got his own goddamn election to contend with. It's always something with him!"

Ah, there it was!

"Chandler?" I sighed, annoyed. "Yeah. It is always something with him."

"She deserved better. I blame Danna to this day—love her dearly as I may—for forcing that issue. Daphne is more trapped than happy. But it might be for the best. Danna and Daphne have always fought tooth and nail since she hit puberty, so they might kill one another if Daphne moves home."

I snickered. "That may be true. How is Danna doing?"

"She's handling it. We've taken time to make peace. I'm having a good day. That's why I called. I have horrible days, too. She's my rock. I love her to bits. But, Cal, she's going to be okay. She will. She's strong."

"She is very strong," I agreed.

I had no doubt Danna could outlast us in a deathmatch.

"I want you to read the eulogy," David said. "I thought about it, but I don't think any of the kids can manage it. I think, instead, you're the best one. I hope you will be the mayor by the day we last speak. And… it seems fitting. I'd be honored anyhow."

What was I supposed to say? No? I couldn't.

"Of course," I agreed. "If it helps."

"Good, then," David returned to local business chatter.

He wanted gossip now more than ever. I didn't mind feeding it to him for a good long hour before leaving. I said goodbye, fighting the urge to get too emotional, and left in my black SUV back up Lakeshore Drive to my place in River North.

"Garrett," I addressed my driver. "Can we go up to Kristy's?"

"Sure," Garrett answered. "Are you sure that's a good idea?"

"I just… need to see her," I said.

We continued along until I sat in a car and dialed her number.

"Cal, you cannot be calling me right now," Kristy groaned.

"Can I come up?" I asked. "Just for a minute?"

She sighed. "Cal, you know better than to do this—"

"I won't stay. Something's happened. I need to tell someone what is going on and you're the only one I trust."

"Sure. But the baby is asleep, so don't knock, just text me. I'll tell them you're welcome in."

The door guys knew me and let me through. I took the elevator to Kristy's floor and stood before the familiar door I long remembered. Before I could even text, Kristy opened it. Dressed in an old robe and pajamas, she invited me in with no pretension. I loved her for it. She didn't have to give me the time of day but would.

"How is Laurie?" I asked.

"She's cranky. Teething." Kristy rubbed her temples.

We stood in the foyer, not sure what to do. It wasn't that we never talked anymore. We did—all the time. I knew a lot about her life with Laurie, the baby she'd had all on her own. I learned about her new place and her new car. I knew about the job she would take after she finished the six months of leave she prepared for. We just never spoke in person because the urge to fall back into bed with Kristy almost always won out.

"What is it, Cal?"

"David is dying," I struggled to stop my tears. "He's got cancer. He might not make it to election day, and… he's dying."

"Oh, Cal, I'm so sorry," Kristy softened. "God, when did you find out?"

"Just now. I'm sorry for coming by. I am. It's just… you know how my family is, and it's not like I can tell anyone else. I don't trust them."

"I get it," Kristy said. "That's sad, Cal. He is one of your best friends. And you are one of his."

"He asked me to give the eulogy," I said.

"Oh, Cal, that's a lot."

"It is," I said.

The baby fussed in the other room.

"Motherfucker!" Kristy groaned. "She's never going to sleep—never ever!"

She spun out of the room to pick up the baby.

"Can I help?" I called.

"Grab a bottle from the fridge and run it under hot water," Kristy returned.

I did as asked, remarking on the disaster that was her fridge. The woman I'd lived with for six years had everything organized. She lived to shop at the Container Store. Now, there were just bags and bins piled up—a stark expression of how parenthood changed people. At forty-seven, I had no idea what it took to be a parent. I stood there, crying about losing a friend while Kristy had just pushed a human out of her body—a human that could not fend for itself.

Kristy returned with the baby. Whether by intent or habit, she swayed to soothe her daughter.

"I stopped pumping," Kristy said. "It was killing me. The mom group acted like I was killing her, but… I wasn't. Well, the formula is fucking great, but I still have a few bottles left from my stash. Hope you don't mind handling boob milk."

I snickered. "It's fine. Not sure if this is warm enough."

"We'll see," Kristy shrugged as I passed the bottle. "Should do okay."

I followed her into the living room, where burping cloths covered every chair and bit of sofa.

"Sorry. The place is a disaster. Welcome to my life—as a single mother by choice. I bet you are grateful you missed all of this."

I sat in a chair while she crashed on the couch. The baby already sucked away gleefully at the bottle. She was bright-eyed over the prospect of food.

"I am not, actually," I said. "It's sweet. You're a good mom. You know everything already."

"I know very little—just enough to be dangerous."

"She's perfect, Kristy. Really. And she's ready to party."

Kristy snickered. "Ah, yes. If she were a college kid, she'd be set to go out on the town. You don't have to stay."

"I'll get out of your hair," I agreed. "Unless you want me to."

"Not unless you want to fold laundry."

"I could help," I offered.

"Mr. Mayor folding my laundry? Don't be silly!"

"I need a distraction. You give me some perspective, okay?"

"The laundry basket is over there. I hope you like onesies and nursing tops," Kristy said.

She didn't mind me helping. I didn't mind pitching in. It was comforting to hear her voice and watch the old movie on TV. I could disconnect and think back to what could have been. After a bit, I left and returned to the apartment we'd once shared. It felt more like I'd been in a dream than anything. It was like going back in time. It wasn't reality. I'd always love Kristy, even if she could no longer love me, but I realized I'd broken the habit. She moved on. She'd found love with this little bundle she brought into the world. I needed to find joy as well.

Going back in time wouldn't fix anything or give David more years. It wouldn't change what happened with Kristy and me or fix divisions in society. I could either put myself to good use and move forward or wallow. I'd lick my wounds tonight, but tomorrow, I would do what I needed to move forward.

* * *

Daphne

"Don't give me that look," Chandler said.

His face, pulled tight in a scowl, said it all. I was asking too much. Chandler wouldn't be happy with what I asked, nor would he be likely to grant support. However, I needed to try. I sympathized with his position. This week was critical to us in many ways. I needed to "be good", as he'd say, and listen. Unfortunately, I felt pulled across the ocean by my tortured heart.

"Dad is declining steadily." I moved forward despite his protesting look. "Mum says I need to come home—that this may be my last—"

"I've heard that three times in the past two months. He always rallies. This is no different."

"Darling, it is. The sound of her voice was chilling."

"I knew it was your mother. Daphne, you will do anything she asks you to do. It's ridiculous."

"Because she is my mother and he's my father!"

"Yes, the Delphines! You couldn't possibly stay away." Disdain permeated his words.

"Chandler, I trust when they tell me it is bad. You don't understand." I slumped on our bed—where nothing happened in a house that remained too quiet apart from constant arguments.

"If you go, Daphne, you will miss this cycle. Again, we will fail to conceive. Think about all the money and time you will have wasted. All because your family—"

I glared, "It is my father! He's dying, Chandler!"

"And that is sad, but you can do nothing to stop it, Daphne."

I struggled to find something he understood. "It looks bad

in the public eye for me to not return home. Davey is dealing with a challenging market and we have a board that needs us to appear *solid* as a family."

"Daphne, I love you. I care about your father, too. I know he's this important and larger-than-life figure. I *also* know your dividends matter and—"

"Don't you think you could just be a little more understanding, Chandler?"

"I have given you a *wide* berth. What more do you want?"

"I've only known he was dying for a few months, Chandler. And when I came home, you didn't do anything differently."

"It's not my fault he held that all back!"

"He didn't want to ruin Christmas," I sobbed.

Dad gave the news while we walked the shoreline on a still day—one I'd never forget. Since then, every time I saw him in between fertility treatments and transatlantic flights, I lost more of him. The man who loved me most was dying.

"Well, I didn't want to disturb the normalcy. We have lives to live. It is very sad to lose your father, but… life goes on. We need to focus on our family now. Darling, you must cut the apron strings. This attachment to your family isn't healthy at all. It's our family or yours."

I reeled with his words. Our family. It was never complete until we carried a child into the long-vacant nursery.

Choosing to leave meant choosing his wrath—the silence, the destruction, all of it. There was nothing I could do to stop him being this way. There was no way to fight it.

"I will go after the embryo transfer," I acquiesced to avoid another argument, more broken objects, and a loss of my safety for one more night.

"Do you think it is wise to travel?" Chandler raised an eyebrow.

"That is the compromise I can give you," I answered. "It's my dad. I love him. He needs me."

"Fine." Chandler turned back to the paper, barely satisfied.

Neither of us was happy, but it was all I could give. My heart was shattered in pieces across the Atlantic while my body suffered here in London—feeling more human pincushion than prospective parent.

PART II

THE END OF AN ERA

11. JUST TEXTING

Daphne

Millions gathered to watch me cry on command the day my marriage ended. They settled before TVs and live streams for a voyeuristic view of a great loss. That didn't include the thousands lining the street to catch a glimpse of the cars carrying us or the media speculation about how we would "move on" as a family. As if my day would not be emotionally difficult or painful enough, I suffered through indignities I couldn't foresee—all to save face politically across an ocean.

"Daphne! I need to come in!"

I stared at my watch, then the door—one more minute.

"Just a minute. I'm using the loo!" I shouted.

Chandler paced outside.

A phone buzzed next to me. Chandler left his phone on the vanity, so I assumed that was why he was panicked. I picked it up, about to say I had found his phone for the third time that day when I spied a message.

NATASHA

Is it over yet?

Natasha. The name didn't ring a bell. I assumed it was a coworker. I knew he wasn't keen on a public funeral—neither was I—but I resented the fact that he was complaining about it to his coworkers.

20 seconds.

Another message appeared. A picture flashed before I could even set the phone down. An image of a woman standing in a bathroom—a bathroom I knew—in a lacy bra flashed across the screen. That was the home of a friend. And while I couldn't see her face, I recognized those breasts. It was over already.

I checked my watch again. It was time. My hands shook for more reasons than before. I lifted the pregnancy test—hostile as ever with only one line. I expected to cry but felt relief. If I were pregnant, I'd have to figure it out. Now, I had options.

I washed my hands, tossed the test, and left, throwing his phone onto my childhood bed. Chandler adjusted his cufflinks, annoyed. I controlled my emotions, not letting him see what I knew.

"There you are," Chandler picked it up. "And?"

"I'm not pregnant," I answered.

He let out a long groan and paced. "Darling, what will we do? Nothing is working."

Unable to help myself, I piled on. "I think it's kismet, Chandler."

"Kismet? Are you mad!?"

"Chandler, I am done. This is a sign from wherever—God, the universe, a goat floating around in space—that we've reached the end of the road."

"How can you say that? We must have children! One cannot be PM without children in this day and age. My star will rise, Daphne, and we have a leadership contest looming—"

"I know," I laughed. "I know. Sucks to be you."

I didn't know why I laughed. It was to keep from crying more tears and to distract from the brutal pain I felt. I should have been able to cry my tears of sorrow for my father's death. CNN said, "The world is in mourning." So why couldn't I? It was because, on top of those genuine feelings, I now knew my marriage was dead.

"Have you gone mad, Daph?"

"No," I answered. "I see now. You. This. It's all a damn lie."

"What do you think you see, Daphne?"

"Check your phone." I gestured.

He looked at it, then looked at me, then looked at it. "Did you…"

"That's Natasha. Paul's daughter?"

"Daphne, I… she has a crush on me. She's been inappropriate."

"So, if I go through your messages, I will not see anything concerning on your end?

"You already have, haven't you?"

I hadn't. I didn't have the heart to torture myself more on this day. I shrugged.

"Daphne, I love you. You are my wife. You are the one I want to spend my life with. It was stupid, and I'll end it all. I will fix it and—"

"There is no time to end it," I said. "Because it's over."

He grabbed my wrist hard. "It isn't over, Daphne! Not until I say it is!"

I tried to free myself, but he held tight.

"If things had not been so bad with the fertility struggles, I would have felt differently."

"Things with the fertility struggles? That's all? That's what you worry about? I tried. I suffered and tried and put myself through hell—all to please you. And this is how you repay me!"

Tears welled, but I held them back.

"You must forgive me."

"I cannot. I will not."

"You will forgive me!"

Not for the first, but the last time, I felt he might strike me. I braced, knowing that somehow, I was done for good after this—somehow, some way.

In my moment of need, the door opened. Dahlia appeared with my baby sister Dora close behind. I made eye contact. She looked at my wrist, then back at my husband. She puffed, emboldened with a need to save me. Dora looked frightened, but Dahlia was ready to throw hands.

"We need to go. The car is waiting. Come on." Dahlia glared at Chandler.

"I am speaking with my wife!" Chandler roared.

"Get your hands off of her and move," Dora said. "Whatever you think is critical right now, it's not. We have a schedule."

She grabbed my arm, pulling me toward the funeral of the century, or whatever cable news called it. People expected big things when the most important person in Chicago died. My sisters' concern for my safety above all remained apparent, but there was no time to dally. Without discussion and as if we knew one another well enough to guess what happened, Dahlia handed Chandler off to Davey.

"Are you… safe?" Dora asked.

"I'm fine," I answered. "It's complicated. Tempers are whipped up. Trust me. It's okay."

Dora was unconvinced, even in her blissful youth. She could feel whatever she wanted or needed, but one fact remained. We had to survive this together as a family. The stakeholders required unity. The nation watched as we laid an American business great and philanthropist to rest.

I squeezed her hand in assurance. "It will be okay. We will

make it through. The Delphines always make it through. We give good face, and we keep it together. That is what today is about."

"Is it?" Dora asked.

"Dora, I promise you it is going to be okay. And I am fine. Or, I will be when this is all wrapped up with a bow."

I patted her cheek and continued outside. I gazed over the small crowd gathered on the doorstep. Davey met my gaze as he circled our flock. Chandler looked ready to pitch a fit, but wouldn't tangle with Davey or Derrick, my younger brother who appeared lost. Dahlia chatted with her girlfriend Susanne, one eye always on Chandler as if ready to punch him. Lanie stared at her phone, endlessly scrolling social media.

Mum stared off into the distance with a lost, directionless gaze. No one dared hug her for fear of losing an eye. We did not make a fuss. Her stiff upper lip mentality prevented it.

I wrapped an arm around her waist. "We're ready, Mum. Just say the word."

Mum nodded. "I'm ready."

Davey read my face and called out., "Let's head out!"

And with that, the Carlisle-Delphines were on their way to lay their patriarch to rest.

12. THE EULOGY

Cal

"I CANNOT IMAGINE WHAT THEY ARE FEELING RIGHT NOW," Joanna Reed, my Chief of Staff, said.

A line of mourners led the procession at Holy Name Cathedral. Joanna—we called her Jo—took it all in. As a former teacher and then alderman, she had seen many things. However, being in a billionaire businessman and philanthropist's motorcade was new. Following David's casket bewildered us.

"Did you call the widow?" My mother asked, exasperated. "You spoke to her, right?"

"I called Lady Danna, yes, of course," I said. "She wanted an overview of my speech, so I sent it. I didn't want to spring it on her. She's okay, though. I get the feeling it's been a process."

"That and she's never been emotional," Mom said.

I turned and glared. My stepfather, Tom, followed suit.

"Lanie is okay," Chloe, my younger sister, said. "She said it's been hardest on Daphne and Dora. Dora is always sensitive. But Daphne seems to carry the world around."

Lanie Delphine was Chloe's best friend. Lord knows our mother tried and failed to separate them. Chloe was twenty years my junior and more like a niece than a sister, as she grew up differently—with everything—and was accepted into society like any heiress. Mom did well for herself over time. She'd built a beauty empire and bought up enough real estate to turn handsome profits, but only after people read her as the teenage single mother.

"Daphne is the oldest daughter," Tom, my stepfather and Chloe's father, said. "Oldest daughters always take the brunt. You'd know, Elise."

I didn't have to look at my mother to see her roll her eyes.

"Danna has so tortured Daphne," Mom said. "No wonder she chose to live across an ocean."

"Hey!" I said sharply. "Danna Delphine just lost her goddamn husband. Can we maybe give her a little respect? Yes, Mom, Lady Danna can have a challenging personality, but you don't give her much of a chance, either."

"It would take her coming down from her ivory tower for me to give her a chance," Mom muttered.

"Mom, it's Lanie's mom and her dad. They've been through hell, okay? Let it fucking go. What is this about? Cuz she didn't invite you to a fucking party twenty years ago? Cry me a fucking river and grow up!"

I looked at Jo, stifling a snicker. Chloe told it how it was. I admired my baby sister's passion for blazing her own path. My mother didn't accept my sister's nomadic influencer life-style, but I found her belief in herself an asset.

We pulled up to the cathedral door and departed. Spring rain poured, so I booked it up the steps. Jo, more than a foot shorter, cursed as she tried to keep up.

"Your mother is… something. What did this Delphine woman do to her?" Jo asked over the organ playing as we slowly filed in.

Thousands lined the aisles—packed like sardines to pay respects to a great man.

"These people are royalty," I said. "A girl who grew up in Stickney and never went to private school cannot hang. You know what it's like."

Jo shrugged. "I guess. Going to private school as the lone Black girl wasn't easy. But you all... I don't want to point it out... but—"

"New money versus old money. It never changes. They are the Astors. We are the low-rent Vanderbilts. And nothing my mother does will make her an Astor. Now, you have nothing to worry about. Lady Danna is plenty welcoming and grateful we are here."

"Why do we call her Lady Danna?"

"Because she was born Lady Danna Carlisle, daughter of a Scottish Baron. And trust me, call her Lady Danna."

"Oh... okay," Jo said.

"I'm not helping you relax, am I?"

"Not at all, Cal."

"You'll be fine."

We made it to the front of the Cathedral. I dropped the family off in our row before going round to the Carlisle-Delphines and paying my respects personally.

"Cal, it was so nice of you to do this," Danna said.

"Lady Danna, it was the least I could do."

She squeezed my hand. I looked down the row of her brood. Davey gave me a kind nod. Derrick, the younger son, stared into the distance. Dora cried on Dahlia's shoulder while Dahlia's partner, Susanne, tried to calm them. Lanie and I hugged.

My eyes settled on Daphne, looking at her hands. I couldn't get over how small she looked compared to our last run-in years before. I observed her inverted posture—more fearful than sad—and wished I could say anything to her. Her husband didn't so much as wrap an arm around her. He looked ahead like you might if called into a meeting that could have been an email.

Daphne

I sat shaking through Cal's eulogy so much that I forgot to listen. As everyone cried for the loss of my father, I wept thinking about a return to London with a man who I no longer felt anything for. This was it—all laid bare. I couldn't deny my suspicions or concerns.

I seethed beside my husband. I longed to grieve and cry at the loss of my father rather than fear my husband's impending retribution, but tears wouldn't run. We followed the casket outside like good little poppets, but resentment poured over me. I pulled my hand from Chandler's grasp, but he held so tight I nearly winced.

Lanie swooped in on the steps. "You're coming back with us."

The glare she gave Chandler suggested he was not invited.

"She and I will travel together," Chandler insisted.

"No. You will go back with the boys. The girls need time to chat."

I stared, mouth gaping while figuring this out.

"Who died and made you queen?" Chandler chuckled, playing his thread off as a joke.

Chandler turned, almost pushing Lanie out of the picture. He gave me a long kiss—one I bristled against, then shot my sister a nasty look as he left.

Lanie took my arm gently and pulled me to where my other sisters waited with Susanna.

"Are you okay?" Dahlia asked.

"I'm… I'm holding on," I fought tears.

My pulse raced from concern about how Chandler might act or what he might—probably would—do to me later in retaliation for Lanie's brave attempt to extricate me. I was emotional, but thankfully, it played well.

We climbed into the waiting car. I held my breath as the driver pulled away. Back on Lakeshore Drive and far from the prying eyes of the press, I lowered my guard. I sobbed, collapsing on Dahlia's shoulder.

"He's cheating on me. I need a divorce, but… I'm scared."

There was a flurry of chatter.

Lanie shouted, "Fuck him with a rusty nail!"

"Really?" Dahlia asked. "After all you've been through *for* his sake?"

"I don't know," I said. "He is seeing an intern. I saw her texts and confronted him about it this morning. It didn't go well."

"I'm sorry," Dora said.

"It's going to be impossible! I feel so fucking dumb!" I groaned.

"You aren't dumb," Dora said from the backseat. "He is. Because you're a winner, and he's not."

"Can't you just hire an attorney?" Susanna asked.

"In the UK. I must find a barrister willing to go up against him."

Dahlia clarified. "Because people will fear going up against a member of the government?"

I nodded in agreement. "And honestly, I cannot even focus on that right now. I worry he will destroy everything I own—as well as the house—in the interim."

"I will break him into a million pieces before I let that happen," Lanie insisted.

"Same," Dahlia added. "He's a fucking mess, isn't he?"

I shrugged. "He's just an older man who does the same thing to every woman he's with. I was stupid enough to think he loved me, and it would be different."

"Stop calling yourself stupid! You're like the smartest person I know!" Dora declared.

Dahlia wrapped her arm around my shoulders and squeezed them. "We've got you. I can take a moment from Paris to ensure you are safe."

"I'm going to have to quit the firm," I sobbed. "They will set me ablaze now."

"Let's cross that bridge when you come to it," Dahlia said. "You can stay with us in Paris if you need to. Promise."

Susanna nodded. "Anytime."

13. DUMB ENOUGH
TO FALL

Cal

"The eulogy was beautiful," Tom said.

Mom nodded. "You're a wonderful communicator. The Delphines no doubt appreciated your kind words."

"I did what I could to remember a man who was very good to me," I said.

"He was. He did right by you. I'll grant him that." By Elise Markham's standards, that was a broad declaration of support.

I looked towards the bar line in the Delphine's North Astor Street House. Like any good Catholic funeral, the after-party had plenty of food and drink. I observed Danna chatting politely with guests—too politely. Usually the life of the party, Danna played along as the world raced around her. She observed it but did not take part. She usually drove the conversation like a queen at court. Today, she stood in a corner, almost bewildered.

"I worry about her," Tom said.

"She needs time."

I wasn't sure if I said it more for me or the widow's benefit. David loved the fire in his wife. I knew how much her temper only wound him up. The two liked to argue like old people, but cancer robbed them of spending their golden years together.

"I'm getting more booze," Mom said.

"I'll join you," Tom agreed.

"No, you will keep me on a leash," Mom clapped back, annoyed.

I stood around awkwardly after their departure until I noticed Kristy hands full with an inconsolable Baby Laurie. I rushed to help her, half-expecting her to fight me.

"Can you hold her?" Kristy asked. "She's a disaster and wants a binky. It's in my pocket, but my hands—"

"I got her." I took the baby.

Laurie transformed from a tiny potato to a smiling *sack* of potatoes since I saw her a few weeks ago at a coffee shop. Her eyes brightened, and she blew me a raspberry.

"You're adorable," I cooed. "Fucking adorable."

"And on my last nerve," Kristy said. "The eulogy was lovely, by the way. You did great."

"Thanks," I said as the baby fussed.

"You have to weave back and forth." Kristy demonstrated. "Alternate with a bounce or two."

"Good to know."

When my mother got surprise pregnant with Chloe, I was in college at Northwestern. On weekend visits, I'd play with my baby sister and mostly ignore the worst parts of parenting. Watching Chloe grow was fun, but this was unfiltered babyhood. Kristy didn't sugarcoat anything.

"I came to pay my respects, but the baby is… complicating matters."

"It's okay," I said. "What if I took her for a walk? You could get some food and a drink and pay your respects?"

"That would be amazing. Here is a binky. Find me if she starts going ballistic," Kristy said.

She handed me the pacifier, and I plopped it into Laurie's mouth. The baby happily sucked away as I wandered the halls until I heard a crash from the hallway. David's study door was cracked slightly. I opened the door to find Daphne on the floor, picking up a stack of books. I stepped in to help.

"I'm an idiot. I meant to move these and... well, here we are."

She looked up at me, confused.

"Did you have a baby, Cal?"

I laughed. "It's Kristy's daughter, not mine. She was overwhelmed, and the baby wanted to take a walk, so we did."

"God, she's perfect," Daphne cooed, standing.

"You're not an idiot," I said. "Go, sit. Where do you want them?"

"You cannot pick up books and—"

"Take the baby." I sensed it might calm her. "Go. Sit."

Daphne complied, scooping Laurie up, and sitting by the window. "You can put them just anywhere. These are the ones I want to read."

I watched her effortlessly bounce the baby before staring again at the collapsed stack.

I held up a book. "You want to read about Soviet jet aircraft?"

She snickered. "Okay, no. It was one of Dad's faves. If I don't steal a few things that remind me of him, I never will get that... I dunno... feeling back."

She played with the baby's chubby hands. "Do you think my life is a joke?"

"I don't. Nor do I envy you. The media attention has to be killing you, Daphne. I'm sorry."

She smiled slightly. "You remember I don't much care for crying on cue, huh?"

I sat by her. "I am well aware. How are you holding up?"

"I cannot even deal with Dad's death yet. I am too focused on what is happening with my husband."

"What is that?" I asked.

"He returned to London—to destroy our house and just about anything in it that reminds me of Dad. So... here we are."

Confused, I turned. Tears welled in her eyes.

"I'm... I'm sorry?"

"We're getting divorced," Daphne said. "I should have seen it coming, but I was the last to know."

"He asked you for a divorce... right now? While you were in this hellish state?" I asked.

"No. I asked him," Daphne said. "I'm fucking terrified to know what happens next. But whatever it is, it leads to me being true to myself. I'm scared as hell."

"But you've never been one to run," I said.

She stared at me, tears running and her face softening. I should have found a tissue, but I needed to communicate she was safe somehow. I brushed her arm affectionately and said precisely what I felt.

"You're going to be better than ever, Daph. You're the strongest sort of person. He doesn't deserve you. And no matter what happens there, it's all just stuff."

"It is," she sniffled, "but right now, stuff is all that is left. And as much as I want to fill that hole and turn back time, I cannot."

"Well, you will get your Soviet planes." I sat the books beside her. "Promise."

"You have your life together. I am so mortified to have you see me like this."

"Like what? Grieving two losses at once?"

"It's a mess."

"Daph, I'm here holding my ex-girlfriend's baby, trying to escape my mother because she's so insufferable."

"Oh my God, join the club!" Daphne laughed through tears. "My mother is quieter than yours, but I sense the judgment."

I propped a box of tissues on top of the books.

"Thanks." Daphne wiped her tears. "At least you brought me a baby. A baby makes me happy. Kristy was sweet for coming. Dad liked her."

"I know. Your parents mean a lot to her. She's worried about your mom."

"She's a good person," Daphne said. "We need more of them."

Daphne held the baby close. Laurie babbled and played with another tissue she'd pulled from the box.

"You better move those, or she will shred them all," Daphne laughed. "I can just see it happening."

"Yeah, you're right," I agreed.

Someone knocked.

"Come in," Daphne called.

Kristy popped her head in. "Oh, there you are. I knew you'd sneak back here. How are you, Daphne?"

"I'm alright," Daphne said. "Thank you for letting me have a moment with your baby—if only indirectly. She's a total doll."

"She's maniacal, too, but we cannot stay," Kristy said. "I am so sorry for your loss."

I transferred the baby to Kristy, and we stared awkwardly at one another.

"Well, good afternoon then," Kristy said. "And thanks for watching her."

She ducked out. It was so odd. Kristy wasn't mine. David wasn't here. Daphne was a crying mess. The world was upside down.

* * *

Daphne

I appraised a book from the stack by me, feeling the soft blue linen cover. Before I even opened it, I knew its smell. I flashed back to our special trips to the Smithsonian Air and Space Museum restoration facility. This book and its tattered, yellowed pages anchored me. I flipped through, taking in the feeling of sitting with my father and talking about MIG engines. I didn't care about MIGs, but I did care about *him*.

"I always knew time was precious." My voice broke. "I just didn't know how much until it wasn't just limited… it was gone."

"It has to hurt. I'm sorry," Cal said. "Do you need a hug?"

"I think for the first time in forever, yes," I sniffled.

Human comfort felt good—even coming from someone I didn't know so well anymore. Cal wrapped his arm around me. He handed me another tissue and sat quietly, taking in my grief. For the first time on this day, I cried tears because I missed Dad.

"I never got to say goodbye properly," I said.

Cal fed me a line of tissues as I blew my nose, saying. "He knew, Daph. He knew. You were his pride and joy."

"Was I? I think in the end; he felt sorry for me. I always wonder if he knew Chandler was fooling around with interns."

"Oof," Cal groaned. "That is a low blow. I don't think he did. He worried about you, but that's how he was."

"I just wish I could have been here. The way it ended felt so wrong."

Cal stood and leaned against Dad's desk. "It was too soon."

"Not just that, Cal." My lip quivered. "He told me over Christmas, and I had to fly right home because of a crisis. I felt like I never had time to say goodbye. It still feels like a nightmare. He never got to even see me react in any *real* way. What if he thought I never cared?"

"He knew, Daphne."

Cal picked up a Cubs ball. Dad threw the first pitch at a game where we rented nearly half of Wrigley Field.

"This place is a time capsule." Cal held a silver picture frame with a photo of my parents at Buckingham Palace with the Queen.

"I know. I love this place still."

"I remember the first time I came here," Cal said. "I remember meeting all of you—all of you except Dora. I think she might have been in bed at the time."

I snickered. "She was still so young."

"This place felt so much bigger then. And it's not like I've *grown* since then. It just seemed so magical."

"Why?"

"This house in the city? I never knew people had places like this. No one does. No one could."

"It's a lot of work. And now, someone has to manage this place," I said.

"Are you coming home?"

"I don't know," I answered honestly. "Part of me wants to. Part of me cannot bear it."

"Things are difficult today, but it will get better."

I smiled at him slightly. "Will it?"

"I tell myself that every day. I hope someday to believe it, Daphne."

"What could you possibly be missing, Mr. Mayor?" I asked. "I made myself into nothing more than a wife of a powerful man. I contorted myself to please him and might have lost everything in the process. You, though? You own this town. You've built your empire—something to be proud of. I said I'd never give up my ambition, but I did. I am so stupid."

"The glass is always half-empty." Cal shrugged. "Every time I see Kristy looking exhausted and run down with a baby in her arms, I feel guilty about it. I have no one to come home to, Daphne. You longed to make it work. I went the other way. Maybe both of us are still just looking for what happens next?"

He sat and squeezed my hand. "Your Dad's biggest fear for all of you was that he'd leave you, and you'd all fall apart. I promised him that wouldn't happen. You all have so much love for each other."

"He wanted me to come back and help. Don't tell Davey," I said. "It would make him so jealous. He's being a prick. Dahlia is still in Paris. Lanie is about to return to LA—probably with your sister."

"They are bonded."

"Derrick's leave pass is up. He has to go back to base. And Dora must return to college. There's nothing more I can do to hold us together."

"It's not all on you. It will work out, Daph," Cal assured.

"I want to help, but I'm so broken, I'm a liability. I don't know why Dad would say he wanted me involved."

"Daphne, I have a secret to tell you," Cal whispered.

"What is it?"

"Your Dad always thought you should have run the show. He always trusted your opinion most of all. Davey knows that—we all do—and it's why there's some tension. I know the two of you can make a good team, though. You can make it work."

I looked into Cal's big brown eyes and shook my head. "What happened to me, Cal? That I trust you know my dad more than I did."

"A man took you far, far away and isolated you. Shit happens. I watched men do it to my mom again and again when I was a kid. But you're young, beautiful, and going to be okay," Cal said.

He tucked a strand of hair behind my ear. For a second, I felt like he might kiss me.

He smiled and stood. "I should get back out there."

"Sure," I agreed.

I should have been relieved to be back alone where I felt closest to my dad. Without Cal, it suddenly felt much lonelier. Was he telling the truth? Did Dad want me to have the business? If so, why was I dumb enough to follow Chandler to London forever?

14. DUMB BALLS

Daphne

BANG! BANG! BANG!

I popped up. Where was I? In three weeks, I'd lived in three countries—the UK, then France, the UK, France, and finally back home in the States. Opening my eyes, I realized I was in my childhood bedroom and the person doing the annoying banging was one of my sisters.

"Daph! Get up! We're going to the gym."

Lanie's voice was little comfort. I was jet-lagged, mortified that my divorce filings were *all* over the news, and exhausted. I did not want to wear tight clothes and parade around the elite athletic club my sister was undoubtedly mentioning.

"Lanie, have mercy on me."

"Nope. Your next life starts *today,* and it starts with an amazing piece of ass named Paolo barking orders at you in the sexiest growl imaginable."

I groaned. I *did* love a good growl, and it had been so long since I'd feasted my eyes on a man worth thirsting over. Hell, just the *thought* of someone touching me to adjust my swing sounded positively lovely.

"Fine," I said. "Let me change."

I put on tennis whites and a pair of new trainers I bought in Paris. While my assets were currently frozen, my mother's credit card would do. Our divorce went from non-existent to downright contentious overnight. Like good attorneys, Chandler and I clawed each other's eyes out. He wanted the London townhome I'd inherited from my aunt and most of my poorly-timed inheritance.

I found my sisters waiting at the steps. Dora smiled as if relieved to see me alive. Lanie looked picture-perfect, taking a selfie as I approached.

"Lanie, can you take a picture another time?" I asked.

"Fine, fine," Lanie said. "But my agent really wants me to up the ante before this audition. It's a huge show. Social media presence is everything!"

We piled in our waiting car—Lanie and I in the middle, and Dora in the way-back seat. Some things never changed. We went to the North Shore Tennis and Athletic Club where our mother served on the board. It was a members-only gem of old Chicago society old-money types. No matter the type of cash in their pocket, one did not simply become a member. They were *invited*.

We filed to the courts, where a very handsome man in a tight polo greeted us. *This* was Paolo. And, as promised, he was lovely. As he bent over to pick up a ball, we all watched, not focused on a word he was saying but his tight little ass.

Paolo demonstrated a serve with Dora, who barely tapped the ball. Not to be outdone, Lanie stepped up and launched the ball hard with a beautiful overhand.

"Try to beat me!" Lanie knew I couldn't.

"Now, you try." Paolo approached from behind to position me and line up the shot. Instead of hitting the ball across the way to Dora, I pounded it into the ass of a poor stranger stretching on the adjacent court.

I wanted to die.

"Ouch! Jesus!" The man cried out.

A man in a suit approached. Someone had a security detail, and I'd hit them? *What the fuck?*

The man pulled back and turned. As soon as even the side of his face was revealed, I knew who I'd hit.

"Cal!" I called. "Shit! I'm so sorry."

Cal's scowl went to a smile as he walked up. "Jesus, Daph, that was… something."

"It was a really bad serve. Blame the jetlag," I said. "I'm so, so sorry. Are you okay?"

"I'm good," Cal chuckled. "Startled. But it's probably good for me."

"Your detail isn't impressed."

"In that skirt? I doubt that is true."

I flushed bright red.

"Fuck. Why did I say that? I… I was making a joke. An *inappropriate* joke. I just got beaned in the ass by a pretty girl and—"

"It's okay," I said, mostly flattered.

Cal trotted to his game.

"Dumb balls," Dora giggled. "What were you doing?"

"I honestly don't know," I said.

"Well, at least it was just Cal."

"Yeah, it was just Cal," I murmured.

Had he been *flirting* with me? A man thought I was *pretty*. Not beautiful. Not lovely. Not wifely. Just *pretty*. Even if part of that was humor, there was enough truth to it, right?

15. JURY AND EXECUTOR

Daphne

WE FILLED THE DELPHINE CONFERENCE ROOM ON THE NINTH floor of its flagship store. Instead of a board meeting, it was time to listen to my father's will. We waited until all of us could return to Chicago—well, all but Derrick, who was deployed. The day was here. My mother stared, gaze steely out at the traffic driving by. I suspected she was only here as a requirement. She knew what awaited her.

Dora held my hand, nervous. Derrick was with us via phone conference.

My father's attorney, Patrick MacDannald, arrived and slowly closed the door. We awaited the news. He pulled seven envelopes from his briefcase.

"Hello, everyone. I will pass these out appropriately, but first, I would like to read the youngest Mr. Delphine's section as he is not here with us."

"That would be me, right?" Derrick asked.

"Yes," I answered.

"Derrick Carlise-Delphine, David Delphine left you 15

family shares and 280 million dollars in a living trust. He also left you his King Air and Piper Cub."

"Oh shit, really?"

"Planes? You're currently getting shot at, and you still want planes?" Lanie rolled her eyes. "Pilots are fucked in the head."

"You wouldn't understand, Lanie," Derrick said. "That's fucking amazing. Thanks, man."

That was simple. All of this seemed painless. If we each got 15 shares, that would amount to 90 shares total. I figured Davey would get the extra ten added to his total for 25 family shares. That would work.

"Now, I have placed what you were allotted in these remaining envelopes for the rest of you. Anyone with concerns may ask to see a copy of the will in its entirety. This was the way Mr. Delphine wished for. Now, Mrs. Carlisle-Delphine, here is your envelope. There should be no surprises."

"Let's wait to open them until they're all out," Dora said sweetly. "Well, minus you, Mum."

Mum opened the seal on her envelope. I watched her go over it as Patrick passed out the remaining allotments. He handed Davey his, then mine. Last was Dora—all in order now. We popped the seals on ours and began to read.

To my daughter, Daphne Eugenia Carlisle-Delphine Walker, I leave 350 million dollars in a trust and 25 family shares of Delphine Holdings. I also leave you the cabin in Boyne, Michigan.

I sat the document down.

350 million dollars. It was an unimaginable amount—even more significant than the inheritance from my grandfather or my trust fund before it vested. The question now was if I would have to split it with Chandler.

"I'm sorry to ask this, but… does it stay there? Can it go in the divorce?"

"I would encourage you to leave it in the trust for now," Patrick said. "Your father… was a bright man. He wanted to ensure you were safe. The trust was put together to not vest for two more years. There are two small payments between now and then you could take. If you take all of the money out now, there is a withdrawal penalty."

I beamed, relief washing over me. *Thank you, Daddy.* I wasn't sure how everyone knew Chandler was a snake except me, but I was grateful for my father's attention to detail.

"Three hundred million dollars," Dora scoffed, turning to Mum as she sat in the corner by the window. "Mummy, this cannot be real!"

"Can I see the document?" Davey asked.

"Yes," Patrick agreed, handing over the entire will.

I looked across the table at Lanie. Tears in her eyes, she looked down at the parchment. She, too, was in disbelief.

"I cannot accept this, Mum," Dora said.

Mum shook her head. "Dora, it is set aside until you are thirty. You will have plenty of time—"

"God fucking damn it!" Davey stood.

He paced back and forth, hands balled in tight fists. I turned, confused. Davey stopped and pointed. "You! What did you say to him?"

"To who?" I asked.

"Dad! What the fuck did you—"

"I didn't say anything to Dad, Davey."

"You got 300 mill and a quarter of the family shares. Mum, do you have family shares?"

"Your father decided that you all would split the shares."

"Why do *you* have more shares? I'm the CEO. I—"

"I didn't say anything, David." My head reeled. *What did he mean?*

"Mum, tell me Dad was wrong! Tell me I am reading this wrong. Daphne did nothing but marry the wrong man and come home with her tail between her legs when she couldn't make it work."

I fought tears. I stood, wanting to run. Dahlia stopped me, wrapping her arms around me for comfort. I sobbed into her shoulder, unable to hide my shame and hurt. Davey's words wounded me in a way I never saw coming.

"Daphne, stop blubbering and sit down," Mum sighed, annoyed.

"Maybe don't, Mum?" Lanie said curtly.

"Well, if she wants to be treated like a child—"

"I'm not a fucking child!" I growled, tone sharp enough to cut glass. "I am *not* a fucking child!"

"Davey's unfortunate remarks—"

"Mirror yours, I suspect," I sobbed. "And they are cruel. What more could I do? What more could I say? I married a man you never let me run from. I did exactly what I was supposed to do—I was a child prodigy! I put myself together well, I married a man destined for greatness, and I tried *desperately* to make a life with him until he fucked someone else. Was I supposed to wait around praying someday I'd get my own happy ending, or... what? Continue to be the focus of all of your abuse?"

No one responded. Davey looked down, realizing that his outburst was wrong.

"Are we done here? Do I have to sign something?" I demanded.

Patrick blinked several times before nodding and pushed a piece of paper towards me.

I found my name and signed—my signature with my maiden name—then grabbed my handbag and disappeared through the back staircase. I wound down several floors before descending into the concierge third-floor crowd.

Here, personal shoppers assisted Chicago's wealthiest patrons. I bobbed and wove through droves of people in a cramped, long outgrown area since we began this service twenty years ago. Seas parted. I was one of the Chosen Few. Everyone knew to spot a Delphine. And given that I now owned about a quarter of the company alone, they should fear me more.

Passing through well-heeled groups of young women, I approached a staircase that would deposit me into where I longed to be. Heels clanging on metal stairs, I descended five more flights into what became the concourse below. I popped out a door next to a ticket machine in the station below, took a left, and ended up on Michigan Avenue in an unremarkable stretch of the block. To my right, a drugstore sold tourist merch. I walked past it, looking at a view of the Delphine storefront's clocktower—complete with the dolphin motif that could be found everywhere in the shop.

I looked at the postcards in the drugstore window. One read, "Greetings from Chi-town!" Though the greeting was cringe—no one calls it that—it made me oddly nostalgic for the "old" version of the city where I'd grown up. Everything had changed. I walked in the spring air, breathing in the ease of the place. The Mag Mile was still quiet at this late afternoon hour. There was nothing all that remarkable about the crowd. I remained anonymous—just a woman in what should be the prime of her life wearing a Chanel suit. I blended right in with the women leaving Bergman-Meyer, our biggest competitor.

I ducked inside with an idea. I browsed racks on the second floor for a moment. Thinking through what they did well versus what we did poorly, I realized the store was bustling in the retail areas, but the clothing options were sparse. I watched a girl looking at cocktail dresses. She grimaced

"Are there any size twelves in the black?" She asked.

I looked through the rack before me. "Nope. A size ten and an eight."

"Of course," she said. "I think it's a conspiracy. They claim to carry up to a fourteen here but only ever have a size ten and below. They don't want people like us here."

I looked her up and down. She was fabulous—tall, statuesque, curvy. Her face was perfectly contoured, and her choice of shoes was amazing. I knew she was right, though. Finding clothes over a size six was a dicey affair for a woman who wanted to look chic. This was ironic, given that the average woman was well over a size six.

"Are there any stores that do carry those sizes faithfully?" I asked.

She thought a moment. "Delphine's does."

"Oh," I tried not to act surprised.

"Yeah. But I never go in there. I probably should. But it's like a maze, you know? I wouldn't even know where to start."

"They offer personal shoppers," I said. "I've used the service before."

"Good luck getting a friggin' appointment," she snickered. "Look, they have a better selection—they even have a plus-sized section! However, it's a labyrinthine task."

So, the shopping experience sucked?

"I just feel it's a bit old," the girl shrugged. "Well, screw it. I'll order it on Net-a-Porter."

She turned and left, but the wheels turned in my brain with this use case. She'd just showed me what the market lacked. And in doing so, presented a clear case if this was our target shopper. The issue was convincing Davey that our target demographic *was* this shopper. I knew more than anyone. I was a woman. However, he denied we wanted to align ourselves with "trendy" young women.

16. THE GALA

Cal

"I do not like that blue on you," Mom grimaced.

"Mom, I didn't ask you to dress me," I said. "And I wasn't asking your opinion."

"Leave him alone," Chloe said. "You should be glad he was even willing to escort you. He wouldn't take me."

We were trapped in a car speeding towards The Chicago Botanic Garden's annual fundraising gala. When Tom fell ill, Mom thought she might miss her shining moment of the year—an excuse to wear a red dress in her sixties with no shame. I jumped in to save her as I planned on attending. Chloe somehow elected to go with a friend of hers. They all rode in my motorcade because Mom liked drama.

"Do not embarrass me—either of you," Mom said. "That is all I ask."

It was Mom's moment to shine. It was expected that her arch nemesis—Lady Danna—would sit this one out due to her husband's death. I attended this early-Summer event to schmooze like a good politician, but my heart wasn't in it. Years ago, I'd shut down party after party with the Delphine

Holdings team. Now, those days were gone. Most everyone had gotten married, had kids, or retired and I was the last lone wolf in the bunch—or would have been had I not been strong-armed into escorting my mother this evening.

At the gardens, we departed to a step-and-repeat.

I recognized a tall blonde ahead of us.

"Kristy!" I called.

She turned, taking a moment to focus on who shouted. She waved and weaved back. She was her normal, vibrant self—looking statuesque in a lilac-colored dress. Unfortunately, a man followed—a younger guy with ruddy hair and a slightly-goofy smile. I stood awkwardly, trying to assess the situation while Kristy and Chloe discussed dresses with Mom.

"Kristy, how are you?" Mom asked.

"I'm good. I'm a little nervous since I left Laurie at home with my mom, but apparently, she's asleep and sleeping better than she ever does with me there."

"They do. They always do," Mom said. "And... who is your friend?"

She turned the screws. I wanted to die.

"Ah, everyone, this is Paul Vello. Paul, these are my dear friends—the Markham's. Chloe, Elise, and Cal, this is my boyfriend."

I could have fallen over if I wasn't holding my mother. I felt Mom's eyes on me, looking for the painful reaction, but I wouldn't grant it.

"You're the mayor, right?" Paul asked.

"Yes," I answered. "That would be me."

"Paul, what do you do?" Mom asked as we moved forward in line.

"I'm an artist-in-residence right now at the Art Institute."

"Oh, cool! What medium?" Chloe asked.

"Oil paints," Paul said.

"Cool."

I said nothing, wanting to crawl into a bush over being the last to know. Kristy never said she was seeing anyone. Leaving this out felt like a violation of trust.

"Oh, there's my date!" Chloe waved her hands. "Anton! Oh my God! There you are!"

She rushed off to join a pocket of young hipsters in pastel suits.

"That's not her boyfriend, right?" Mom asked, concerned.

"Uh, Elise, I don't think any of those boys are going to be dating Chloe anytime," Kristy snickered.

"He's a choreographer," I confirmed. "One of them is his boyfriend."

"His boyfriend? Then why is he with her?" Mom asked.

"I have no idea," I said. "I am guessing it has to do with social media."

"How do you know this?" Mom demanded.

"I follow on social. I never have any idea what she is doing otherwise."

We waited at the top of the step-and-repeat, watching Kristy and Paul stand together, looking deep in love. Paul stared as if she was his entire world. My stomach churned.

Finally, they left. I smiled and took a few photos with my mother before stepping aside to watch her shine. Elise Markham was fire incarnate. My mother often annoyed the shit out of me, but I was always proud of her. She was the girl who started a beauty brand out of her grandparents' basement when no one believed in her—a baby on her hip and no man to help. Now, glittering in diamonds, Elise Markham had it all. I wondered if I would ever feel half as accomplished in nineteen years when I was her age.

* * *

Daphne

"You look so pretty," Dora brimmed.

I squeezed her hand. "Thank you. You look divine."

I wish I *felt* pretty. It wasn't that I felt ugly. It was that I felt *odd*. We pulled up to the line of cars dropping off attendees for the Chicago Botanic Garden Gala. Dora and I were sent as the family's emissary.

"I wish I could do this more," Dora said. "You know, I just want to feel fabulous. I am sure it's great. Maybe next year in London?"

London. My home. The place I saw myself living forever.

"We'll go together sometime," Dora tried to cheer me up. "When things are better. You can show me all the good parts."

"Lanie knows the exciting parts better than I do," I said. "Dora, I'm sorry if I'm dulling your shine tonight. I don't mean to. However, Daddy is barely in the ground and... I haven't had the time to cope. You all got months to adjust to the news and say your goodbyes and I've been back a week and still cannot get over waiting to hear his voice in the house."

The door opened. Dora stepped out, holding her hand to me. I grabbed it, rising to my feet.

"I feel the same," Dora admitted. "Yeah, I'm a little further along, but I still cried a little this morning just taking the dogs out in the garden without him."

I held her arm tight as we proceeded towards the VIP entrance. A woman with a clipboard greeted us.

"Miss Delphine and Mrs. Walker," she said. "Right this way. Unless you want to take photos?"

Mrs. Walker. I hated it. Every time someone said it, I felt owned by a man who had frozen my assets and trotted out all my failings in the press.

"I'd like to take photos," Dora said. "I never get to do this."

"It's not appropriate," I said. "Unless maybe we do it with the rest of the board."

Dora glowered.

"That will happen later. I am sure the photographer will take some of you, Miss Delphine."

"Thanks," Dora backed off.

We followed the organizer through a string of men in tuxes who looked at my pretty, naive sister as if she were steak on legs. Dora completed her transformation from awkward, sweet teenager to unbelievably kind, stunning young woman. She was an it-girl with Mum's beauty and Dad's patience. I felt she was a bit precious and longed to protect her.

The organizer brought us up to a special bar for distinguished guests where Dora and I began drinking.

"That's John Calbert," Dora whispered, nodding toward a tall, lanky man with cornsilk blonde hair. "He is so hot."

"We have different opinions on that, sweetie," I snickered. "Who is he?"

"He is a climate activist. God, he's so great!"

"Keep your panties on, Dora," I giggled. "We aren't here to flirt."

Dora pouted. "I feel like I am going to turn into a pumpkin."

"We are here out of obligation to the charity. This isn't a social call. Daddy just died. We're supposed to be somber."

I spotted Cal Markham approaching in a dashing navy-blue suit. The lantern lights made it hard to tell, but he wasn't wearing black. His salt-and-pepper hair was freshly cut in a way that made me want to run my hands against it to feel it tickle my palm. *Why* did I have that impulse? As I just told my sister. This wasn't a social occasion. It was an obligation.

"I'm going to go say hi to Adelaide," Dora left.

I stared at Cal as he sidled up to the bar.

As he moved aside and met my stare, I fussed with my drink and tried not to gawk.

"Daphne, how are you?" Cal asked. "I didn't expect to see you."

"Mum insisted someone from the family attend to support her board," I said. "So, she sent me with Dora because she didn't trust Dora."

I nodded in Dora's direction.

"Dora is growing up," Cal said. "I remember when she was a baby who crawled around your dad's office. How did we make it here?"

"You couldn't possibly remember that," I giggled.

"I did. I was on his staff out of my MBA, and she was a toddler," Cal said. "I'm old, Daphne. I'm a sad old man."

"Cal, you aren't *that* old."

"Well, I'm old enough that when a pretty girl hits me in the ass—hard—with a goddamn tennis ball, it smarts for a bit."

"I'm sorry about that. I just wanted to die, Cal."

I stopped. Wait. *Did he call me pretty again?*

"It's all good. I'm mostly giving you a hard time. How does it feel to be back out? Are you okay, Daph?"

"No," I answered. "I'm holding it together for everyone's sake, but I'm not great. I miss Dad like crazy. Honestly, the next person who calls me Mrs. Walker is gonna get a slapping."

Cal nodded. "Yeah, I think they should stop doing that immediately. You're Ms. Delphine. He doesn't deserve to take your name away."

I smiled. "Thanks for saying that. I feel as though it's a perpetual punishment for his bad behavior."

"You shouldn't be punished for the sins of a dick like that."

I snickered. "Should you speak like that in public, Mr. Mayor?"

"Everyone knows I wasn't a well-bred member of this crowd. You cannot teach an old dog new tricks, right?"

"Well, you've got us all fooled."

"Not at all, princess. You don't have to pad my ego, Daphne Delphine."

Princess. The last time he'd muttered that; he sent me into orbit.

"I'm not one of you. I get to be one of you for the evening, but when I go home, I'm still a lurker. I was lucky to learn the ropes from David, but I'm always an outsider."

"Sometimes, that's an asset," I admitted.

"What do you mean?"

I didn't finish. A short, round man in a poorly fitted tuxedo nearly ran into me. Cal pushed me aside, protecting me from the oblivious man. I shivered as he rubbed my back, his hand resting there too long. My eyes met his and he let me go as a boyish grin crossed his face.

"You alright?" Cal laughed. "I thought he would take you out."

"I'm good, yeah," I fought the flush that ran up my face. "I just meant I'm in my family, but am at everyone's mercy. I cannot make choices for myself."

Cal shook his head, carefully choosing his words and giving me more space. "I don't believe that for a second, Daphne. As long as I've known you, you've been your own person."

I shrugged. "Maybe?"

Cal sipped. "Your father wanted you to have the business. He doesn't trust Davey. He would have left it to me in your absence, but I turned him down."

I gaped.

"I want you to know that, Daphne—as an outsider. You're not helpless. Your father believed in you. I'd think it'd be a goddamn shame for you to think all this time you don't deserve a place at that board table. And if I could be any help, let me know.."

"What… how…"

"Davey would be smart to keep you close. The whole thing needs an overhaul. Get under the hood. Look at the financials. Use your head. After handing it over to your brother, your father did his best in his old age to help guide it. Davey isn't imaginative. He's not the strategist you are, Daph."

"You don't know that—"

"I've seen you both in action. I know you both—as an outsider. If you ever want to talk, just let me know."

"But you cannot do—"

"I cannot do much, know. But I *could* be a sounding board if you needed it.."

"I cannot get ahead of myself, Cal."

"Are you getting ahead of yourself or just getting in your own way?"

I considered. "I have ideas. I have a concept, even, but have no idea what to do with it."

"Oh, do tell," Cal arched his brow.

"Mrs. Walker, I need you for a moment." The organizer approached. "Just for a moment."

I gave Cal a said look.

He patted my shoulder. "We'll continue this conversation later."

17. THE BRASS TAX

Daphne

"WELCOME HERE, DAPHNE," DAVEY SAID. "CAN WE ALL SAY hello to my dear sister who has decided to stick around on her return from London?"

The faces around the conference table nodded politely. I was a guest—he made that clear.

"So, the first matter on the agenda is our partnership with Levoy Brands," Bernie Crow, the president said.

I recrossed my legs and peered out the window. If I paid too much attention to his feeble attempts and dilution of our brand, I might explode. What I wanted to do was call him out, assert my ownership stake, and correct this trajectory, but doing so would badly undermine my brother. I moved chess pieces gently and kept the peace.

"We think value drives customers," Bernie said.

I looked to Davey to call any of this out, knowing we were losing money hand over fist in this segment.

"So, I have plans to expand these capsule collections in quarter three."

I interrupted. "And that proposal with the influencers

Davey thought up? Is there any plan to use them to market the new products?"

Davey looked deer-in-the-headlights. It *was* his proposal, but clearly, he didn't want to talk about it. He shifted in his chair.

"I… uh… we talked about it, but Bernie thinks legacy media is the way to go."

"We'll target more middle-aged customers that way, though," I said. "It's a segment we already have. I thought the goal with these capsule collections was to target a younger demographic?"

"Influencers are hard to manage," Bernie said. "We expect that working with some cable providers—"

"None of the millennials you want are on cable." I looked to Davey.

He *knew* better. Why wasn't he speaking? He was beyond help. My brother knew better. He cared, didn't he? Why wasn't he fighting for what he wanted?

"Maybe you can talk to me more about that strategy," Davey said. "Later, Daphne."

"Or, I could speak with Bernie? I have plans—"

"With all due respect, Mrs. Walker, you don't know anything about U.S. retail," Bernie nearly scoffed.

I shut my laptop with a definite clap and stared at Davey.

"Bernie, Daphne has been on the acquisition side of retail for years. She has worked for several major firms in London. She's also *in* our target demographic. It might help to explore what she is thinking."

Might help. It was so passive!

"I could try to understand, I suppose," Bernie said. "Let's connect another time."

I nodded, trying not to let on I felt humiliated. I knew this company. I knew what it *had* been and *could* be, but Davey let this new, ineffective president walk all over him. After the meeting—boring and pointless—ended, I followed Davey back to our father's office.

"Sit, please," Davey gestured to sit before the desk my father used to call home.

I looked at the sports memorabilia that replaced my father's family photos on his bookshelf. My stomach churned.

"Thank you for coming," Davey noted. "I realize things have been... tense."

Because you made *them that way.*

"And I just wanted to say that my reaction to your... windfall... was inappropriate and unlike me."

I set my jaw. "It wounded me. And I know Mum told you off about it, so let's leave it there. She's apologized—in her way—and I will chock it up to heightened emotions, this once. But if you're about to ask me if 'we're all good', I will say fuck no."

"Daphne, I brought you here to bury the hatchet, not start a fucking war!" Davey paced, annoyed.

"I want to make the company better, Davey. That is why I am here."

"Fine, let's get to brass tax, then. You should respect my judgment in meetings. Daphne, I am in charge. Like it or not, you chose Chandler over the family and your career."

"I tried to run away the week before my wedding, and Mum drug me back kicking and screaming, Davey! You were there! You told me to run!"

The week before my wedding, I fled my family's home in London with the help of my brothers. A teenaged Derrick got wildly drunk as a distraction while Davey helped flee. Unfortunately, my parents found me at our aunt's Paris house and convinced me to return.

"Then why did you come back? Why? I helped you leave, and you fucking came back."

I grabbed a tissue from his desk. "Because I was scared. Because I knew if I didn't go through with it, I would embarrass all of us. I owe you immensely for trying to help, David. I will always be so grateful to you. It just… you have taken it out on me since then. Do you think I liked feeling subordinate to Chandler's whims all this time?"

"You want me to believe that a woman with an Oxford education felt powerless to leave her stupid oaf of a husband?"

"Have you ever faced that sort of thing, Davey?" I asked. "Because you get so beaten down and hurt that it doesn't matter anymore. Fighting only hurts worse."

"And I was your big brother trying to save you," he nearly whispered. "I tried."

I sighed, sensing he really felt remorse and worry all this time. Davey's anger always came first, then remorse.

He sat across from me and palmed his head, "You're right, I took it out on you. I should have understood. I should have asked."

"Then stop blaming me. Let that go. I'm here now, Davey. I may have made poor choices in my personal life, but I am excellent at my job. I was a star. And I want to be again."

"I was going to offer you the head of Organizational Development. It's open and—"

"What is that?" I asked.

"It's in HR. They lead the training team and—"

I stood up. "Davey, that's fucking nuts! I don't know anything about *any* of that. I am an attorney—"

"Not in the U.S."

"Well, I have serious experience with acquisitions—"

"We are focusing on our core operations. There's not much to play with in that space."

I walked to the corner bookshelf and found the one remaining family photo Davey kept. I stared at my father's broad smile and my mother's more subdued grin. I looked at all of us as we proudly stood before our Michigan house, happy and together. I missed those days.

"What do you want, Daphne?" Davey groaned. "I am trying to give you something. I don't have much on offer."

I turned, and chuckled. "Make me president."

"Daphne, Bernie knows what he is doing."

Picking up the photograph, I turned. "No. He is running this place like a fucking discount store—which is where he came from—"

"He plans to bring in a wide variety of customers and make the place accessible, Daph."

"No. He will continue to dilute the brand. Our sales floor is a disaster. We are hemorrhaging money in kidswear. Our overperforming divisions are jewelry, formalwear, beauty, and personal shopping. We have more interest in our concierge services than we can accommodate. I have a plan—"

"Yes, I am sure you do, and I am open to hearing it."

"Bernie isn't. He wants to take this down. I want a job where I can *do* something."

"This team is good. They are on autopilot—"

"That isn't what I want, Davey. I want a job that will *challenge* me. I don't want that. Tell me I wouldn't be good at the job. I know this store—its history, what it can be, and... I can do that if you let me try."

Davey rubbed his temples and groaned. "Daphne, give me time to think, okay? Yes. There are changes we must make. I am working on them, but I need to know you will be a team player."

"I'm always a team player. I'm on Team Delphine. I want to see this beautiful place survive—"

"Well, that's the offer. Please take it, Daphne. You need the money."

I shook my head. "I don't. I do not need money. I will figure it out. What I *do* need is the respect of the people around me. You're putting me in a ridiculous role so I can fail rather than shine. Dad would never—"

"Dad may have loved you most of all, Daph, but that's not my fucking problem," Davey's voice vibrated through the room. "This is for your own good. I am protecting you—"

"You know what? I'm sick of people telling me what is good for me, David!"

"Where are you going?"

I turned to leave, the picture in my hand. Shaking, I opened the door, my body halfway in the hallway.

"Home," I said. "Because you can take your job and shove it up your ass."

I said it loud enough for accounting to hear it. I wanted it to sting. I wanted to embarrass our precious CEO as much as he'd embarrassed me.

18. RELIEF

Daphne

I found Mum in the living room. She turned off the TV as I entered, a concerned—but not angry—look on her face. I had no idea what Davey told her, but I was about to go off in a legendary way. If she threw me out, I would have nowhere to go, but I still had my pride. If I accepted defeat, the last bit of self-worth flew out the window onto North Astor Street.

"I don't care what he's told you," I said. "But it's all bullshit! And I'm not taking his stupid job. It's all one big plot to embarrass me. Hasn't there been enough of that? Why does everyone in this family fucking hate me?"

Mum furrowed her brow. "Daphne, what are you talking about?"

I crossed my arms and moved from one ball of my foot to the other. "Davey isn't sic'ing you on me?"

"No," Mum said. "What happened?"

"I rejected his job offer, and he went off on me. We need to fire the president. I would make a very, very good one. I have ideas, but he doesn't want to hear them. He thinks I am an idiot. And—like everyone else in this family—he wants to blame me for the abuse I suffered at Chandler's hands."

"Daphne, what are you—"

"What? You're going to deny how badly he hurt me?"

I hoped she would understand the implications without me getting into the details of what happened.

"Darling, I had no idea he laid hands on you. Why didn't you say anything?"

"Because of Paris," I sobbed. "Because of you breaking me down. He'd already started to throw me around about three months before the wedding. He didn't hit me until a few months *after* we were wed. The other abuse started around the time I wasn't getting pregnant. He loathed me by the end and took it out on me daily."

"But it never showed."

"He was good at hiding it—like most abusers. He'd hurt me where you couldn't see it. He'd always say he'd never bruise my pretty face because the only good part of me would be gone."

Tears welled in Mum's eyes, but I was done crying.

Not a hugger and always restrained, Mum kept to herself. Dad was the touchy-feely one. However, on this occasion, she stood. Wrapping her arms around me tight, she cried. And then, the gates opened. We both cried in the living room together for a good few minutes. I didn't realize how much I needed to let it out. We both did.

"Darling, I am so, so sorry. I have many regrets, but upon realizing how bad things got with Chandler, my greatest is going to Paris. Before this, I had my suspicions—ones I shared with your father at the end—but this is worse. Sweetheart, you leaving him at the altar would have been bad. I worried it would ruin us—and you. I had no idea what was happening. I was concerned about all your prospects—"

"Did it ever occur to you I could be happy unwed? That I could make a life for myself and my own happiness? Even now, I am on the cusp of it, and everyone is trying to drag me back down! Davey sees my return as some version of weakness. He punished me for staying with an abuser. I couldn't leave! It's very complicated and—"

Mum shook her head and wiped my tears. She wrapped her arms around me tight, holding me close and shushing.

"I love you, and I am so sorry, my darling girl," Mum cried.

I bristled. We did not often get an I-love-you, even if we knew she loved us all very much. But now, she was crying into *my* shoulder.

"Truly, Daphne. I regret it very much. I… I have struggled to watch what Chandler has done after your filing. And… I am so sorry, sweetheart. I don't expect you will forgive me, but if you choose to—"

She pulled back, "If you choose to, I will try to start over from a better place."

Her face, streaming with tears and pulled tight in contrition, made me break back into tears. We held one another, sobbing. As we calmed, our breathing synced, bringing me comfort and relief.

"I… I have been so angry with you for so long," I said. "I am… it will take me time to trust you again, Mum."

"I know, sweetheart. I know," Mum sniffled, pushing a stray swath of hair behind my ear. "And I will wait. I am so sorry all of this happened. I just thought it was cold feet. I got cold feet the week before I married your father, and—it was different. I see why Davey fought so hard to save you. It's why I don't understand his reaction now."

"You took that out on him for *years,* Mother. It translated into his broken relationship with me."

"I don't recall—"

"Dad carefully navigated Davey and I not getting along and your anger at Davey. Now, he's dead, and I'm here trying not to go to war with Davey as he runs the company aground —all to fucking punish me."

Mum shook her head. "I'm sorry. I am so sorry."

"Apologize to Davey," I said. "I don't owe him one. However, you do. It might help things for me."

Mum nodded. "Does he know about Chandler?"

"He does now. But he still will not move on what he sees as a challenge to his authority. So, now I have no job, no money, and—"

"Do not worry about the money," Mum insisted. "I don't want you to ever worry about the goddamn money. When the courts have had their say in a few months, you will again be a very wealthy woman. As for Davey, I can—"

"As much as I appreciate you potentially intervening," I said, "I think I need to take care of this one."

Rather than wallow, I headed upstairs to research next steps. I already pulled all our board materials for the last five years. It wasn't quite enough. All I had was public financials. I missed too much and needed more. I sifted through the papers Davey handed me for onboarding, then grabbed the full copy of my father's will, drawn to the one person I knew could get under Davey's skin better than anyone else.

Cal Markham. I ran my finger down the page. He got my father's heirloom pocket watch—something Davey loathed— and then something *much* more valuable.

"Thirty shares!" I covered my mouth.

Family shares were worth double non-family shares, but that was still a ten-percent ownership of the company.

Together, we could manage a third of the company. Instead of worrying about what Davey might *grant* me, I would play his game better than he could. If Davey didn't believe in me, I had to. The information on where all the bodies were buried was right here in the company portal and I had the beginnings of what I thought might pressure Davey into doing the right thing.

19. THE PLOT

Cal

"Sir, there is a call for you," Susan, my assistant, said over the intercom. "Daphne Delphine."

Confused, I said, "For me?"

"Yes, sir."

"Put her through. Hold my four."

"Yes, sir. Here she is."

"Daphne," I said. "What do you need?"

She was tentative. "I need to talk to you about the will."

"Is this about the pocket watch? If it means that much to Davey—"

"No," Daphne said. "Davey doesn't want you to have the watch, but I don't care about that. I know about the shares. How did you intend to manage them? I figure you will start up an LLC and grant them to some sort of manager, but I have something I'd like to propose."

I didn't realize *she* knew, but was aware I shouldn't have this conversation over the phone.

"Daphne, can we talk about this at another time?"

"Cal, after what you said at the gala—"

She thought I fobbed her off.

I emphasized, "Off the record."

"Oh… shit. Yeah. Sorry, I got ahead of myself."

I chuckled. "It's okay, but you're not just dialing my cell. I'm free this evening if you wanted to meet up."

"I don't want to do this here," Daphne said. "I've been combing through papers, and I have questions I think you can answer. I'm just a little worried about doing it at my place."

"You could come to mine." I hoped she didn't read that as too presumptive.

"Ah… the press could find out. I don't need this to come up. I don't want to cause you trouble."

"It's no trouble, Daphne." I lied, curling the phone cord around my fingers.

"Well, I don't want to be the one who gets you embroiled in a scandal neither of us can afford right now."

"Could I just stop in?" I asked.

"I don't want to involve Mum. I'm not sure this is worth driving to Michigan for, but we could meet there. I promise you… it's strategy. You don't have to stay but maybe that works?" Before I could even answer, she said. "That's stupid. Don't even—"

I cut her off. "I have no plans this weekend. I'm skipping a tennis competition. Mom wanted us all to enter. If I'm not around, she cannot guilt me."

"It would definitely be easier to duck the press," Daphne agreed.

"Even my Chief of Staff won't complain," I said. "It would be good to speak without any interlopers, Daph. I think I have something important to say and need space to say it."

"You're welcome to stay," Daphne said. "Again, no ulterior motives. But if you're travelling all that way—"

"I'll think about it," I was unsure about throwing myself into a boiling pot with a newly available Daphne Delphine.

* * *

Daphne

"I'd like to speak with you without any interlopers, Daph."

Cal's words hung in my head. I'd invited him to our lake house—against my better judgment.

It was nine before Cal's car pulled into the circle drive outside the family farm's main house. The Delphines owned this place for years—having bought it as a wedding present for my great-grandfather. It contained miles of fruit trees, bushes, and a vineyard unmatched in Western Michigan. In short, it was a piece of heaven. Cal knew it well, as my father hosted leadership meetings here several times a year.

I held the door for Cal, an overnight bag over his shoulder. Two men met my gaze, leaning against a black SUV that followed his sportscar up the drive.

Cal chuckled. "They don't bite, and they don't talk."

"Are they going to need a room?" I stared at his security entourage.

"Nah," Cal said. "It's taken care of. Look, I could sleep in the pool house if that's better. But driving back—"

"I made up a guest room for you. It's silly for you to drive back."

I stood awkwardly in the foyer, words failed me. I sensed Cal loathed me for choosing Chandler. It colored every meeting thereafter. He nervously ran his hand through his salt-and-pepper hair. He waited for me to speak, while standing with his hands in his jeans pockets.

"Have you eaten?"

"I am famished," Cal said. "But I don't want to impose."

"It's okay. I made a chicken bake for dinner. If you don't mind leftovers—"

"That's great. Thanks," Cal said. "Should I run this upstairs—"

"I'll put the food in the oven," I said. "And you can run your bag to whichever room you want."

"Thanks."

Cal disappeared while I put the casserole dish in the oven and poured wine. I needed something to give me the courage.

"You don't owe me any wine, Daph," Cal said.

I snickered. "But I feel whatever we discuss is better with wine."

"For you for or for me?"

"Both? But have mercy on me." I sipped and relaxed on the bench to his right.

"I promise you this… it's not going to be painful. I really don't mind seeing you."

My hands sweated as I worried he *had* gotten the wrong idea.

"Oh! No, no, no!" Cal shook his head. "I'm not here to… you know."

"What?"

"To… seduce you or whatever. This is not a repeat of Hawaii. This isn't just business, but that's not my intent, Daphne. I care. Just go. Tell me all your plans."

I took a deep breath. "So, I know you have ten percent of the company. Together, we own thirty."

"Fine. What is it you need then?"

"Well, can you tell me what you plan to *do* with your shares? Because I—"

"Daphne, you're killing me," he groaned.

"No, just listen. I have an idea!"

He grabbed my hand. "Before I say what I am going to, just know that I'm so happy to see the way your eyes light up like this. It's a relief. But given my conflict of interest as mayor, I should say nothing about what I truly feel about the company."

"Say nothing, then. Just listen."

He sighed long and nodded.

"Davey is trying to shelve me in this shitty role. With your shares, I'd stand a better chance to force his hand and make him fire our disastrous president."

"Given the shape the company is in, you'll need more than that, Daphne," Cal said.

"It could work if you put your shares into a management agreement. You could elect someone—"

"I already have an idea about that, but I'm not going to say more. However, I will caution you."

"Why?"

"You're suggesting a coup, Daphne. Even with my shares, it's not enough. You must either ask your family to chime in or get the other non-family members of the board to side with you."

"It's not a coup!" I laughed defensively.

"Uh, it is. You're asking your siblings to choose. And, Daphne, he's the CEO. He has been running it."

"Dad wanted me. You said—"

"Daphne, he may have, but you've been gone. You need a solid plan."

"I know that. I also know that you are better aware of the board members than I am. I need to impress them and make them trust me."

"So, you want me to do your dirty work?" He rubbed his temples. "Oh, Daphne, you're killing me!"

The buzzer beeped, signaling the preheated oven. I put

the casserole in, shaking my head. I did the math. It was a coup, but could I win? I could—only with his help.

As I closed the oven door, Cal said, "I have some ideas. I shouldn't meddle, but you have my ear."

I turned, beaming. "Good. Because I'd like to tell you about my plans to save the company."

20.HARD CHOICES

Cal

Daphne returned to the breakfast nook.

"Cal, I have poured over the financials. They aren't good. And I know there are probably a million reasons for that. You're going to tell me that I'm trying to revive a zombie. Retail is—"

"Mom is seeing *big* returns in retail right now," I said. "Retail isn't dead. But as Davey sees it, luxury retail is a thing of the past. Have you looked at comps?"

I shouldn't give her any help, but I suspected Daphne did the research. Like her mother, she held her cards so close that I never got a read-in. What did she know?

"Of course, I have. You know me too well," Daphne answered. "The sector—as a whole—is challenged. It's problematic for most."

"But there are bright stars."

"Beauty is doing very well," Daphne said. "Which is why Elise M is over-performing."

"No, it's not," I insisted. "It is because while Mom can complain about Chloe's lack of a 'job', influencers are selling her product for her. It's grassroots, guerrilla marketing—driven largely by Chloe being Mom's biggest hype woman—making it work."

She looked down at her wine. "I want influencers and luxury collections—not value fast-fashion. Even Davey does. Sadly, Bernie doesn't."

"Influencers can be complicated, but they also bring in younger people. You're right. It worked for Mom. And Mom's stuff isn't even *luxury*. It's just *good*, right?"

"Her newest line is trying. And certainly, the anti-aging stuff is. It's hella expensive, but I swear the under-eye serum is amazing."

I snickered.

"Don't judge me. I'm getting old."

"Daphne, you do not *know* old. You are not even middle-aged yet. Your skin is impeccable, and I am sure every woman your age hates you for it."

"You are the first—and last—straight man to tell me that, so thank you."

I laughed. "Fair, fair. You're lovely, though. Can you name a major competitor that is outperforming?"

"Selfridges. Bergman-Meyer. Both have reduced their store footprints and retail stock to focus on a very specific customer. Bergman-Meyer has a similar price point and has the sort of American consumer we'd like to have. I did some research there."

"And?"

"I talked to a shopper—she had no idea who I was. She's our ideal customer—fashion-forward but not into fast-fashion, twenties or thirties, and the type to seek out stores with similar values to hers. She was looking for a size twelve but couldn't find one. We carry a wider range of sizes, so I asked if she'd tried Delphine's. She said, quite frankly, it's a maze. It doesn't feel like a luxury experience.

And while she wants to use our personal shoppers, they're never available."

"So, what is the concern then? You have the beginnings of a plan. Why not think about the possibilities?"

"Because everything is complicated. Davey and I had a *massive* fight. He gave me a job I'm not qualified for and did not want—a director's position when I've already been an SVP. It was a huge insult all to 'protect me'. Doing anything about this will only make it ten times worse. Please, Cal. What I need are introductions—social ones. Nothing more. Let me get the ears of the people who I need to convince. Do it... as a friend?"

She gave me the sweetest, most pitiful look.

"If you want to save the Company, I will support you in any way I *legally* can. Your father would want it to remain solvent, Daphne. And... I will always have a soft spot for you."

She blushed. "Do it for Dad. Leave me out of it."

"I could never leave you out of it," I said, too honest. "Give me exactly what you need, and I will tell you what I can do and not lose every shred of integrity when this becomes public."

She dropped my gaze, stood, and paced. Still ruminating, she opened the kitchen French doors to let in a lake breeze.

She returned, nostrils flaring, "Tell me who we need and let's do the math."

"What is your ownership stake?" I asked.

"I own 25 family shares. Davey only owes ten. None of us had them before. Dad kept them until his death."

"So, twenty percent of the company?"

"And you own—"

"Thirty," I said. "So, that is almost a third of the shares."

"Yeah, so you need to get a proxy."

"I'm working on it. I have an idea of who can step in," I

said. "Honestly, you might not even need me. There are two other non-family investors. Daphne, I am glad to set up meetings if that would help you. That is all I can do."

And if anyone found out, it would *still* look bad—very bad.

She paced more before agreeing. "Okay, these are hard choices, but... if I am to save the company, I will have to risk it all. Well, if you can guarantee me one thing."

"Yes?"

"If I end up homeless over this, you'll take me in."

She joked, but I realized it was a possibility. Daphne was in a precarious situation if she was as dependent on her family's money as she expressed.

"I promised your father I would look after you and your mother," I agreed. "That promise will be honored, Daphne. I don't think I will *need* to honor it like *that*, but if I do, I will."

"Good, then where do we begin?"

"It's not *that* simple," I said. "Daphne, there is one thing your brother is right about. It's that you will need time to work through this. I can make the connections you need, but you must work on your business plan. You have it in you, but you gotta come prepared for the fight. I cannot help you there."

"I will put in the work," Daphne promised.

* * *

Daphne

"Dad asked you to look over all of us, right? Not just me." I asked Cal.

"Your Dad asked me to watch over Danna because he was leaving her. But he knew the brunt of keeping things together would fall to you. I don't think he sees either of you as a damsel, Daphne. If that is what you are worried about, that wasn't his read."

Maybe he should have. Part of me wondered if I'd have run to my father if he stepped in to save me. Would I have listened? Could I have seen it then?

"Then what?"

"He never trusted your ex, Daph. He loved and supported you. He wanted it to work—I am sure most people did."

"Who didn't?" I furrowed my brow.

Cal nervously chuckled, then cleared his throat. "For one, I remember some people being salty about it."

"Some people?" I raised my eyebrow.

"Yes, some people."

I held his gaze defiantly and for too long. "Like you, Cal?"

Cal's gaze fell to his wine.

The timer beeped, and I let it go. He never answered it. His silence said it all. He regretted Chandler coming back on Sarah and Erik's wedding day. I took out the oven dish and grabbed plates.

"I hated seeing you with him that morning," Cal said.

I stopped, hands gripping the dishes and processed it.

"It felt unfair, Daphne. And if your dad hadn't offered me a major real estate investment that morning, I might have been less of a coward and told you how I felt. Is that what you want to hear? That I wasn't brave enough to possibly upset the apple cart? That money seemed more important than a fling? Because I know what you're thinking—"

I spun. "Cal, I don't blame you or see it that way. You know I was railroaded into taking Chandler back. Sleeping with me was a bad idea."

I lowered the plate. I peeled back the dish foil, trying to ground myself in the moment.

"It *was* a bad idea. I risked a lot—stupidly," Cal said. "But unless you saw it as predatory—my only *real* concern—I don't regret it."

I brought plates and silverware back to the table.

"I was a grown woman," I said. "It was stupid based on your position in the company and that you were my father's confidant. Nothing about it was *bad*. Of course, I'm sure you just returned to sleeping with whomever you were sleeping with, right? I was a blip."

Cal scowled. "Daphne, that's not my MO."

"You don't have to lie," I snickered. "I'm a big girl. This was ancient history, Cal."

"Daphne, that isn't me. You're… that's not me."

Cal took a bite, annoyed.

"You don't mind leftovers?"

He chuckled. "No. I was raised on them—as a latchkey kid. I couldn't be picky. I wasn't raised like a princess in a tower. I had to fend for myself while my mother built her business."

I crossed my arms.

"Daphne, you're a good cook. Relax."

I hated that shit. He didn't get to talk down to me like I was some petty little girl.

"I'm spoiled, but I've been through hell in the past decade, okay? I tied myself to an asshole who abused me in every way imaginable for the duration of our marriage. I assure you I wasn't treated like a princess. Don't infantilize me, Cal."

"I wouldn't," Cal said. "You should have been treated like a queen. You deserve all of that and more, Daphne. I am sorry, Daph. For all of it."

"Then don't speak to me like that, Cal."

"Sorry. You hit a nerve."

"What nerve?"

"I'm not a player, okay? Or at least… I wasn't. Now, that's impossible. And someone my age probably shouldn't run around like that. But that's never been it. I don't do one-night stands."

"The legendary Cal Markham doesn't do one-night stands?" I laughed. "Never?"

"Never," Cal said.

"What were we then?"

"It didn't feel like that, Daphne," Cal said. "This is a mistake. I shouldn't have—"

He looked uncomfortable, making me reconsider baiting him.

"Cal, don't," I said. "Sorry. I just assumed all men who remain in your current position are just chasing women left and right. I never… considered… you know?"

"What? Considered what?"

"Considered it could have felt like *more* to you. I assume you're a perpetual bachelor without judgement."

"I haven't been. Kristy and I were together for six years. I loved her."

Cal showed vulnerability and sweetness not seen since the library.

"It *did* feel like more. I didn't expect that. I expected to fuck you and move on. Instead, it was some of the best sex I'd ever had. I don't fuck people I have no interest in. I guess it takes some connection to… go there, Daph."

I was confused, "So, why'd you do it? Because doing it would have gotten you in major trouble with my father—"

"Probably," Cal said. "I didn't think it through."

"Because you were thinking with your dick. And… I didn't think—"

"I wasn't. I mean, partially. I am ashamed to admit how much I'd enjoyed working with you and how badly I'd wanted to wipe that serious look off your face all summer."

I suddenly forgot I was nervous or wasn't supposed to

feel like this. It had been years since a man talked to me like that.

"You're gorgeous, Daphne. Tempting. But you were taken—and off-limits. I don't know why I gave in. It seemed like we had a moratorium as long as we were in Hawaii. After that night at the office, I'd sworn it off. Then, we were in paradise and everything felt different."

My face flushed, surprised by his forward statements. "I know what... I know what you mean."

"It was the wickedly funny, chaotic side of you that drew me in, honestly. You were a mess—and I couldn't help but want to make you *more* of a mess. It was a wild time. I dunno."

"Blame my mother for that—always. Well, we're working on it right now. She encouraged me to leave town because she is trying to put some space between Davey and I. Chaotic is a good word."

"I like chaotic Daphne Delphine," Cal's voice was deep and hungry. "She's great."

Cal's eyes lingered too long. My palms grew sweaty as I dropped his gaze.

"You really thought it was that good?"

"Was it not good enough for you?" Cal said.

"It was..." I looked for words.

"You can be honest, Daphne."

I've never had so many orgasms in one weekend. I nervously laughed, afraid to tell the truth.

Cal focused on his food, unsure how to read me. I wanted to tell him everything.

"Be honest," Cal repeated, "but don't leave me hanging."

"It was more than satisfactory," I played coy. "I should have taken you up on it at least once more."

21. BAD CHOICES

Cal

I LOWERED MY FORK, TRYING TO READ DAPHNE. SHE WAS THE most confounding woman. I hadn't come here to seduce her but as she bit her lip, it was over. She could ask for whatever her heart desired and I would have given it.

"Satisfactory? You think it was satisfactory?" I asked.

"*More than*. It's a limited sample size, Cal," Daphne said. "You must admit, it could have been a flash-in-the-pan."

I set my fork down.

"You done?" Daphne asked. "I need to run the dishwasher."

"I am—"

I went to stand, but she rose instead, picking up the plate. I hated it.

I grabbed her hand. "No. Sit down. I'm a big boy. I can bus my plate."

"You're a guest," Daphne said.

I shook my head, loving the defiant look on her face. Dumb and braver for the glass of wine we'd imbibed, I pulled her into my lap. The look of surprise on Daphne's face was more than enough reward for my misdeed. I thought for a moment she might slap me. She merely stared, mouth gaping.

"I don't need you to wait on me like a servant, Daphne. Someone should take care of you."

Her face flushed. Speechless, Daphne shook her head.

I tucked her blonde hair behind her ear. "You don't think you deserve that?"

"I… I can do fine on my own," Daphne quieted.

"That's not what I asked," I said.

"I… why do you even think that?"

"Because you're amazing, Daphne. You know that deep down, don't you?"

She nodded as if mystified.

"Now, what do you want? What can I do for you, princess?" I asked.

"I… I don't know," Daphne whispered.

I pulled her chin towards mine, unable to resist, and leaned to kiss her. But before my lips could even meet her, she gripped my shirt and pulled me closer, her lips pressed hard against mine. Her greedy kiss hit every note it needed. I needed more of her. I ran fingers through her hair and remembered how I felt when we kissed on the balcony years before—how free we felt. Gripping the roots of her wavy hair elicited a low moan.

I pulled back slightly, our faces almost meeting, and her hot, rapid breath told me all I needed to know.

"Can I try to get into the 'exemplary' category with you, Daphne?" I asked. "I'll do whatever you want me to do."

Daphne nodded.

"I need you to say it out loud, princess. Say it."

"Yes, Cal. I want to try. I *need* to," Daphne pled.

I swatted her ass. "Then get upstairs, Daphne. I'll come find you."

"Oh… okay," Daphne said, confused.

She slowly stood before me. I rose, gazing down at her. She was desperate to get off. It had been so long since I touched anyone like this. I was dying for it, too.

"Go, go on. I can figure out a dishwasher, Daphne," I assured.

"Oh… okay," Daphne murmured.

I watched her leave. I should have taken the moment to shake myself out of it. Before, my risk was losing my career opportunities. Now, I risked an angry public and the loss of image. I should have said no. Our relationship wouldn't play well in the press, but I craved her.

* * *

Daphne

I paced in my room, unsure of what to do. Did I run? Did I tell Cal no? I felt my body's betrayal—due to years of fertility treatments and wishful thinking—deep in my bones.

Cal appeared in my doorway. I looked over, unsure where we went from here.

"I… I have no idea what I'm doing," I confessed. "And… I worry I'm just going to be a grave disappointment."

Call approached, pulling me to him with a firm grip on the small of my back. He owned me in these moments. And yet? I knew, somehow, I had absolute control.

"We can do whatever you want, Daphne," Cal said. "Whatever you want—or nothing at all. I cannot imagine a day where you are a disappointment."

I wrapped my arms around his neck, kissing him. Each time our lips met; I grew braver. I wanted him but was terrified I'd ruin it. What *it* was, I didn't know. I just knew he'd do anything to please me in the moment. So, I let go of my fears. I breathed him in and let him walk me to bed.

Cal threw his clothes aside as I fell into it. We were older and, perhaps, wiser, but *damn*. Cal Markham was still gorgeous. He aged like fine wine.

"You aren't going to meet me halfway here, princess?" Cal chuckled.

I sat up, pulling my t-shirt off and revealing my very utilitarian sports bra. I desperately wished it was sexier. But, as Cal pinned me, his body pressing into mine the best way, I didn't care. I tried to slip out of my jeans. Cal stood, whipping them off. He traced the outline of my panties with his index finger. I shivered.

"What? You good?" Cal asked.

"I..." I had no words.

I repositioned myself on the bed to grant more space. He read the room, climbing back in. He lay beside me, running his hand down to my center again. Rather than pin me, he longingly looked at my reaction as he ran his fingers on my clit—just over my panties.

"Oh, God," I let out a little moan.

"That's all it takes?" Cal asked.

"I didn't say stop," I panted. "Did I?"

Cal kissed me as he slipped his hand into my panties. My pussy was slick. The heat of his kiss sent me reeling. I bucked my hips towards him. Cal slipped one finger, then two inside me.

"Oh fuck," I gasped.

"You like that?" Cal asked. "Do you want more?"

I nodded.

"I need you to say it, Daphne."

"Yes, please," I begged.

Cal kissed down my body, pulling my panties off. He cast them aside, then gently parted my legs. I worried about the difference between twenty-four-year-old me and my present self. I feared I'd disappoint him in the moment. Cal dove between my legs, slowly kissing my clit. I threw my head back in total disbelief that this was happening.

He had no idea how many years it had been since anyone had gone down on me. It seemed an eternity now. The way he slowly, torturously, sucked on my clit, and licked deliciously made me want more. Though I never preferred it, I didn't want him to stop. I gripped his hair to steady myself.

"Oh, God. That feels so good, Cal," I gasped. "Fuck!"

It only encouraged him more. Cal slid two fingers back inside. The sheer pleasure sent me into another dimension. I squealed. Why was he *so* good at this? As if magic, every stroke of Cal's tongue and each thrust of his fingers drove me closer to the edge. I was desperate to get there, grinding my hips now.

"Please, please," I begged. "Oh God, please, Cal."

I gripped the headboard behind me as I gave over to the rush of pleasure his touch gave. I shrieked a line of inaudible words, unable to control myself. I couldn't stop it. I felt like the gates opened. As if a light within me turned back on, I came to life.

Cal met my gaze as I looked down. "Was that good?"

"That was exemplary," I said. "Fuck!"

Cal chuckled, kissing his way back up my torso. I felt the full length of him pressed against me as he kissed my neck. I wanted all of him inside me, but I knew there was an issue at hand—one I needed to broach before we got carried away.

"Cal," I panted. "I… I want to do this, but I'm not on the pill. And…"

He pulled back, looking down at me. "Oh, shit. If you don't believe me, I honestly didn't plan anything—"

"I'm sorry. I've spent the last five years trying to *get* pregnant. And it's not like I expected you to show up and do what you just did."

He chuckled, then kissed me slowly and sweetly. "I will have to suffer the atrocity of waiting until the drugstore opens in the morning. I mean… if I'm allowed to stay."

"You're allowed to stay," I said. "I could—"

"No. This was about you, Daphne. I wanted to give you what I suspect you haven't had in years. I will get mine eventually. And it will be sweet… when it happens."

Cal rolled onto his back, pulling me into his arms. I rested my head on his chest, listening to his heartbeat as it calmed. I never had a man deny himself an orgasm for me. What was this sorcery? I waited for the other shoe to drop, but it never did. I drifted to sleep to the sound of the waves, cuddled up on Cal's warm chest.

PART III

AGAINST ALL REASON

22. INCOGNITO

Cal

Daphne was asleep when I drove to the local pharmacy, arriving early to avoid a crowd. I may have been out of state, but I was where every well-heeled Chicagoan retreated to on summer weekends. Clad in a Cubs cap and dressed down, I hoped I was sufficiently incognito. My security guy minded the front of the small pharmacy-cum-grocery in this sleepy lakeshore town. I knew he probably judged me, but I didn't care.

I tried not to think about Daphne's happy moans as I ducked into the appropriate aisle and grabbed the first acceptable box of condoms. Trying not to make a big deal, I added a pile of snacks and pushed them across the counter towards the clerk. She looked at me as she rang up my purchase, trying to place me. Internally, I melted down.

"Are you…"

I held off finishing the sentence. *Play it cool, Cal.*

"One of the Vanderveens?" She finished her thought.

"Oh, nope," I waited for the total. "Sorry. Just visiting a friend here. Not a local."

"I swore you were Robbie Vanderveen's kid. Well, you've got a doppelganger."

"Interesting." I was disinterested.

I tapped my credit card to pay. She handed me the bag, and I raced out, hopping into my car and dashing back to Daphne's where I found her cracking eggs in the kitchen into a bowl, the smell of bacon tempting me.

"Daph, you didn't need to make breakfast."

"I'm in a good mood," she said. "So, sue me!"

I grinned. I'd never woken up with her before. It was a treat.

I kissed Daphne's forehead. "You're too kind. I promise to make up for it."

"Oh, I'll take you up on the offer, Cal. If you can make the toast, that would be great."

"I can handle toast," I said.

"Can you cook?" Daphne asked.

"I am fully housebroken, and, yes, I can cook," I chuckled. "My mom cannot. I learned so we had something to eat that wasn't out of the microwave. Tim is the cook in the family. Chloe would burn the house down."

Daphne giggled. "That's sad. Mum doesn't cook. Dad always did. I'm making his 'famous' eggs."

"What makes them famous?"

"Cheese," Daphne answered. "But he tried to teach us all to cook. It worked for Davey, Dahlia, and me."

"Ah, Dahlia. Well, she's a pro."

"I know," Daphne said. "I wish I could convince her to come home."

"She could make the place a trendy spot, you know?" I said.

"The food hall could be amazing, right? If I gave her the reins, she'd make it fabulous."

"Chloe would hype the hell out of it."

"Influencers are a big part of what we need," Daphne said. "Davey doesn't see the point. Dad didn't, either, but they need to wise up. Influencers are walking billboards. Our customers spend most of their time on social media. If you have no social media footprint, do you exist?"

"Nope," I said. "It was a big part of my campaign."

"Did Chloe hype you?"

"Chloe wasn't my target demographic. It was young community organizers. I had a cult-like following and just ran with it. No clue how it worked. It was organic."

"We need that. Cal, can you set up meetings so I can work on all of this? I am serious. I want to do it."

"Of course," I agreed. "Absolutely. And just to be clear… it has *nothing* to do with what happened last night."

She bit her lip. "I know. But last night was… lovely. Thank you."

"Oh, I plan to take full advantage of this moratorium on normal life today. I'm prepared."

I nodded at the bag.

"Good. I'll let you if you want to spend all day in bed after this. However, if I do not eat something, I'll be hangry. Always feed me breakfast. I don't take kindly to being hungry."

I snickered. "Noted."

Daphne bit her lip. "Of course, I don't have to start the eggs for a minute, and the bacon has twenty minutes, so we have some time to kill."

"I like the way you think, Daphne," I said.

* * *

Daphne

I didn't see myself as the type of girl to get it on in her mother's conservatory. I also didn't think I'd be the person to do it astride my late father's best friend on an expensive heirloom piece of wicker furniture. Mother had only recently reupholstered it custom-printed Swedish fabric. And if Lady Danna saw me right now, she'd lose her goddamn mind.

"Well, are you going to come over here, or am I just going to sit here in my most vulnerable state?" Cal asked.

I kicked off my shorts and panties as if defiantly announcing I was ready and climbed onto the couch. I slowly lowered myself down on top of Cal, easing into my pleasure.

"You alright?" Cal cupped my face in his hands.

"I'm great," I kissed him.

I slowly ground against him, feeling how deep he filled me as I did. It felt glorious! I was going to get off *twice* in two days. That was more than I'd gotten off in as many years! I bit his lip as I slowly bobbed.

Cal pulled back. "You are greedy, Daphne."

"You like me greedy," I said.

Words poured out of me. When within five feet of Cal's beautiful and available cock, I turned into a different woman altogether.

Cal ran his hands to my breasts.

"Take your top off," he pled.

"Why?"

"Daphne, in all the times we've done this, I've never seen your nipples. I bet they are glorious."

Nervous to be completely naked—even with a man who had had all of me in other ways—I peeled my shirt off. I hadn't put a bra on this morning, so my breasts bobbed freely as I ground on Cal's hard cock.

"Fucking hell, Daphne," Cal groaned. "You are the most beautiful thing. Why didn't you—"

I cut him off with a kiss. He met me, playing with my nipples.

He leaned down at an impossible angle to suck my nipple before I could even stop him. As Cal gently licked, then sucked, my eyes rolled back. Why did that feel so good? As he sucked one nipple, he thumbed the other with his hand, enhancing the sensation.

"Oh, fuck, that feels so good," I gasped. "You don't think they're... odd."

Cal dropped my breast and met my gaze, eyes assured. "Odd? They're fucking perfect."

I tossed my self-doubt aside and gripped the back of the couch forcefully. I wanted to take him deeper, so I ground harder. My breath quickened as my sweaty palms gripped the couch for dear life. Cal never gave up, focused entirely on my beautiful climax. He read every breath, every moan, and every twitch of my body to see how he could better serve me.

"Cal!" I cried, gripping the couch. "Oh my God. Oh my God!"

I came hard, feeling like I couldn't breathe—but in the best way. As I began to scream, Cal pulled away, silencing me with a kiss. I moaned into his mouth as I came down, his right hand still rolling my nipple gently. I pulled back, eyes somehow heavy with overwhelm.

"I fucking *love* listening to you cum, Daphne. You're such a bad girl."

"I... oh... fuck." Nothing made sense. I was beyond help.

"What, princess? Cat got your tongue?"

I nodded.

Cal kissed me again as he bobbed me on his lap like a ragdoll. He used me, but I'd never felt so good about *being* used. I threw my head back, gripping his shoulders.

"You're going to cum again, aren't you?" Cal asked.

"Uh-huh," I panted, close again.

"You better go soon, Daph. Because with your tits in my face, I'm not going to last."

"Think of the Cubs or something," I said. "Think of them losing the playoffs."

"You're cruel, Daphne."

"Cruel or…" I was close. "Cruel or… realistic."

"I don't want realistic, Daphne. You're a fucking fantasy."

I found that hard to believe but very flattering. And the more I watched Cal watch me, the more I grasped he wanted me—this—more than ever before. I was a goddess suddenly in charge of her pleasure. I could use him as much as I wanted to get off. He handed me this in a way no one ever had.

"Oh, fuck," I moaned. "Oh, fuck! Fuck! Cal!"

"Yeah, cum for me, Daphne," Cal growled. "Make a mess for me, princess."

He drove me mad every time he called me princess. I was already too far gone, screaming for mercy to whatever God I prayed to. I dug my nails into his shoulders as Cal bobbed me and buried his face in my shoulder. As he came, I moved my hand to feel his heart racing. I'd done that to him. I'd unwound him.

Cal smiled. "Daph, you are… fucking amazing. It was just as good as I remember it being."

"You… remember it?"

"You don't?" He looked offended.

I giggled. "I do. I tried not to for years. But… I did."

Cal smacked my ass. "Let me take care of this. Jesus, woman. You're too much."

23.OLD HABITS

Cal

I HEADED HOME SUNDAY MORNING, NOT WANTING TO LEAVE Daphne. She waved goodbye from her front door, wearing little more than short-shorts and a tank top. I hated to leave her. We spent the weekend in bed scheming about the list of people she needed to court if she wanted to shake up the C-suite.

As I returned to Chicago, all chaos broke loose. Once in my apartment, Kristy texted an SOS.

KRISTY

I am so sorry to ask but can you take Laurie
for a couple of hours?

The baby? Why would she ask me that?

ME

Why? What do you need to do?

KRISTY

I have to run my sister to urgent care. And I don't want to expose her to whatever ick is there. Can you take her? I can drop her off with everything she needs.

I don't have anyone else to call, Cal. I'm sorry.

How was it that Kristy had a boyfriend, but I was her fall-back? Sadly, I wanted to help Kristy and remained a sucker for a happy, fat baby. So, I gave in. I had no idea what I did, but I was doing my best to try to help her. She'd been there for me when I needed her.

ME

Fine. I can take her for a bit if you bring her here.

Kristy appeared twenty minutes later, handing the baby off with a very full diaper bag. I was left staring at a bright-eyed little human who rolled around on my floor, delighted to eat her own toes.

"You are very awake," I noted. "And very happy."

Laurie smiled, then giggled adorably, rolling over and kicking her legs. When my doorbell rang, I turned on the TV to catch up on a cable show. Assuming it was Kristy, I hoisted the baby and proceeded to the buzzer.

Albert, the front desk guy, said, "Sir, Miss Markham is down here requesting to speak to you."

"My sister?"

"Yes, sir."

"Uh… send her up," I sighed.

Before too long, my sister appeared clad in a bright pink dress and heels a mile high.

"Chloe, what the hell?" I asked.

"Why are you holding *a baby?*" Chloe tossed her handbag onto my kitchen island. "Do you have a love child, Cal?"

"God, no!" I said. "This is Kristy's baby."

Chloe approached, looking at Laurie like she was observing a rare specimen. "Nope. She doesn't look like yours."

"Chloe, she's not mine. Kristy used a sperm donor. I was *not* the donor."

Chloe shrugged and tossed her shoes aside, losing half a foot in height.

"What are you up to?"

"I went to a polo match, but I got bored. You said you wanted to talk, but we were out of town all weekend in some mysterious place. What do you want to talk about?"

I returned to my living room and sat the baby down. Chloe plopped on the couch beside me.

"Why is the baby here? Are you and Kristy—"

"No. She had to run her sister to urgent care. Something about needing stitches or something."

"Oh. Well, she's fucking adorable."

"She is, yeah," I said while the baby rolled to Chloe, blowing bubbles. "Reminds me of you at that age, kid."

"What do you need, big brother?" Chloe groaned.

"Uh… I need you to become my proxy."

"For what?"

"For my shares in Delphine Holdings. David left me shares, but I cannot exercise them as the mayor. I have a huge conflict of interest. I want you to take them over."

Chloe giggled. "Why? What?"

"Because I trust you to represent my interests. And… I think you and Daphne are about to fuck shit up."

"How?"

"Well, it's a little complicated, but Davey is running the company into the ground and refuses to listen to Daphne."

"What, Davey being a chode? Never!" Chloe laughed.

"He needs to be taken down a peg."

"So, how did you hear this hot dish? Lanie has said *nothing*."

"I heard it from Daphne. Long story."

Chloe raised her eyebrows and tilted her head. "Are you… the two of you?"

"What? No!" I lied.

"Uh-huh. I *totally* buy that."

"That is a *ridiculous* idea."

"Yep. Ridiculous." Chloe looked at her nails, then playfully blew a raspberry at Laurie.

How does she know?

"You're an idiot. All men are fucking idiots! Cal, you spent the entire gala talking to her—hanging on her every word. And yes, she looked *impeccable*, but how you looked at her pained everyone around you. You got it *bad* for her."

"She's too young for me, and she's David's daughter."

"Yes, because any of that matters when she's over the age of thirty and your bestie is dead. What is he going to do, reanimate and come cut off your balls? Get over yourself. Fuck her or don't, but if you don't, you're stupid. She's hot and needs a rebound, so you should hit it."

Chloe stood.

"Chloe, I… I don't know what to say."

"You don't have to. I know how it is. I'll take your shares. When you want to talk about the next steps, contact me. I'm off to London next week, though."

"Cool," I said. It was not cool. I didn't know what to say. "It has to go through probate. Then, when it is, I will let you know."

She saluted, picked up her shoes, popped her handbag under her arm, and vanished. I'd never understand Chloe.

She was more aberration than person. She appeared and disappeared when she wanted, not when you asked.

I looked at Laurie. "Kid, if you haven't guessed, my life is a disaster."

She gave me a two-tooth grin and babbled before forcing her entire hand into her mouth. I turned my attention back to the television, relaxing while Laurie gnawed on her chubby hands and feet.

After a couple of hours, two diapers, and a bottle later, Kristy arrived back at my place. Kristy's presence delighted the baby, who screamed for her mother.

"How did she even know it was you?" I asked.

"Oh, she can smell me. It's milk. She won't calm down unless I leave the house sometimes."

Kristy picked the baby up, kissed her on the cheek and settled on the couch.

"So, how is Preston or whatever his name is?"

Kristy scoffed. "Paul. His name is Paul, Cal. And he's in New York."

"Ah. Does he watch Laurie a lot?"

"No," Kristy answered. "He has no clue about children. I have struggled to let him have any contact with her without me right there. Call it mom guilt or anxiety or whatever."

"And yet… you're desperate enough to leave her with me."

Kristy shook her head. "Cal, you're different. I've known you forever, and I trust you."

"You don't trust Paul?" I raised my eyebrows.

"It's… we aren't there yet, okay. I trusted you once with my medical directives. Paul is new. And we're not exclusive or… anything."

"Ah."

"So, you know, you shouldn't feel *guilty* if—"

I shook my head and moved away. "Kristy, please tell me you aren't coming onto me."

"He's been out of town for a week, and it could be fun, Cal."

"There is a baby involved," I said. "And that is enough to tell me no."

"I'm still a sexual being, Cal. Don't act so opposed. You fucked me when I was pregnant—"

I cleared my throat. "Yeah, well, that was *different*. My circumstances alone have changed."

"Oh… are you *with* someone?"

How did I answer that? Was I honest?

"It's new, but yes," I said. "And even though we're not exclusive, I'm not that guy, Kristy. And I don't like to share. You *know* that."

Kristy sighed. "I know. Monogamy is *boring*, Cal."

"Well, so sue me. I am a boring old man, Kris."

She smiled. "That's fair. I wish you the best. Let me guess, she's younger?"

I snickered. "What? You really think I am looking for someone younger."

"Well, I was. So, no shade."

I rolled my eyes. "She's a bit younger than you."

8 years your junior. Thirteen years younger than I am.

"Knew it! But are you having fun?"

"Yes, Kristy."

"Am I freaking you out?"

"Very much so," I said. "I am… not at all ready for this."

"That's fair. I will take this little bug out of your hair. Thanks again. I promise not to—"

"It's okay." I smiled. "I do not mind her at all. She's pretty sweet."

24.COUPLES WEEKEND

Daphne

WHEN SARAH ASKED ME TO VISIT IN TRAVERSE CITY FOR THE weekend, I grudgingly agreed to drive four hours north. Traverse City was lovely, but I suspected there was more to this request than a weekend at their family's sprawling lake house. No sooner had I arrived than I realized everyone was paired. No amount of fresh lake views and winery tours could make up for the awkwardness—not even the relatively handsome offering that I was immediately introduced to.

Sarah pulled me over to a man wearing khaki shorts and a blue t-shirt. He had a baby face, but his wrinkles suggested he wasn't all that young. We were probably well-matched in age. He was handsome but short and slender—not my type.

"Daphne, this is Ken. And Ken, this is Daphne, my cousin. Daphne, Ken is an attorney—just like you."

So was Chandler. I swore I'd never date another attorney.

Smiling weakly, I extended my hand. "Super nice to meet you."

Ken gave a firm handshake. "And you. All Sarah says

about you is that you are smart, and she's so excited you're back in the States."

"I would selfishly love to give her a reason to stay *permanently*." Sarah winked.

Fighting an eyeroll, I smiled slightly and sipped wine.

"Okay, wine tour in ten!" Erik announced. "We're waiting on one more."

I wanted to die. Instead, I visited the cheese plate.

"They go all out, don't they?" Ken asked nervously.

"They do, yeah," I agreed. "Sarah's mother is very theatrical. She gets it from her. Erik is also a social butterfly. This is how they've always been. How do you know them?"

"Horton and Newland works with us sometimes," Ken said of Erik's firm. "And I golf with Erik a lot. My ex knew Sarah first, ironically."

I looked around, concerned.

"I got the friends in the divorce. You can calm down," Ken joked.

"I get it. I am… still trying to figure all of that out. Thankfully, most of my close friends are my sisters and cousins. That's the nature of a big Catholic family."

"You're recently divorced?"

"Divorc-ing. He's also a barrister—in the UK."

"Ah, well fuck. That is *rough*. My apologies. We're the worst people to divorce."

"Your ex is a lawyer?"

"Nah. Yoga teacher."

Well, there was *no* way this worked. She had to be some nubile waif of a girl. I was *not* that woman.

"It gets easier," Ken insisted.

I nodded, unsure what to say. My divorce was one thing. This experience was another. Whenever I visited a winery, I thought about our dad's deep interest in our own. If I thought too hard, I'd start crying. I had yet to go to our family's winemaking operation. Mum encouraged me, but it was too painful. Some of my best memories were of harvest time. It felt so free and calm. It felt so *normal*. And now? Now, it felt too vulnerable and nostalgic. I wasn't ready. Today would be rough.

"Thanks," I said instead.

"Hey! Mr. Mayor! Making us late!" Erik declared loudly over the din of adult conversation.

I stared over, heart stopping, and made full-on eye contact with Cal Markham. Between the rolled-up shirt-sleeves and his excellent stubble, I could not look away. I only envisioned the look he gave me when he ducked between my thighs and ate me out. One weekend of debauchery stirred up so many big feelings—a continuation of the things I felt for weeks after the first time he had me. The sexual chemistry was unmatched, but I wouldn't risk a hookup here.

"And Cal joins us," Ken sounded happy. "Do you know Cal?"

"Cal was one of my father's best friends," I said. "I am well acquainted with Cal."

I tried not to stare as Sarah introduced Cal to the only other single at the party—a socialite. She and Cal were well-matched. She was pretty, tall, and had shiny chestnut hair. They made a *much* more handsome couple than we ever would.

"Let's round up and head out!" Erik declared.

We piled into the waiting limo bus for our multi-stop wine tour. I decided it was time to get drunk. If I was to survive watching Cal flirt with this brunette and as I pretended to care about Ken—a lovely man I wasn't interested in—I would need something to dull the pain. I listened to Ken carry the conversation, talking about Big Law and his partnership buy-in. I couldn't have cared less if I tried. I was so over work talk, and sad I missed that key part of my own life.

We filed out to the first winery for a tasting of primarily dry wines.

"Bone dry. Your favorite," I heard over my shoulder.

Turning, I spotted Cal.

"You are correct."

"So, you were offered up to the Ken Doll," Cal said.

"And you are the match for Brunette Barbie, Cal."

Cal, breath hot on my neck, whispered. "Not interested. I should be grateful for being forced into this pity-arrangement, but all I can think about is watching you cum."

Fuck. Why did he do this? Why did he constantly torture me?

"We cannot…" I lowered my voice. "We cannot *do* this, Cal. This is not something—"

"You're going to tell me we'll spend the whole weekend *not* doing anything?"

I swiveled, needing to face him. "Do you want to risk this, Cal?"

"I shouldn't, but damn, I want to."

I rolled my eyes. "You are barking up the wrong tree, Mr. Mayor."

"And your resolve will weaken, princess. Mark my words."

* * *

Cal

At the third winery, we were treated to wine amid fruit bushes. Daphne immediately decided to thwart less-than-stellar wine and beelined it for the berry baskets the owners offered. I could see the wheels turning as she went to hunt blueberries on her lonesome. She needed a break. I saw an opportunity and followed her with a basket into the field.

It took me a minute to find her. She loaded her basket with blueberries.

"I knew I'd find you out here," I said.

Daphne said. "Blueberries are the best, okay? The Riesling was a grave disappointment, however."

I tasted a berry. "So, how do these rate?"

"I prefer the ones at our farmstand."

"You're quite the critic, Ms. Delphine."

"I know better. Can you blame me? Why drink shitty light beer when you can drink Blanc de Blancs?"

How she pursed her lips made me want to do everything to her. Why did she tempt me so much when she looked like this and spoke her mind so freely?

"I would only want the best champagne if I could have it."

"And why can't you, Cal?" Daphne slowly ate a blueberry, never dropping eye contact.

"You tell me, Daphne," I growled, pulling her towards me.

She gazed at me, green eyes boring into my soul.

"You really cannot resist me, Daph," I ran my thumb over her chin and lower lip.

As if out of a fantasy, Daphne took my hand, sucking my finger. Now, rock hard in public, I knew better than to do anything. I also wanted to fuck her and wasn't going to have an easy time beating down my impulse to run her off to any place at all.

Daphne let my finger go. "You're hard, Cal, aren't you?"

I pressed her hand against my erection. "Yeah. You did that. You're just going to torture me?"

"Cal, we're in public!" Daphne scoffed, pulling her hand back. "This is fun, but—"

I pulled on the hem of her dress, running my hand up the

outside of her thigh. I whispered sweetly, "You don't want me —not at all."

She replied, "The vision of you eating me out on the kitchen island lives in my mind rent-free, but that's not what we're—"

She grew speechless as my fingers rubbed the side of her lacy panties.

I kissed her now, delighting in the vibration from her slight moan as I pulled her panties aside. She played coy, but the option to get off always won out with Daphne. She was easy to please and desperate for more.

"You want to cum on my fingers, baby?" I whispered.

"Yes," Daphne panted as I slipped two fingers, then three inside. "Oh, fuck."

"Yeah, you like that?"

"You're a bad boy."

"And you're a naughty girl, Daphne."

Her head fell back as my fingers dipped inside her, the same thumb she'd sucked on moments before slapping against her clit with every thrust. Daphne's hips couldn't have pressed harder against mine. I ran my left hand down her hips to her ass, allowing her to brace against me. She moaned louder.

"Quiet," I whispered. "You don't want to be discovered, do you?"

"Oh, God, Cal. You are *so, so* good."

"Yeah? Do you want to cum, princess? To make a mess?"

"I want to cum so badly," Daphne said breathlessly. "Please, Cal."

I wasn't one to deny her an orgasm. I persisted, kissing her again so she could stay quiet. I soon felt her pussy pulse around me as her nails dug into my shirt. She bit my lip, then pulled away, looking truly satisfied and a little deviant. I slid my fingers from her wet pussy, again denying my pleasure for hers.

"You really should stop coming onto me," Daphne whispered.

I reran my right hand over her chin, spreading her wetness as I did. I worried she might bristle, but she didn't. Instead, she again took my thumb in her mouth, sucking once more and never losing eye contact. It was the sexiest thing she ever did.

"You like that?" I asked.

"Uh-huh," Daphne replied.

"Good. Sit on my face later, and we'll call it even," I said, hoping to do much more.

25. ALL YOU NEED

Cal

It was late when Daphne and I finally found time to sneak down to her cousin's boathouse for a bit of fun. My supposed date decided to run off to bed with hers—perfect timing—leading us to play the sad loners. She "took a walk" while I turned in—only I couldn't turn in. I eventually followed her down to the boat house where she waited for me on a workbench, desperate for more.

I pulled her towards me and kissed her. I didn't need words. The desire on her face said everything. Each time we did this, I realized how compatible we were. Daphne knew what she wanted and I knew what she craved. I always gave her what she needed. Her moans and deep kisses said more than the sweetest prose.

"You remembered a condom, right?" Daphne gasped, pulling back.

"Yes," I said. "I put it in my wallet earlier."

After our bit of fun in the bushes, I'd decided my new thing was to pack condoms in my wallet. I wouldn't get caught without one again. It was odd that this was my arc in my late forties. After years of being partnered and exclusive, then incredibly single, it was about a decade since I'd needed to contemplate prophylactics. But, for Daphne, I'd come prepared.

"I swear I'll get on the pill, but I have to—"

"Shh," I cut her off. "Don't apologize. You don't need to feel bad for asking me to do the bare minimum to protect you."

I kissed her neck for a bit, delighting in the feeling of her rapid pulse against my lips.

"I don't want you to think I'm some sort of demanding bitch, Cal."

I stopped kissing her neck and stepped back slightly.

"I would never say that about you, Daphne. Never."

Daphne cocked her head. "Why? I mean, you could have—"

"I want *you*. I shouldn't, but I only want you," I said.

The words rolled out of my mouth, dropping like a bucket of water spilling into the lake. The water sloshed against the dock a few feet away as I waited silently for Daphne's reaction. She stared, befuddled. I'd just admitted this wasn't a game.

"I'm sorry," I shook my head. "I should go and—"

She grasped my wrist tight. "No, Cal, don't. I... I don't know what to say. I'm dumbfounded, not offended."

I curiously awaited an explanation.

"Cal, it has been years since anyone told me they wanted *only* me. I've spent years feeling compared to anything on two legs with big tits and a nice ass—anything in its twenties. You really *could* have anyone you wanted. You're Chicago's most eligible fucking bachelor. You're wealthy, powerful, and you have chemistry with a wall. Why me? I just... I don't know what to say."

"You don't buy it?" I cupped her face. "Daphne, you are so

beautiful. You're smart. Somewhere in there, you're driven beyond measure. Recently, I saw that spark return—the one that always impressed me. Where is that girl who had me so wrapped up eleven years ago—the one who drove me wild? Because I want her to stay here—to always come out and play."

"I… I am so broken right now, Cal. You cannot fix me."

I shook my head. "I don't want to. I don't need to. You're going to fix yourself over time, Daph. I will be there for you while you do. You need space and time and I can give you that. I can also promise you as much attention as you'd let me lavish you with."

"Why, though?"

"I don't fucking know. I know what you need. I read you. And damn if you don't give me everything I want right now."

Tears welled. I didn't know what to do. She was *crying?*

"I… fuck… I'm sorry. You… no one has said anything like that to me in like… a million years. I don't deserve this."

"Daphne, you deserve *everything*. After what you've been through, you deserve to be treated like a queen," I protested. "And maybe I cannot give you enough. Lord knows I'm complicated and this is messy as hell."

"It really is!" Daphne giggled.

"But could I try? Would you let me try?"

I pressed my forehead to hers, our noses touching and listened to her breath. She brought herself back to earth. Her hands softened in mine and her body relaxed. The anxiety of the moment abated. I kissed her forehead. In the moment again, Daphne squeezed my hands and met my gaze.

"Cal, I cannot promise you much. I'm looking down the nose of a complicated divorce, my family would flip the fuck out of we ended up together, and I don't think the press would look kindly on it."

"Let me worry about that," I said. "And… we can keep this under wraps for a bit. I promise you."

"Okay," Daphne agreed with a little nod.

"I want to try, Daphne. That's all."

She slowly kissed me, offering me something—though neither of us could name what—then wrapped her arms around my neck. I pulled her to the very edge of the bench, again pulling her skirt up. She had no panties on.

"No panties?" I joked.

"I tossed them… earlier. They were a disaster after our little run-in. And, I wanted to be practical."

"You are such a bad girl," I said.

Daphne bit my lip as she unbuckled my belt. "And you love it when I lose it."

"I do," I pulled out my wallet.

The definite sound of my zipper stiffened my cock. I tossed my wallet and phone on the bench. I ripped the condom open hastily as she efficiently tugged my pants and boxers down. I rolled the condom over my cock as Daphne kissed me. Slowly, I pressed its head against her entrance. She moaned into my mouth and clasped her legs tight around mine, pulling me in deep.

It was a sweet relief to be back inside her. I'd enjoy getting her off again—this time feeling her pussy pulse around my cock. Pumping—each thrust making her breath more ragged—I took her in. She glowed in the boathouse's low light. Daphne was such a beauty, even if she didn't know it. I pulled down the straps of her dress and bit her right shoulder.

"Cal," she gasped. "What are you doing?"

I pulled the top of her dress down, revealing her pretty pink nipples. Her breasts were perfect. I had no idea why anyone would want more than this—more than she was and more than I deserved. I played with her nipples with a gentle roll of my fingers. Torturing Daphne was my favorite thing these days.

"I wanted to see you. And you're not wearing a bra."

"It has a built-in—"

Daphne moaned and threw her head back. She braced against the workbench with her wrists. She never finished the sentence.

She screamed, "Oh, God! Fuck! Cal, don't… don't… stop!"

She climaxed. Her eyes rolled back as she tightened, pulsing and writhing. I thrust harder and faster, a rush of energy hitting. Every time I unraveled her, I felt like I punched a card. Someday, I told myself, I'd feel like enough for her if I could just keep bringing her to this place.

"You are so good at that." Daphne returned to the surface, breathless.

"Yeah?" I panted. "You liked that?"

"It's so good. Your cock feels so fucking good!" Daphne dug her hands into my lower back to steady me.

I thrust more erratically until the urge to let go was inevitable. I came—falling against her shoulder and breathing into her neck.

"You're unmatched," I whispered. "In a league of your own, princess."

* * *

Daphne

Cal bit my ear and pulled away. I couldn't fight the urge to kiss him again. Every time I brought him to orgasm it felt better. I mystified him in a way I never had with my ex-husband. It was so hot to watch this powerful man descend into glorious pleasure under my spell.

Cal stepped back, sliding out, still erect. I tried to fix

myself up and look less like a total disaster. However, as I pulled my dress up and covered my breasts again, I looked over to see Cal's panicked face.

"Daph, I… uh… I'm sorry."

"What?" I asked.

"The condom broke."

"What?"

In all my years, I never had this happen.

"Yeah, it's… shit."

He grabbed a shop towel to wrap up what was left of the condom, then tucked his deflating dick back into his boxers. He pulled up his pants as I sat, stunned and in disbelief.

"Well, I need to get Plan B," I said. "Cal, I'm not on the pill at all."

"I am well aware. I don't want you to panic or think I'm not… supportive."

"Cal, this is *not* the time for me to be pregnant—not that it probably matters. At this point, I'm fucking doomed."

"I doubt that. You're still young, Daph. You still have time. I'm the old fuck. And that's for the best, right?"

I shrugged. "It's still in the realm of possibility."

"I'll go into town to grab you Plan B tomorrow," Cal offered.

"That's silly. If you get found out, it won't be good. I will do it. If the press—"

"Shh," he pressed a finger to my lips. "The press this, the press that. I get it. You're right. My goose *would* be cooked if things came out and we didn't have time to massage the details but let me be clear. My concern about this is for you—not my image."

"Maybe you should be more concerned about that, Cal." I shook my head.

There was a buzz on the table. I looked over to see Cal's phone.

"Someone called The Boss is calling you?" I said, confused.

"Oh, fuck. I shouldn't—"

"Answer it," I said, suspecting this person would *keep* calling him.

Cal complied, picking up the call. "Yes, Jo?"

He listened for a moment, then rubbed his temples. "Right now? You realize I'm in Traverse City, right?"

This was work-related. I could smell it. And it wasn't new. I'd been deserted over far less by Chandler. I wouldn't have minded it so much if I wasn't also possibly just inseminated by a man who had no claim to me and wasn't obligated to stick around. My skin crawled at the idea that I could have suffered five long years of infertility, only to get pregnant in my cousin's boathouse with a man I shouldn't want. Shame hit me like waves swallowed a lighthouse.

"Yeah, okay. I will call a car or something. Get me a flight, okay? Thanks."

He hung up. "That's my chief of staff. We have an issue with a police officer."

I sensed he couldn't say more.

"Daph, I am so sorry. I feel like a total dickhead leaving you to deal with this."

"It's… it comes with the territory, alright? I can handle it. I'm a big girl. Go deal with your chaos, Mr. Mayor."

He shook his head, then gave me a long kiss. "Let's talk when you get back. Let me know if you need something. I'll miss you, Daphne. I'm sorry."

"Don't apologize," I said. "Shit happens."

It did, but seeing him rush away so soon after this incident felt lousy. It gave me pause. Could I ever rely on Cal to just *be there?*

26. THE PILL

Daphne

The day after the boathouse incident, I feigned period cramps and rushed to the pharmacy for supplies. When my pain supposedly got "too bad", I elected to drive home, and no one stopped me. On the six-hour drive back, I fought terrible cramps but thankfully no bleeding. My period was due in a week and now began the countdown in hopes it just *happened*. I'd waited years to see happy, positive lines on a test, but this wasn't the time. I padded upstairs and threw myself into bed.

I avoided my mother, who would leave early for Lake Geneva the next morning with friends. Next, I booked an appointment with a concierge women's health service. After talking to the doctor about my options, I felt better. She assured me I did the right thing. Since my cycle was regular, I was unlikely to have conceived so late. I knew this, but it confirmed things. She wrote me a script, and I went home in a better mood. I left to get groceries.

Returning, things fell off the rails. My mother left a note.

Daphne,

I did not go to Lake Geneva. Patty fell ill, so we are taking a raincheck. I will be home for dinner.

Great. I pulled out my laptop and watched reality tv, spit balling how I'd get out of it. I scrolled until I saw what Cal was dealing with on the front page of the *Chicago Daily Tribune.*

The Mayor's Office and Chief of Police have different versions of what happens next. Following the elevated response to an assumed school shooting at Roosevelt High School, Mayor Markham's office believed a tape should be released for the purposes of public transparency. However, the police union and Chicago Police Department refuse to release the footage. Evaluating this, it appears Mr. Markham's office is outhorsed. Inside sources suggest tackling policing will be more difficult than expected.

As I finished reading, Mum appeared.

"Things are hairy out there," she gasped. "Don't go. I predict there will be demonstrations."

"What is this about?" I asked, concerned.

"Cal's office is—along with Black leaders—demanding they release a tape. There was a school shooting just before your father's death. CPD made it sound very dangerous. They used tear gas and rubber bullets on students. Well, they *say* it was a shooting, but I'd say it was a student who brought a toy gun to school to appear cool. The boy was wounded, but teachers said he did not appear to wish harm on anyone. Other students said they felt *less* safe after CPD's response— not more."

"So, Cal inherited this?"

"He did. And he ran on a reform platform, so good luck to him," Mum sighed. "It will be a mess. Bishop Yates is going to hold his feet to the flames."

I winced. "He should, but that sucks for Cal."

My parents and Bishop Yates, a social justice leader on

the South Side, formed an alliance in charity work. Mum thought the world of him. Yates was generally good-natured, but I suspected he had a big hand in getting Cal elected and wasn't afraid to hold him accountable.

Mum rolled her eyes. "It does. CPD is corrupt. They are goons. At least the administration is. I suspect the Chief will be sacked—as he should be—but only after people march."

"That's awful."

"The good news is, I was able to get us some essentials and pick up your prescription from the chemist. I needed to fill my migraine medication, after all."

I panicked.

"Is there anything you need to *tell* me, Daphne?" Mum asked with a sly smile.

"Why?" I wondered.

"I know what the tablets are. They are birth control. Lanie was on them for enough years."

Lanie was the first to go on the pill before leaving the house. Dahlia only dated girls—even if she wasn't *out* yet. I was a late bloomer. Lanie didn't subscribe to Catholic guilt. She and Mum went round about it for ages before Dad told Mum to back off and Lanie got her pills. I would have stepped in to mail them if need be. The last thing I wanted was for my baby sister to end up pregnant at sixteen.

"I don't need the guilt, Mum. People are on them for a *variety* of reasons."

"Yes, well, Daphne, I doubt that is what this is."

I sighed. "Mother, I have a right to privacy—"

"I know. But I want you to know that… you're a grown woman. I am not here to judge if you have a man interested in you. All I ask is that I meet him and approve of him before he starts sleeping over."

"I sincerely doubt that will be a thing, mother," I protested. "I'm just… prepared."

"So, there is no man?" Mum looked disappointed.

"There is a man. It's not a big deal. I don't want to talk about it. He also owns a place and lives alone, so I don't see us retreating to my childhood bedroom."

I suspected the very idea of fucking me in my childhood bedroom would turn Cal off. Or maybe it wouldn't? Was that a kink for men? I didn't know. What I *did* know was that I was not going to make Cal do a walk of shame from our house in the morning and risk getting caught on camera.

"Well, if it happened, that's all I asked. You have a whole wing of the house to yourself and are a grown woman."

"Yes, I've already been sullied by the atrocity of divorce—"

"Daphne, I don't think like that," Mum said. "You always assume I am fanatical. Maybe I was close-minded with you and Davey. You were so young even then. But when Dahlia told us who she was, we realized we didn't have all the answers. I don't agree with everything the church does, alright? What worked in *our* marriage wouldn't work in yours. Neither of us was saintly. I took time for so much introspection in your father's last months. I got therapy, alright? And, darling… I wish you would, too."

I looked out the window, shaking my head.

"Daphne, I have grown. I know it will take time for you to bloody well believe me. That's fair, but I'm not here to judge you. Father Tony isn't, either, sweetheart. You are welcome anytime at mass. I would love for you to go with me."

I sighed. "Mother, I wasn't even married in the church. You only want me to do this for you. I cannot take communion—"

"I am aware," Mum said. "But it gets lonely."

"You aren't lonely. *I* am lonely. Church won't fix that."

"Sweetheart, I am so lonely. I miss Daddy every day. I come home to a silent house and it feels so awful. I sit in a pew all alone. I know you have lives. And I know this situation doesn't please you, but… I was hoping maybe I would get to know you again. You've changed. I want to know the grown-up Daphne. We were never close. You were your father's child, but I need you, Daphne."

She longed to connect. I forgot she could feel isolated. I had only seen her go, go, go after Dad died. Even when I wanted to lie in bed and cry, she was at the gym or seeing friends. But it was all a distraction. She did these things to occupy her time. It validated me to hear she wanted to see me—really see me.

"I will try," I said. "Look, I know you say it's chaotic, but I think I feel good enough to duck down to the store. I can make us some dinner, okay?"

"That would be nice," Mum agreed. "I would like that."

"And… about therapy," I said. "You're right. I do need to see someone. Dahlia and Lanie keep harping on me. They're right. I didn't know you were seeing someone. That's a good thing, I guess. It's brave, Mum."

She smiled. "It's smart, not brave. And as clever as you are, sweetheart, I am sure you will find the right person to talk to soon."

27. THE PROTEST

Cal

"You don't want to say anything to your sister?" Mother demanded, harsh.

"Mother, what Chloe does is up to Chloe."

"You didn't arrange this?"

"I cannot tell Chloe what to do, Mom. Honestly. She is out there protesting and engaging with people her age. While her politics and mine align, I have not coached her or asked her. She has not talked to me. You know how she is. I know more about her life on social media than I do from anything she says to me."

"I hate that part," Mom said.

"Chloe is her own woman. I am not getting involved. I don't even have *time,* Mom. I'm headed to a charity event."

We were deep in the middle of a days-long protest hoping to smoke out our police chief while watching people tie up Lakeshore Drive in a fit of rage. Deep down, it pleased me to see people like Chloe—privileged people who could otherwise ignore these problems—were out walking with protestors who felt their lives were at risk daily. Citizen protests were the only way I saw my administration's path changing in its relationship with law enforcement. To date, the protests had been organized and largely nonviolent, but something had to give. Everyone felt the tension.

"Fine. But I don't like it."

I rolled my eyes.

Jo stood before me; arms folded in annoyance. I was running late.

"I gotta go."

"Don't get hurt," Mom said.

"I am a big boy. I can handle it."

I hung up, tucking my phone in a tuxedo jacket pocket.

"You know, I'm all dressed up, looking like a million bucks, and waiting on your ass to get off the phone," Jo said.

"I know. My mother is panicked over Chloe. And yes, you clean up nice."

"That girl is pigheaded, but she's right," Jo said as we boarded the elevator. "Doesn't your mother want to be on the right side of it?"

"She doesn't want her friends bothered because Chloe stands for something."

"You ran a reform campaign and were always surrounded by Black folks. I'm not sure what else there is to say. Did she forget about that?"

I snickered. "Mom gave up on me being chill long ago, but we're different. Chloe is her precious angel baby who had everything from day one. I had to be tough. She wants Chloe to have it easy. Yes, there is some implicit bias there, but Mom's main point is, why fight so hard when I ran so you could walk? And why not make money with all that privilege?"

"Must be nice to be a rich white lady."

"It's easy," I admitted. "To be white, I mean. Now, what do I need to know about this event?"

"Alderman Lewis sees this as the crowning jewel of his summer, Cal. The charity raises money for summer camp, but it's his pet project. Make an effort. Write a check. Make nice with organizers. It's the same game it always is."

I zoned out, going to my Making Nice place. Deep down, I wanted to refresh my browser nonstop to see if the union or chief had news. I wanted him to step down. It's what the community needed. It's also what *I* politically required to get the council to change the appointment rules. Despite the stress, this was a convenient way to press my agenda.

We arrived at the venue for the banquet shortly after it began. I was never early—always late, but not in a rude way. I gave good face—something David taught me. He thrived on social interaction and I always led with that. We had been so alike in that way. Danna could be an ice queen, but David had to be personable. I never understood how it worked. It just *did*. I wondered if I would ever have someone in my corner to settle me as she did.

As we entered, I spotted Daphne at the bar. I knew her wild blonde hair a mile away. She left it down, as I liked it. I approached, ignoring Jo's pleas to beeline it to the host and I spotted a bejeweled clip she'd used to tuck hair behind her ear. The urge to kiss her and pull the hair at the base of her head overcame me. I smelled her perfume before she saw me —floral and sweet. She was sexy as hell in a pink gown that accentuated her round, firm ass.

"Hi," I said. "You're here."

"I came with Mum," Daphne answered. "She said she was lonely. I'm trying to be supportive. Of course, she's ditched me for a friend."

I chuckled. "That's how I always feel escorting my mother or sister anywhere."

"Well, I am glad to see you," I spotted Jo's annoying waves from the left of Daphne's head.

"I'm… I'll be back. I'm sorry. Jo is about to land a fucking plane over there. I have to go see the alderman."

"Got it," Daphne said. "It's okay."

The way she smiled melted me. The urge to kiss her grew stronger. Her gorgeous green eyes begged for more. I couldn't do it, though—not here.

"I will be back. Promise," I said.

I stepped to where Jo stood.

She pulled me in, "Is there something you want to tell me about Daphne Delphine?"

I did a double take.

"The minute you could, you went straight to her—"

"She's just a friend," I lied.

"Well, I will remind you that you're making a speech at the DNC in a couple of months—the speech to end all speeches. I busted my ass to help get you the keynote. The last thing that people want right now is to see you with a much-younger woman who isn't even divorced and is the daughter of your notable dead best friend."

I winced. "I am doing my best to keep it under wraps."

"Mind yourself. Keep it quiet for now."

She knew me too well. I worried that if Jo already knew, other people were soon behind. She was right. This was about to be my moment. Any concerns about conflicts of interest, would wait.

* * *

Daphne

I watched Cal work the room like a champ. I knew how to be a politician's wife. I was used to being left to my own devices

—as I had for the best part of the decade. This was different, though. I was the girlfriend no one knew about. It felt a little shameful, but a lot hot. I only agreed to attend for the chance to see Cal in a tuxedo.

When Cal returned, he looked winded and needed a drink.

"Need something to wet your whistle?" I joked.

"I'm so parched," Cal admitted. "All the talking, you know?"

"I do," I said. I didn't want to admit how much I knew.

We approached the bar where I ordered another gin and tonic. He took a glass of champagne and took a long sip.

He kept his voice low, "You look downright stunning, Daph."

I blushed.

"Don't play coy. You *know* how good you look."

"I'm… well, glad you like the dress."

"I do. But it's not the dress. It's everything."

"I had a minor win today," I admitted. "That is giving me some encouragement."

"What is that?"

I nodded toward a woman in an expensive lace shawl. "Carlos and Caroline Menendez are interested in my luxury-focused concept. Thanks for giving me that heads up."

Cal beamed. "That is great to hear. I want a full report later."

My face dropped as I thought about *later*.

"What, Daph?"

"Later in a biblical sense, right?"

Cal sighed and looked around. "I don't want that, Daph. Let's say later as in… well, when can you get away?"

"Cal, you have a shit ton of—"

"Daph, when? I owe you given my rude departure last weekend—"

I took a deep breath. "I could get away tonight. Mum knows I'm seeing someone."

"How?"

"She found my pills."

"Pills?" Confusion spread.

I rolled my eyes.

"Oh, *those* pills," Cal got it. "Ah. Well, does she know—"

"I'm not daft, Cal. She has no clue who it is. She thinks he's a stranger. All she knows is that I have no intention of bringing him back home to North Astor Street."

"Good," Cal said. "Things are more fun on Superior. I will be here another couple of hours—mostly circulating. I'm not ignoring you. It pains me even to contemplate that. I'll text you, but it's not just… well, I want to hear about everything."

"Okay," I agreed. "I'll try."

I longed for him to brush my lips with his thumb the way he did or to kiss me gently. I wanted him to acknowledge me —really show that he was here for me. Instead, Cal faded into the background. As I watched him disappear to do his job, I spotted my mother on the other side of the bar.

I approached, sick of standing awkwardly alone.

"Mum," I said. "I'm going to head out later tonight."

"For what?"

"I have a date," I said. "Sort of last minute."

"A date? Still to come?" Disapproval spread.

"Yeah. He's still at work, but I want to see him," I said. "I am going to go to his. Don't stay up. I just wanted to let you know I'm not going anywhere yet."

She nodded. "Well, at least he has a job. A real one, right?"

"A real job, yes."

My mother was convinced politicians didn't *actually* work. She saw it as a silly job that made no money—likely because Chandler never made any and he never did much other than politicking. Unfortunately, Cal *was* a politician.

But he didn't need my money and was currently trying very hard to hold a machine city's police union accountable for endemic policing issues.

"Alright, well, don't do anything stupid. Ring me if it goes south," Mum said.

"I will."

28. SQUEAMISH

Daphne

At Cal's building, I was immediately permitted to go to the elevator that granted penthouse access. It wasn't unusual for people to recognize me, but it was odd to see Cal's security guards jump at attention to direct me to his floor. I sensed he'd explained how important I was to him, which warmed my heart and made me feel less like a girl going for a booty call.

The elevator doors opened to Cal drinking a beer at his kitchen island. He was still in his tux pants and shirt, but he'd tossed aside his jacket and tie. His shirt sleeves were rolled in a way that made me find him irresistible. Sadly, I was nervous to report my bit of news that was sure to halt this fun.

"Hi," I said. "Your door guys are really on it."

"I told them to expect you," Cal said. "You took the dress off."

"Long story," I winced. "Besides, if I am going to leave here on a walk of shame tomorrow, I won't want to do it in an evening gown."

"Good point." Cal paused, then pulled my chin towards his lips.

He leaned, planting the sweetest kiss. I lost myself again, intoxicated with the way he made me feel.

Casually, he asked, "You want a beer?"

"Uh, sure," I answered. "Why not?"

Cal opened a pilsner from a local brewery and handed it over. "Summer beer, you know?"

I sipped. "It works."

"So, do you have enough votes yet?" Cal got down to brass tax.

"I think I will as long as your guy comes through."

"My guy will strike as soon as probate signs off. Don't move before," Cal said. "And my guy isn't a guy."

"Can you introduce me to them?"

"I can set up a meeting soon," Cal said. "I want to be mindful of how this all works."

"I understand. The Menendezes are good. They want to see the store go back to a luxury op. I am designing a full business plan for my board deck."

"So, you know what you're asking for?"

"I want to be named president. I am going to give David the chance to do that. If not, we'll go to the board. But I don't want anyone in the family to say I railroaded or humiliated him. I will broach it when the time is right."

"Hopefully, I'm through probate soon," Cal said.

"I have your watch in my room. It's in my safe," I said. "Once it's done, I will bring it to you."

Cal pulled me close again, kissing my forehead. "It's okay, I'm more worried about you."

"Me?"

"This is a lot, Daphne. And I know you said you were dealing with your attorney—"

"Chandler is a dick," I sighed. "But I've known that for going on fifteen years. It's fine. I'm okay."

"And… the pills?" Cal asked.

"Ah, that. Well, I'm starting them, seeing as how my body has picked *this evening* to spot and have a period. I'm not pregnant. So, stop worrying about a love child with a Delphine overshadowing your mayoral tenure."

Cal's brow furrowed, as if I struck him. "Daphne, I wasn't worried about that. I was worried about *you*. My concerns were for you—not my hide."

"Be that as it may—"

He cut me off. "No. Daph, you're the one I care about here. I can take things on the chin. I don't need you to worry about me. I'm a big boy. You're the one with a bunch of simultaneous storms overhead."

"Cal, you have protests—"

"And they benefit me politically. Chloe is out there marching. If I felt concerned about it, I would have called her home. Not that she'd listen, but I would *try*. I'm not worried about it. Yes, it's stressful and there's a lot of chess maneuvering, but I was mostly worried about you thinking I was a fucking asshole."

I smiled slightly. "No. I didn't. And now, we won't have to worry if it happens again, okay?"

Cal took my beer, setting it on the counter beside his own. He kissed me once more, enveloping me in his arms. As his tongue tangled with mine, my whole body tingled. I wanted him to run me to the bed and do everything to me. Unfortunately, that would *not* be happening. I had to push him away before things got too out of hand.

"Cal, I told you… I am on my period," I said.

"And?"

"Well, we should wait."

"That doesn't bother me unless it bothers you."

I stared in disbelief.

"What? Did you see a ghost? Did I overstep?"

"No. I just…" I shook my head, voice trailing. "Never mind."

He ran his fingers through my hair. "Daph, I've waited too long. I want to please you, to unwind you, and, unlike last time, to hold you."

He said all the right things to make me want him.

"It's going to be a murder scene."

"It won't be that bad," Cal laughed. "Come on, princess. Let me get you off."

I trusted him. He'd done this before—somehow. I undressed, tossed my tampon, and climbed onto the towels he'd laid on his bed. Usually, I'd be too embarrassed to try this, but Cal piqued my curiosity.

I lay there vulnerable, but feeling safe as he slid a condom over the head of his penis and down the shaft. He gently pinned me to the bed, kissing my neck and pressing against my entrance with my legs slightly parted.

"Cal, I won't cum this way," I protested. "It's nice, but."

Cal parted my legs further with his body. "Why don't you let me try? No one ever made you cum with their mouth before me, did they? That's why you avoided it?"

I nodded.

"Let me try."

"I'm afraid you'll freak out. Like what if I start bleeding or—"

"I can always stop," Cal said. "And you can always say no, Daphne."

He comforted me. I loved his protective streak. It put me at ease.

He kissed my neck again. "Let me worship you, princess. Let me try."

I gave into his pleas, grinding my hips against his until his cock slipped inside. My fears fell aside as he thrust deeper. Slowly, he rocked his hips as I rocked mine. Desperate, we worked together to try and bring me to the point of no return. I doubt it was possible, but damn I hoped he'd succeed.

"Does that feel good?" Cal asked.

"Yes," I whispered while digging my nails in his back. "You always feel good."

Cal kissed me as he thrust deeper. I moaned, unable to keep it down.

"She likes that after all," Cal growled. "Cum for me, Daphne."

With every thrust, he hit a spot that made my toes curl. I thought I might end up with a terrible leg camp, but persisted. Cal's right hand found his way to my left nipple. He rolled his fingers over it the way that sent me into orbit. I bucked my hips to his.

"Oh, you're greedy, princess," Cal laughed.

"Don't stop," I pled. "Oh, God, please don't stop, Cal!"

* * *

Cal

Daphne's pleas didn't fall on deaf ears. I had never watched her cum from this angle. As her orgasm grew, her body flushed, and nostrils flared. She looked beautiful anyway when she came, but watching her body shift with every thrust and feeling her toes curl around me felt like I'd cast a spell over her.

"Oh my God! Oh, fuck me, Cal! Fuck!"

She dug her nails deeper into my back, dragging them as her eyes rolled back. She may have left my back scratched, but I didn't care. Her screams of pure satisfaction made up for any minor discomfort. I kissed her, wanting to be as close as I could at that moment. I breathed it in—how her chest rose, how she felt, the sight of her eyes rolling back, and how she smelled. I knew I just did what she claimed was impossible. I'd just brought her somewhere no one else had.

I pulled her hands behind her head. "No more scratching my back, Daphne. You're poorly behaved."

"I have… impeccable manners, Mr. Markham," Daphne panted. "I find it… abhorrent you'd…say otherwise."

"Abhorrent? You look utterly delighted, princess. Try again."

Daphne bit her lip, encouraging me to fuck harder. Unable to do more, I pulled her ankles around my ears. Now, with every thrust, I got a tiny moan. But what was more, her tits bounced beautifully. With persistence, I managed to fuck her well enough that she came again, making little sense and resorting to unintelligible screams as she gripped the pillows for dear life.

"Oh, good girl," I said. "Very good girl."

I couldn't fight the urge anymore. Every fiber of me needed release. The visual was too strong. I fell forward, pinning her once more as I gave her one last, hard thrust. I lay there, pressing into her. Her rapid breathing and mine synced for a moment before I slowly released her.

"Mmm," Daphne moaned as I pulled back, sounding almost sleepy. "You win."

"I win?" I laughed.

"You were right. I just thought I was hard to get off."

"You are easy to get off, princess," I said. "Which tells me past lovers have never done much work."

"Lovers?" Daphne snickered. "Cal, I've only been with two people. You and my ex."

I did a double take. "You… lost your virginity… to him?"

It didn't compute. She was too young for *me* when we

first slept together, but at least she was a fully-grown woman making her own money. The timing of her partnership with Chandler Walker was hazy, but I remembered it happening several years before we hooked up. It didn't seem right.

"Don't judge me," Daphne said.

I'd killed the mood. She recoiled back to her insular self.

"No, Daph, I didn't mean it like that. Only that… well, you were so young."

"You don't need to make me feel bad."

"Daphne, baby, I don't mean it like that. I am more worried—"

"Worried?

By now, I tried my best with damage control in more than one way, using a towel to mop up the bit of blood present. I wasn't squeamish, but soon realized Daphne was.

"Oh, God. This was a bad idea!" Daphne grabbed a towel from the bed and raced into the bathroom, slamming the door.

I pulled the towel around my waist and knocked.

"Daphne, are you okay? I'm not angry, but I am worried I've upset you. If so, baby, I'm sorry."

"I feel so gross and this was all a mistake. I've fucked it up," Daphne sobbed "I… I don't know."

"Can I come in?"

She paused, then squeaked, "Yes."

I found her curled up by the bathtub, looking upset. Trying to diffuse the situation, I turned on the shower.

"Why don't you wash up? Okay?" I asked. "Not that I need you to. I'm not bothered by any of this. Promise. It's just… I think you would probably like a minute. I could join you if you'd like."

"No ulterior motive?" Daphne sniffled.

"No. You have drained my tank for the foreseeable future,

Daph. No motive other than I want to make sure you're okay."

I reached out to help her stand. She nervously dropped the towel and went into the shower. I sensed Chandler often shamed her. I didn't want to ask too much directly, since these things triggered her. I did, however, want to ensure she felt safe.

"Washcloth," I handed her one from my linen closet. "If you need anything else—"

"I'm okay. Just… don't look at me while I get cleaned up."

I waited back to the wall in the cold until Daphne relaxed.

"I'm sorry for going off. I just… I saw all the blood. It freaked me out. I didn't want you to hate me."

"Daphne, I could never hate you," I turned, unable to ignore her. "And it was barely anything."

Daphne didn't shout at me. Instead, she moved aside so I could soak up some hot water.

"I know what you meant. I think," Daphne said. "And to some degree, I never paid any attention to the… circumstances of why I ended up with him. He was my supervisor. I was an intern. We never did anything while I was on his staff, but he took me out immediately afterwards… I dunno. I think he fetishized the fact that I lacked experience. And I figured initially you wanted the same when we hooked up. Well, until you told me I was in charge and did whatever I wanted you to. That was all new to me."

"I am sorry for that, Daphne. For the record, I wanted you because I wanted you. I didn't want you because you were young and I wanted to dominate you. That was never it."

"I know. I get that now. You treat me like an equal—you always did. I told myself that was the case with Chandler, but it wasn't. He loved that I was younger because I got to be a trophy. Then, when I didn't give him children, I just became an old, dried-up husk of a woman he didn't want anymore."

I shook my head. "Daphne, none of that is true. I hope you know that. You are vibrant. You're smart. I love your fire. There is nothing dried up or husk-like about you, baby. And I'm sorry he was so bad at appreciating you, but given my body count is a *lot* higher than yours, I can say you are no cold fish."

She blushed.

"You're magnificent, okay? Don't let anyone tell you to settle for less. You deserve it, Daphne."

"Thanks," Daphne said. "And while that was pretty great—not gonna lie—I don't think I have the stomach for period sex. I will have to disagree with Lanie and Dahlia on this one firmly. It may have been fun, but I've tried it and I'm not really into it unless you have to have it."

"It's fine," I said. "But if you aren't into it, I'm not either. Daphne, you can always say—"

"I wanted to try something different, Cal. And you taught me that I could get off in missionary, which is a pleasant surprise. But, can we hold off a bit?"

"You lead the way. In the meantime, I will soak up whatever time I have to hopefully wake up next to you in the morning."

Daphne smiled. "I would like that."

29. THE SPEECH

Cal

My first major speech as mayor came after the "voluntary" resignation of the Chicago Superintendent of Police. How willingly Reggie stepped aside is still debated, but he eventually left. It took two weeks of protests for me and activists to smoke him out and get what we wanted. But once it happened, I was ready to go. My only limitation was the assumption I should be subdued versus the way I felt—ready to jump for joy over the breaking of chains.

I was the mayor of a machine city—*the* machine city in the eyes of many—about to end a decades-long way approach to policing. I knew my moment awaited me at the city hall podium. I fought a smile while looking over a room of reporters. We did it.

"Thank you all for coming," I said. "I can confirm my acceptance of Superintendent Ramsey's retirement after over thirty years with CPD. In the past twenty-four hours, I've spoken with leadership within the force and community organizations about next steps. After much discussion, I have asked Sherry Wilkes-White to step in as interim superintendent. Chief Wilkes-White previously served as Executive Director of Community Policing and the First Deputy Superintendent in the same bureau. She is a licensed clinical social worker with over twenty years of experience on the force."

I looked at the small group of police willing to share a stage this morning. I was the most hated man in the room to them right now. I appreciated that Sherry bravely broke rank to join me. Her detective husband's steely gaze indicated he wished she told me no. There were no guarantees this would be a permanent gig and there was a considerable risk of personal harassment.

"This is an interim appointment. I have faith in Chief Wilkes-White's abilities to shepherd CPD in this turbulent time and will let her tell you about her plans for the next week of critical changes. Before that, however, I want to state how we will fill this role permanently."

I composed myself, taking a deep breath. Here was what I waited for.

"As I promised when I was elected to office only weeks ago, I will deliver on a new appointment scheme for future Police Superintendents."

There was chatter.

"As is outlined in the plan you received in your briefing, this reform ensures *all* stakeholders have a say in the appointment of Chicago's top policing official—from our students to our neighborhoods and clergy on up to our city political institutions. I want to thank all the community organizers, religious leaders, school officials, and policing experts who have engaged in a dialogue about the way forward. And for the many citizens who expressed their concerns for policing and safety here in Chicago, your voices will be heard. I know my administration will always strive to listen—even if we don't always get it right the first time."

"Sir, will you release the video?"

I didn't answer. "With that, Chief Wilkes-White, would you like to take over?"

Sherry took the helm. "Thank you, Mayor Markham."

I disappeared into the hallway, letting Sherry earn her keep.

"She's going to be eaten alive," Craig, Jo's assistant, sighed.

"She's tough. She'll be fine," Jo said. "Better her than the mayor."

"That's not why I took off," I said. "I didn't want to undermine her. How bad would it look to appoint our first female superintendent only to mansplain over her?"

"It's a bad look," Jo agreed. "And she can be the one to own the fact that we are releasing the tape. She's taken enough heat from both sides. Now, we begin the next campaign. And focus on the vote."

I champed at the bit—salivating over a chance to hit the initial part of my agenda within my first hundred days. It was historic and boded well for my chance at a second term. I was about to do a rare bit of gloating before my phone distracted me. I spied a text from Daphne.

DAPHNE

You did great. She did, too.

ME

It's a new beginning I hope.

DAPHNE

So, tonight's the night?

Tonight's the night? What did that mean?

ME

?

DAPHNE

The big meeting with the council. What did
you think I meant?

I chuckled.

ME

I was hoping it meant I got to see you.

All of you.

Daphne typed. Had I flustered her? We'd not sexted. We
never discussed it, but it seemed she avoided it. I wasn't sure
if that was on purpose.

DAPHNE

You really expect me to drop everything?

ME

If you want to.

DAPHNE

And if I was to drop by, what do you expect?

ME

Absolutely nothing.

We returned to the office. I sat, waiting for her response.
Had I expected to see Daphne tonight? No. Did I want to see
her *every* night? Yes. It wasn't possible, but I wished it was.
Nights with her far surpassed nights in a quiet penthouse
alone. It didn't matter what we did. She made me smile.

DAPHNE

What do you want, Cal?

ME

Oh, I get to choose now?

DAPHNE

You've been a good boy.

What do you want?

ME

If I get to choose... you on your knees, princess.

I waited. This could backfire. She'd never blown me. Daphne was trepidatious about certain things, so I never pushed. Instead, I suggested things and saw where it landed. Sometimes, it worked. Sometimes, it didn't, but if we were honest, neither left unsatisfied.

DAPHNE

Tell me when

The next twelve hours would torture me, but I hoped the payoff was worth it.

30. VICTORY LAP

Daphne

"I'M STEPPING OUT," I WHISPERED. "I NEED TO GRAB something quick."

"What is it you are looking for?" Dora asked.

"I need to break away for a minute," I said. "Can you just cover for me?"

We browsed racks of clothing in our private shopping area at Delphine's. Mum was enmeshed in a rack of dresses fit for a Sunday. I went with her to Sunday mass and already had enough. Dora, a good girl, never complained. In contrast, I talked Cal's ear off about how little I enjoyed pretending everything was fine. It wasn't.

I heard from my divorce attorney that Chandler's attorney had added yet *another* roadblock to what should have been a simple dissolution of assets. We had no children. He wanted spousal support and my house—which I inherited. He wanted me to grant him *use*. The judge would deny it, but it added time. I offered him a very handsome settlement, instead. Mum complained initially, but I wanted to be free. I'd make the money back with my business shares if there was value left after Davey finished running it into the ground.

"Why? You're acting so weird. Can you bring me with you? I want to see what fun you get up to!"

"It's not fun, Dora Elizabeth. It's boring."

It wasn't *fun,* but it was a release. I made plans with Cal for the evening—plans that somehow had me riding high like some sex goddess. However, my underwear drawer reflected my reality—one made for a woman married for a decade and divorcing after a frigid last two years. Nothing matched and my panties were utilitarian at best.

"I'm going with you."

"No, Dor—"

"Mum, we're going to look at something else. Be back."

"Daphne, you have a rack of dresses to try on," Mum protested.

"I can do it later," I groaned, pulling Dora out the door.

We ventured to the fifth floor, which was luggage—something that didn't sell well—and lingerie. I expected we'd find the floor surrounding the boutique, luxury collections busy. Everywhere else, it was dead.

"Why are we buying luggage?" Dora asked.

"We aren't. We're looking at… underwear," I said.

"Oh? What are you doing?"

"I need some… staples."

There was nothing *more* awkward than approaching the luxurious piles of naughty, lacy panties with your kid sister. I suspected Dora had limited experience with men *and* lingerie, but knew the difference between basic clothes and things one wore for titillation.

"Are you seeing someone?" Dora gasped.

I sighed. "Dora, I am seeing someone, but it's not your business, and I'm not saying more."

"Is he hot?"

"I don't describe people my age as *hot*."

Yes. I wasn't going to deny the base attraction to Cal. With Cal, I couldn't resist the idea of doing naughty things.

"Okay, but like… are you…" she lowered her voice. "Are you sleeping with him? Or is this your first big date, and you want to be prepared?"

She was so sweet and naive.

"Sweetie," I laughed. "The train left the station. I want to embrace singlehood and enjoy life."

"What about this?" Dora picked up an incredibly scandalous, strappy bodysuit I'd never pull off.

"No. I want to stick to something *simple*," I said. "I am too old for shit like that."

"I like it. It's sexy."

"Then buy it for yourself," I laughed.

"I could *never*!"

"Okay, well, I couldn't, either."

"So… it's good, though?"

I beamed. "It's so good. Like ridiculously good."

I couldn't hide it. I didn't *want* to.

"I'm happy for you."

I was in the process of setting a chemise aside when my worst nightmare arrived. A man cleared his throat, expecting something. I ignored him, assuming he was rude and expected me to move. He could go around.

My baby sister excitedly announced, "Davey! What are you doing here?"

"Mum said you were up here," Davey answered. "I saw your names on the schedule. I get a bit of a tip off."

I ignored my brother.

"Daphne, can we… chat?"

I kept ahold of the lacy garment, hoping to mortify him and sighed, "Last time we chatted, things went tits up quickly."

Dora giggled. "Tits up! I'm dying! Given…"

Davey's steely gaze at me quieted her exuberance.

"David, whatever you need to say, you can say with Dora here."

Davey shook his head, looked down, and scratched the back of his neck. "Daph, I wanted to apologize to you."

"Oh, really?"

Davey sighed, "Daph, I was out of line—"

"Again."

"Yes, again. I will find you something. Give me time. We can talk about the discussion we had earlier. I am… working on it. But you need to give me this quarter—"

I played it cool, but deep down I guessed I'd won. He may have needed another few weeks to fire the president, but Davey would come around eventually. I'd give him a few more weeks to make progress while lining up my ducks. I still needed the votes to secure a spot as president or a place in the c-suite. And, unlike my brother, I wasn't keen to be caught with my pants down burning bridges.

"I can do that," I was firm but fair. "But you need to be kind to me in the interim. We want the same thing. We both want everything to work."

"In the meantime," Davey said. "Come up with your plans. No matter what happens, you need to show me—and everyone—how serious you are about this. Nepotism isn't enough."

I nodded, my heart leaping. I had plans—loads of them. "I can do that. I am a team player."

"I know," he agreed. "I will… leave you to… this."

He blushed and fled.

"God forbid we buy frilly things!" Dora snickered. "What is going on with you two?"

"We fought. He was an ass," I answered. "And I suspect

Mum harangued him over it. But let's hope things improve now."

"A fight about what?"

"Handling the estate," I answered. "Boring business stuff. You're not missing anything."

"Just all the fun," Dora sighed. "Is it silly if I just buy that ridiculous red thong just for me?"

"Why else would you buy it?" I asked.

"For a man?"

"Dora, a man will not care if you are wearing panties—more than likely. If it makes you feel beautiful, buy it. Make yourself happy first. Don't rely on a man to do it for you, okay? That's where I got lost with Chandler and now, I get to spend another ten years playing catch up."

Dora grinned. "I think you'll make up for lost time much faster with whomever this dude is. Seriously. Who *is* he?"

"I plead the fifth," I snickered.

"Oh, so he *is* an attorney?"

"Lawyers don't talk like that, Dora Elizabeth. No, he's not. You'll get nothing more from me."

* * *

Cal

"You better put down your drink," Daphne said.

She came in like a hurricane—a woman on a mission. Before I knew it, she stripped down to her bra and panties.

"Slow down," I said.

"I am single-minded and I've been thinking about this all day."

Daphne kissed me, unashamed by what I might have described as desperation. It was the type of desperation I could get behind, though. Her hands went straight to my belt, unbuckling it.

She bit my lip and pulled back. "You want my mouth around your cock, right?"

Did I ever!

She unzipped my pants.

"Daph, you don't have to—"

"Oh, I will unless you tell me not to."

"I won't *stop* you, baby," I confessed. "God, you are... possessed."

Daphne tossed the dress she'd been wearing aside, revealing the blue-green set of underwear. The bra was barely-there, mostly see-through, and the panties covered little. *Damn.*

"This is... unexpected."

"I went shopping," Daphne kissed me slowly and deeply. "I know what I want, okay?"

"Yes, princess," I gasped as she ran her hand over my cock through my boxers.

I was rock-hard in anticipation as Daphne freed my cock and dropped to her knees. Holding it in one hand, she looked up obediently but held *all* the power. I wanted to be inside her pretty mouth. I fantasized about it plenty, but now it was *here*.

"There are rules," Daphne said. "If you try to push me or thrust into me without my consent, I'm done. Full stop. That's a hard boundary."

"I won't, then."

I didn't mind rules. Negotiation was a big part of sex—especially with Daphne.

She licked the head of my cock, keeping her green eyes on mine. I moaned and played with her hair, pulled into a loose ponytail.

"You could take your hair down," I said.

"It makes all of this more complicated. Trust me."

I wanted to tell her I never thought about that before. I shuddered as she took me in her mouth—only a bit, then all of me. She went torturously slow, then sped up. I suspected she did that for effect, pumping her hand on my shaft in a beautiful rhythm. I held her head, not forcing it. I needed to believe it was real. She was straight out of a fantasy.

"Daphne, you are… fucking great… at this," I panted.

She tickled my balls, as if taunting. I threw my head back.

"I'm gonna cum if you do that much more, baby."

Daphne pulled back, her fingers rolling slowly over the head. "Call me princess. And isn't that the point?"

"I'd like to savor this," I admitted. "And still fuck you."

"You can fuck me in a bit," Daphne said. "And you're on bided time with my jaw, Cal."

"Oh, I… I get that." I shuddered as she took me back in her mouth. She took me in deeper and deeper. It felt delicious.

"Just like that, princess. I'll cum like that."

Daphne increased the intensity of the suction and ran her tongue over the tip of my cock with each bob of her head. She stroked my balls. I couldn't do more than pull on her ponytail to steady myself as she brought me closer to climax. Was there nothing she couldn't do well? Maybe she claimed to be sex-starved, but I unlocked the unexpected naughty side of her.

"Oh, fuck. I'm—"

There was no finishing the sentencing as I came in her mouth. She gagged, then spit me out and wiped the remaining bit away.

"Sorry, I wasn't… fully prepared," Daphne grimaced. "I should have told you; I sometimes cannot swallow. It's…"

She looked for words.

I finished her sentence, tilting her face towards me.

"Amazing and I don't care. Let's clean up, princess. You're such a good girl."

Daphne's mischievous grin made me want her even more. She stood as I fetched a kitchen towel.

"So, tell me all about your victory," Daphne said. "And I'll tell you mine."

"Does it have to do with that bra?" I snickered.

"No. Well, sort of. I was browsing the lingerie racks when Davey found Dora and me. It got awkward—and I'd suspect it would be much *more* awkward if he knew my real reason for buying lacey things."

I grinned and mopped the cum off the floor. "He'd shit a brick, Daph."

"Well, he told me he's going to fire the president. He asked me to give him the rest of the quarter. And by then, I know we'll have our ducks in a row. So, can I meet your guy?"

I took a deep breath. "I will try to make it work."

"How does it feel to be the Reform Mayor in a machine city?" Daphne gripped my shirt.

"Oh, stop it," I snickered.

"I will not. I'm proud of you. You outsmarted people who refused to listen or cede power. They endangered the lives of *children* and refused to see their errors. You're trying to fix it. Don't forget this day. And don't apologize for the win. It's a turn-off if you cannot own your success, Cal."

"Then what is a turn-on?"

"Your ruthless embrace of being a complete badass when it happens, Mr. Mayor," Daphne said. "Don't apologize when you nail the landing."

31. THE GUY

Daphne

CAL INVITED ME TO MEET HIS "GUY"—SAYING I SHOULD prepare for an afternoon at a horse barn. Slightly confused, I donned a pair of Lanie's breeches and a polo. I drove to a posh barn in Lake Forest. I wasn't sure what this had to do with the "guy", but assumed it was a good cover to keep us out of hot water. My confusion only increased as I reached the barn aisle and saw Cal talking with Chloe as she tacked up a big grey with two bold, big socks.

"Daphne, you made it," Cal said.

I didn't greet him with a kiss. I never dared do that in public. It was an odd contrast. I'd been in his bed the morning before, but now we were only friends. Chloe was my sister's best friend, so I didn't worry too much. In a way, it made our trysts a little naughtier. If shagging your late father's business associate and friend was forbidden, being the mayor's favorite distraction in private didn't make it feel less cheeky.

"Hey," I said. "Chloe, who is this?"

"Malcolm," Chloe said. "He's my grand prix prospect. A new toy."

"A very *expensive* toy," Cal said.

"He earns his keep with the ladies," Chloe said. "We imported him. He's a baby still—only five—but there aren't any studs with his lines in the US yet. We're doing a lot of business. I gotta grab his wraps. Gimme a sec."

She disappeared. I whispered, "Cal… where's the guy?"

Chloe returned from the tack room.

"That's my guy," Cal whispered, nodding at Chloe.

"Chloe?" I asked, confused.

"Yeah?" Chloe asked.

"Sorry. He just said… you're the guy?"

"Nope," Chloe answered. "I'm the badass bitch who is here to back you, Daphne. *That's* what I am."

"Noted," I said.

"I'm glad to discuss whatever it is we need to. But I figured you could take out my schoolmistress, Claire, while we talk. She's a bit of a pain, but she's less spooky than this annoying prick."

She patted the stallion's shoulder.

"You're good to ride, right?" Chloe said.

"I am. I have a helmet in the car. Based on what your brother said, I wasn't sure what the assignment was."

"It is secret squirrel stuff. Grab your hat. We'll go out on the trails. This is the easy day for this one."

I agreed, returning to my new car—a gift from Mum—to grab my brain bucket. When I approached Chloe, Cal held a bay mare with resting bitch face.

"Daphne, this is Claire. She's sometimes a cunt, but she's nice to ride. Promise," Chloe explained.

"Typical mare," I said. "Are you joining us, Cal?"

"I am opposed to horses. As you can see, they loathe me."

"No, that's just her normal face," Chloe giggled. "He's a wuss."

"I'm aware of my mortality. We're not all rubber like you, kid."

Chloe fastened her helmet. "Well, go up to the lounge and have a pop or something. There's always snacks. We won't be gone forever."

We took the horses outside to a waiting mounting block near one of two massive indoor arenas. It was a horse palace. It put our nice, but much simpler stables outside London to shame. I rode there for years before going through IVF. I sold my horse when it became clear I wasn't around enough to enjoy her.

Chloe swung up on her massive horse without issue. I looked at Claire like she was a fire breathing dragon. This did not bode well. Cal held her as I swung astride her and grabbed my reins.

"You good?" He asked protectively.

"I'm good," I promised.

Cal patted my boot and left. I followed Chloe across the parking lot towards a break in the trees. A wide path greeted us. It was nice to see a show barn with trails. It spoke volumes about the care the horses received outside daily training.

"This place is gorgeous," I caught up.

"I love it here. The coach is amazing, too. She's working wonders with Malcolm. And Claire is in a part-lease with a teenager who thinks she hung the moon. It makes me happy to know they are cared for. Of course, Mom comes out to check on them. She's not one to ride, though."

"What does she do?"

"Oh, she just lived to be a horseshow mom. Cal is terrified of horses, and I don't think it was within the budget when he was young, but the minute I wanted a pony, Mom was there to buy it."

I smiled. "She always wanted one?"

"Always. I got to live the dream. I always had everything I needed. I am very spoiled, I realize."

"Yeah, but you're doing your own thing, too. I won't judge you for making money through some unconventional means."

"Good, cuz I forced Cal to take my 'What I wore to the barn' post and he totally rolled his eyes. Can you work on that?"

"He loves and supports you," I assured. "But I cannot do anything to control him, Chlo."

"Oh, really?" She raised her eyebrows. "That's cute you think I believe any of that."

"What?" I feigned confusion. *How did she know?*

"Don't lie. He says he's sleeping with someone. I beat that out of him. And then you're just… here and he's trying to save the company and prop you up? Oh, sweetie, I'm a lot smarter than that."

I didn't want to insult her.

"Look, this stays here, okay? We haven't told *anyone*."

"I never tell anyone's secrets—not even Lanie's."

"I am not asking to know anymore, Chloe. But it would be…" I wasn't even sure what to call it.

"A media firestorm? Yeah. It would be *something*. A Delphine and Markham collab? It's a joining of two dynasties —an empire to build. People would lap it up."

"But it would *not* help your brother."

"Oh, really? I see my brother has a hot, younger girlfriend from a legendary old money family quite beloved in the city."

"A girlfriend in the middle of a contentious divorce. I have no idea what my squirrely ex is going to do."

"I doubt it would change opinions on you two dating. Are you dating or just… hooking up?"

I wasn't sure how to answer. "We're exclusive, but it's not like we can actually *date*."

"Uh-huh. Just you wait!"

"Chloe—"

I didn't finish my sentence. A deer hopped out of the brush. Chloe's horse spooked. She sat her horse's reaction well. Claire teleported. I knew I was about to lose my seat. Despite holding on for dear life, I quickly lost my grip, falling hard.

* * *

Cal

"Just rest, okay?" I asked.

"Cal, this is an imposition for you all—"

"It's really not," I assured Daphne. "Just rest. Dad is making food. I'll wake you for dinner, okay?"

"I still worry about sleeping—"

"The doctors said it was fine, Daphne. What you need is *rest*. You're a bad patient."

She growled, "I hate this. I don't want to be fawned over."

"Well, you don't have a choice, princess. Sleep."

She mumbled something while curled under the covers. This place was usually occupied when I visited Mom and Tim north of the city and didn't want to drive home. I left Daphne to sleep, returning downstairs. Chloe was in the kitchen devouring an entire cheeseboard while Tim prepped cocktails. Mom was at a tennis lesson.

"So, is she calming down?" Chloe asked.

"She's fine," I answered. "She's resisting rest, but I think she will calm down eventually with nothing else to do."

"I feel so bad she fell. Claire was a total baby about something silly."

"This is why I don't fuck with horses," I said. "Make fun of me all you will, but Daphne is worse for wear."

"She doesn't even have a concussion, brother. Calm down. God, you're too protective."

I rolled my eyes. "I'd like not to start a war with the Delphines, okay?"

"Uh-huh. That's totally what it is."

Tim snickered.

"I don't need you piling on, Tim," I said.

"She's a nice girl," Tim said. "But you brought her here."

I did. I figured the alternative was to drive her home and deal with her mother. Forced to pick a matriarch to deal with, I'd pick mine. I didn't need to tell Danna Delphine anything we were up to. That wasn't our dynamic. I figured Daphne would want to handle it more delicately than in her current state with two bruised ribs.

"Who did you bring here?"

My mother arrived, still dressed in tennis whites.

"Claire wasted someone. We're trying to patch them up," Chloe said. "You look… accomplished."

"I just beat Danna Delphine quite triumphantly," Mom said. "Her sour face was so satisfying. I unseated the Queen unceremoniously."

Chloe burst into a fit of laughter. Tim made eye contact with me.

"Oh, fuck!" Chloe patted my back. "Well, *this* is awkward."

"She just lost her husband. Could we *try* to be nicer?" Tim asked.

"For all the years she tortured me, I doubt it, sweetie."

That was debatable. I gathered Mom and Danna felt they were the victims in this feud for the contest of Hostess with the Mostess in Chicagoland. Neither was the winner. They had different niches. Mom never got a fair shake given her status as a "new money" working woman. Danna only had to manage domestic matters for an old money husband, but she was often vilified for having strong opinions in a way a man never would.

"So," Mom said. "Who did Claire attack?"

"Well, she teleported and bucked her off," Chloe said. "But you should ask Cal since it was his *friend*."

I cringed.

"Wait, is it Kristy?" Mom's face brightened.

"No. Kristy doesn't ride," I answered. "Chloe, I'd like to strangle you."

"Who is it?" Mom grew impatient.

"Daphne Delphine," I sighed. "She went out with Chloe and—"

"I'm sorry, but… you brought one of the Delphine girls back here?"

"Lanie is here literally all the time, Mom." Chloe rolled her eyes.

"But not at your *brother's* invitation."

"I made an introduction. That's all," I lied. "Chloe is taking over the shares David willed me for the company."

"David willed you shares?"

I winced. I left that out.

"He did."

Mom shook her head. "And you're… what? What is this? Why are you helping that girl?"

"Because Davey is running the damn company into the ground."

"Yeah, that's all it is."

I slapped Chloe's arm playfully. "You're really testing my patience, kid."

"Kid? Daphne's what… eight years my senior? Get over yourself, Cal."

"What is going on?" Mom grew serious. "Calvin, if you are… entangled with that girl… so help me."

"If I am, it's none of your business, Mom."

"No, it *is*. Because you brought her into my house, she's still married, and she's just as pretentious as her mother. You couldn't bother to find someone… less complicated?"

"Last I heard he wasn't engaged to her, so calm down," Chloe said.

I said, "I will remind you that Lanie is a frequent guest and you don't react this way to her."

"Lanie and her mother do not get along. She's different. I don't think she is a spy. Daphne is—"

I countered, "What, Mother? A well-educated, ambitious woman trying to do right by her family's company? I would expect you'd *respect* that as a woman who had to—"

"I built a brand from *nothing*. She was David's precious favorite child—a princess. She's never worked for anything. What did she do? Lie on her back and play politician's wife to no avail for years? I heard she couldn't even give him a child and that was—"

I pounded the kitchen island with my fist. "Mother, so help me if you say another unkind, false thing about Daphne, I will lose it! I will leave and I won't be back."

She fell silent, surprised I spoke up. I rarely got animated. Usually, I was a good boy who let her rant. Daphne was different. She did nothing to my mother and deserved none of her anger.

"Be kind," Tim reminded. "Sweetheart, she's just a girl. You'd hate anyone to describe Chloe like that, right?"

"What do you see in her?" Mum glared, ignoring Tim's reasonable question.

"She cares about me," I answered. "And… I have feelings for her. So, you can give up your hope that I will move on."

Mom groaned.

"As for her marriage, he was an abusive dickhead. And the reason she didn't have kids is not any of your business, but it is *deeply* painful for her. She's good to me. Would you rather me be lonely, Mother?"

Mom sighed, annoyed. "When Danna finds out you're having an affair with her precious daughter—"

"We're not having an affair," I said. "That's a silly way to describe a consensual relationship between two unattached adults."

"She's *married.*"

"She's separated," I said. "And the divorce is messy. She deserves so much better."

"I think she doesn't deserve you."

"You think that about every person we bring home!" Chloe rolled her eyes. "Get over it. Don't be an asshole, Mom."

"I worry about your career."

"That is *mine* to worry about, Mother!"

"What does Jo think?" Mom asked.

"She's not wild about the idea," I admitted. "But I'm not wild about ignoring real feelings for someone who cares about me. We are careful. Being open doesn't help either of us."

Mom grabbed an apple, shrugging. "Fine, whatever. You're a grown man. However, I'd remind you the Delphines will never see you as an insider. If there is any chance to flip this around on you, they will."

"This isn't a calculated move to end my career," I scoffed. "Daphne and I have feelings for one another. It's not about some game of chess."

"It is *always* a game of chess with those people," Mom sighed. "It's a bad omen. If she can bring you down, she will."

I didn't debate my mother because she wasn't wrong. I wasn't an insider. I did, however, know Daphne's heart. And, either way, her downfall was tied to mine. We had much to lose by playing our cards too far from our chest.

32. THE KID

Daphne

My phone rang. I couldn't ignore its vibration and light in the dark room at Cal's family home. Annoyed and assuming it was my mother, I reached for it. My chest and back suffered stabbing pain. I panicked when reading who rang.

"Meredith?" I asked, confused. "What do you need?"

My attorney calling from London at what was already late evening there—on a Saturday—had me confused.

She got into it immediately. "I have bad news and want to say it before it leaks. Although, given Chandler's ability to self-preserve, who knows?"

"I'm sorry?"

"Chandler has impregnated the intern."

"What? How? There's *no* way. His sperm were—"

"Somehow, he's managed it, Daphne. This comes from his attorney. He's pressuring us to accept these bad terms to spare you quickly."

It hit like a brick wall. He got her pregnant—something he never could with me. Why did she get this and not me?

She was a *child* in comparison. She was the other woman. I realized now I hated myself for that impulse, though. This wasn't *her* fault. She was a pawn in his manipulative game of world dominance just as I had.

"Spare me?" I asked. "Spare *him*. We're coming up on an election. He doesn't want it getting out. As I see it, we have a move to play—the one to win."

"Explain."

"Meredith, he's the man who cheated with an intern and impregnated her. Now, he's dragging his ex-wife through the mud. He wants to marry her and end this quickly. If so, we have *him* over a barrel."

"Daphne, your goal was to minimize press attention—"

"Sure. But I want freedom more. I can go underground for a month or so."

"It could backfire—"

"It could, but what more can I do? Either way, when the news comes out, it will be a scandal for the press to salivate over. That's a given. Let's let them know before he can organize a way to attack me. I refuse to give him anything more than I've offered. I don't care how he feels about it."

"Take a deep breath and think about it."

I couldn't breathe deeply. The bruised ribs complicated that.

"Ring me tomorrow. On Sunday, we can do whatever you like, but I strongly caution you that this could backfire."

I was resolute. I wanted to do this. Rage won out. As Cal's face appeared at the doorway—so full of worry—I wanted it even more. I needed to give us a chance. No matter how challenging this was, I longed to *try* with Cal. He signaled a future I never thought I'd get. And with him, things looked *hopeful*. If I wanted to rid myself of Chandler, I must play dirty. If I wanted more with Cal, I'd have to shoot my shot—even if it backfired.

"You're up," Cal said.

"I am," I said. "Cal, there is… I need to talk to you."

"I'm sorry. I feel so bad. Chloe does, too."

Cal sat on the bed.

"No. It's not about this, but… something has happened with my ex, and… it's messy."

"You can tell me anything, Daphne," Cal said.

I smiled, knowing it was true.

I squeezed his hand, affirming, "That's why I trust you with this."

But before I could share, Elise appeared.

"We will soon have dinner. Will Miss Delphine join us?"

The way she said it made it clear she wasn't happy about that prospect.

Cal turned, reading my mind. "I think I'll take her home and put her to bed instead, but thanks, Mom."

Relief rushed over me. The last thing I needed right now was Elise intervening. I didn't need her thirty-year feud with my mother to bubble over while I was broken and battered in more ways than one. I needed to feel safe and that would never happen at a table with a woman who had a personal vendetta against my family.

"Suit yourself, then." Elise left.

Cal whispered, "I will explain it later."

"You don't need to say anything. I am grateful you're taking care of me. That's all."

I kissed him, though it hurt. His lips pressed to mine reminded me I needed to choose me—to choose happiness— and ignore those who'd rain on my redemption arc. I refused to apologize for feeling joy.

"I'm assuming she knows?" I asked.

He brushed my face. "Unfortunately."

"And she's not happy?"

"Also, unfortunately not."

"We're grown-ups, Cal. I don't care. I need to tell Mum, though. Before she finds out from yours."

"I doubt she would ever admit I was schtupping David Delphine's daughter. It would suggest an alliance."

I chuckled. "Well, we shouldn't put it like *that* I suppose."

"No, we would have to be honest—to tell everyone that Cal Markham fell for Daphne Delphine a million years ago and that he loves her."

The words took me by surprise, but felt *so* right. I shouldn't love this man. I shouldn't feel so strong. Until now, I hadn't thought I could even name the feeling. Now, as he cupped my face, his eyes so kind and sweet, I'd never deny my feelings.

"And I'd have to admit that—despite my better judgement —I love Cal Markham."

* * *

Cal

I tucked Daphne into a comfy nest on the couch. After we devoured dinner from a local pizza place, she wound down. I couldn't have been happier with my choice to bring her back to mine. She was safe. I stood up for this woman—who I loved. I got brave by saying I loved her. I told her the thing I held in for weeks. She loved me back—so purely.

"Are you comfortable enough? I can get you another pillow or—"

"I'm fine, Cal," she laughed. "You're so worried. It's sweet, but I'm not made of glass."

I bent to kiss her forehead. "I just want to take care of you, baby."

"I know," I said.

"You don't," I shook my head. "You need someone to take

216

care of you. I want to show up. I need you to know you can always call, Daphne."

She looked down, unable to accept this declaration head-on. She'd believe I loved her. She'd believe I *wanted* her. However, she struggled to trust me. All I could do was keep showing up and proving my genuine need to protect her. That is what Daphne deserved and never got.

"I love you," she turned to me. "I appreciate that you care so much, but I swear I'll mend."

"Well, I'm going to load the dishwasher. Shout if you need something."

I bussed and cleaned our plates, happy with the evening's domestic simplicity. It was nice to have her around. I worried about suggesting she leave some things here, fearing she'd run. Truthfully, I wanted her here all the damn time. This place felt lonely and cold without her—always so sad and off. I never felt more at home than with Daphne on my couch, tucked in with a movi*e*.

And, just as I thought about that, interlopers entered as they always did. The front desk buzzed.

"Sir, Kristy is here with her child. She is wondering if you would accept a visitor?"

"Right now?" I grimaced.

He handed the phone over. "Cal, I'm sort of in the middle of a disaster. My sister is back in the hospital. My mom can pick up Laurie in a bit, but she's driving in and I don't have anyone to call. The babysitter is in Cancun."

I wanted to say no but doing so felt unkind.

"I have a guest, Kristy."

"Oh… okay. Well—"

She didn't want to hear that. "Oh, shit, sorry, I—"

"No, no," I said. "Let me ask if it's okay."

I raced to the living room.

"So, complication and I'm sorry. Kristy's sister has a

medical emergency and she has no one to watch the kid. Do you mind if the baby joins us for a bit? I feel awful, but you don't need to say—"

"Sure. If you have it handled, I cannot lift a baby right now."

"Thank you," I kissed her head. "You're so sweet, Daphne."

"No, you are. This is above and beyond what I'd do for an ex."

I shrugged. "She's a friend, Daph."

I raced back, "It's fine. Come on up."

Kristy appeared on my floor a few minutes later, baby on hip and diaper bag over her shoulder.

"Hi. I'm so sorry. I didn't know what to do," Kristy looked shaken.

I reached for the baby, but Kristy stampeded into the living room and deposited the baby on the floor before I could stop her or explain what was happening.

"She just got sick and called me from the ambulance. I have no idea how long she'll be at Northwestern or—"

Kristy's eyes fell to Daphne who already cooed at the baby from the couch.

"You're even cuter than last time," Daphne said.

I waited for an implosion—my past and present colliding.

"Daphne," Kristy said. "When Cal said you had a guest, I didn't realize—"

"Sorry. I wasn't planning on it."

"Chloe's horse booted her. She has bruised ribs and... I'm—"

"Playing nursemaid, I guess," Daphne said. "To more than one person now. Thankfully, this one is much sweeter."

Kristy laughed nervously. "Sorry. I thought when you said you had company, you were on a date or something. I didn't realize you were taking care of the wounded."

Daphne didn't protest or point out it was more. It felt like she avoided it out of worry, shooting me a look to stay calm.

"I mean, if she weren't injured, we would have," I said. "Damn horses."

Daphne's face flashed surprised. *Had she expected me to deny it?*

"Then I apologize for the cockblock," Kristy joked, sounding hurt. "I will text you when Mom says she made it in."

"They'll call up. I'll have them let her in to get the kid," I said. "Don't worry. I remember all the instructions from last time. She'll be fine."

"Thanks a million—" Kristy moved to kiss me out of instinct, then stopped herself, shaking her head. "Sorry. Thanks."

She darted out as the baby rolled to face me. I lifted her and sat on the edge of the sofa.

"You're stuck with us for a little bit, Laurie."

"I'm sorry if I made that awkward," Daphne said. "You could have denied it. She seemed shaken up—"

"I didn't want to," I said. "I didn't want to deny your place here and act like it was nothing."

"Why?"

"Because I love you, Daphne," I sighed. "So very much. I don't want people to assume I don't, okay? That's cruel."

Daphne smiled. "And that is why I am telling Mum when I get home. But, Cal, it might be difficult to love me after I tell you what I meant to tell you at your mom's."

"Okay? Tell me."

Laurie fussed. I put her on the floor, trying to give Daphne attention while ensuring the baby didn't do anything dangerous. I didn't know how parents always did this or how children survived infancy. They were so tricky.

"Chandler got the intern pregnant," Daphne said.

"What!?" I settled on Daphne's face. "Are you okay?"

"No." Daphne wiped tears. "It's a slap in the face."

"If the baby is—"

"No. In a way, it's fine. A balm. And… I cannot just wallow in self-pity right now. Chandler made a severe miscalculation by threatening me to settle faster over this. He thinks if this goes public it puts me in a bind—"

"But it makes him look bad? How has he managed to cover it up?"

"The election is coming," Daphne said. "The Tories protect themselves the same as anywhere. Party leadership trades favors and stories to cover it up with the press. Regardless, I'm not a Tory and I don't give a fuck about their stupid election. If he won't settle, it's mine to run with. This is my best attempt at blackmail. If he settles, I won't leak it. If he lets the cat out of the bag, he could lose it all. I intend to play this game."

I grinned. "Now, *that* is the Daphne Delphine I know. You should. I'm sorry, Daphne. I know how hard that news is to take."

"I… I don't want to focus on it. And it's not like I can do anything to remedy it."

It hurt watching her twist in pain—like I watched Kristy tormented by the choice years earlier.

"I know you don't want kids," Daphne said. "So, I don't want to get too mushy and freak you out. I'm not looking to force you into anything."

"That's not true, Daph," I protested.

"What isn't?"

"I *never* said I didn't want kids."

Daphne glanced at Laurie as she held a cord.

"Shit!" I hopped up to secure my laptop charger. "I didn't say I was ready for parenting. Clearly!"

"No one is when they become parents," Daphne giggled.

"But you desperately want kids, don't you?" I asked. "I can tell. Kristy wanted this baby so much—"

"And you didn't. That's my point."

"No, that wasn't it." I lifted the baby, handing her a book to flip through.

"She's just going to tear the pages out," Daphne warned.

"God, what can I hand her?"

"Does the diaper bag have a teether?" Daphne asked. "A toy?"

I sorted through it to pull out a little lamb. As I handed it to the baby, she grabbed it and put it immediately in her mouth.

"See, you're good at this—even on narcotics," I joked.

"I love kids, but so do you, Cal."

"I do. And that's why I wouldn't rule it out—although, at my age, what is the point?"

"Dad was older than you when Dora was born," Daphne said. "Stranger things have happened. And Chandler magically got his girlfriend pregnant, so… who knows? Maybe it's just my luck?"

I took a beat, unsure what to say or how to articulate my feelings.

"Daph, it wasn't babies. It wasn't that I didn't want kids. It was timing—going into the biggest race of my life—and Kristy not wanting to get married. I cannot just pop babies out and not be married—even now. People wouldn't take kindly to it, Daphne."

"So, wait? Your main issue was getting married—not babies?"

"Don't judge. I also think Kristy never could have stood to have me—and only me. She's free. We'd tried a little bit of nonmonogamy, but once I set my eyes on running, that had to end. Even just that change bothered her. She's in an open relationship with that artist of hers. And I don't know… I won't judge because I love her—as a friend—but it would never work for me. Having a child and still seeing multiple people? No."

"I couldn't do it, either, even if that's what Chandler wanted. He never wanted to fuck me. I wasn't good enough. I was a cold fish he had to service."

I furrowed my brow. "You? Nah. Never. He didn't try, Daph. He never deserved you. You are too good for him, baby."

She smiled. "I wish I believed you—but knowing he knocked her up hurts so much. I hope this is acting out of strategy and not blind rage."

"That's fair. As a political animal, I would do the same thing. If I were you, I'd want freedom. If you want my selfish opinion as the man who loves you and would like to love you openly, I want this wrapped up so I can finally shout it from the rooftops."

"Cal, we still have to worry about my board prospects, the shake-up, the coup—"

"If we can finalize this much, Daphne, we're one step closer to me being able to let out the truth and love you in daylight. I want that. I selfishly want that above all else," I said.

She brushed my face. "I want to love you in daylight, too, Cal Markham."

PART IV

A NEW DAY

33. COPPING TO IT

Daphne

Cal dropped me at home for the first time—babying me as I stepped into the foyer. This morning, my entire body ached from my unceremonious booting off a cagey flight animal. It wasn't the first time I'd come off a horse by a long stretch—but it was the worst yet. Getting old was a bitch.

Mum rushed in, frightened at my disheveled appearance.

"Oh, my goodness, Daphne Eugenia! What happened!?"

"I fell off a horse and got a little banged up. I'm okay. Or I will be."

Standing there, I prayed she didn't ask me why I was in a pair of scraped-up breeches and one of Cal's shirts. My breeches got a run through the washer last night, mostly removing the stains, but my polo was toast.

"What do you mean?"

"I went on a ride with a friend and came off," I said. "I have a couple of bruised ribs. Other than that, I'm okay."

"Bruised ribs? Oh my God!"

I braced, as she hadn't yet acknowledged Cal's presence. Her eyes flitted from me to him, and I winced internally. If I were Mum, I'd have *questions*. I'd want to know what was going on. While I'd feared this moment, I knew it was time to come clean. I couldn't love Cal in any meaningful, good way without at least telling Mum. I lived with her. She was owed an explanation.

"How did you get roped into this, Cal?" Mum laughed. "Last I heard, you hated horses."

"I still do—especially now," Cal chuckled nervously. "It was Chloe's horse. I took care of her following the incident. My whole family feels terrible, Lady Danna."

"Darling, why were you with Chloe on her horse?" Danna asked.

"She... invited me out." I looked at Cal with trepidation.

"Well, Cal, thank you for taking care of her. I'll take it from here. I feel bad for you getting roped into this. You must have better things to do."

"Not really. It's a Sunday. Even I get to take a day off sometimes." He shifted, looking at me.

It was now or never.

Breathing as deeply as my ribs allowed, I choked, "He's sort of obligated—"

"Because of Chloe's mad horse?"

I could have let it go and laughed it off, but I'd deny everything.

"No," I said sternly. "Because we've been seeing each other. This is the guy."

"The one you went on the pill for?" Mum stammered. "The... the man you've been spending *all* your free time with?"

"Yes," I answered.

Mum glared at Cal. "You know better!"

"I, I'm sorry—"

"You better be. If David were here, he'd still knock you

down. Daphne? You could have *any* woman—a grown woman your age—"

"With all due respect, Lady Danna, Daphne is—and has been—a full-grown woman. I've never done anything to hurt her—nor would I!"

"And you'd just risk everything with this scandal following her?" Mum groaned. "I love her. She's my daughter. I know her heart is good, and Chandler is a twat."

Where did that come from? My mother's colorful language surprised me.

"But the press… your supporters? Would they be so kind?"

"I don't know. I also… I don't care."

They wouldn't. Cal could deny it. He lied to himself that this would be fine, but he already had enough public scrutiny to sink him. Perhaps if he wasn't so charming and good at rhetoric, it would have. Until my divorce was settled, and he was further into his term, we weren't going public. It wasn't to protect me. It was for his own good.

"You should. You gave up a very lucrative position as David's first choice replacement—"

"He what?"

I stared past my mother, spying Davey. Fists balled, he strode in.

"Nothing." Mum shook her head, trying to cover her tracks.

"No, you said Dad asked Cal to be his replacement. His first choice! Did you or did you not?"

"I… that is the past, Davey—"

"I wasn't his first choice," Cal said.

"So, I was? Then why ask. I accepted." Davey didn't buy it.

"Your sister was," Cal sighed. "Then me. Then you."

Davey flew forward, knocking me down in an attempt to punch Cal. I ignored the scowl, sobbing in pain. The cold marble was a cruel reminder of my fragility. I could barely breathe.

Suddenly, everyone turned. The idiot men stopped.

Mum bent to comfort me. "See what you did? See what everyone's childish behavior did!?"

The men stood silent, afraid to say or do anything. Finally, Cal dropped and helped me sit.

"Are you alright?" He glared at Davey.

"Can everyone just fucking stop?" I demanded. "I'm in tatters. Cal has done nothing wrong, and Davey has the fragile ego I've come to expect."

"Says Dad's favorite child!"

"Yeah, well, maybe he had a fucking point since you are running the thing into the ground!"

I didn't know where I found my voice, but I didn't expect to see it on my mother's foyer while in great pain.

"Davey, your head is *anywhere* but with the retail side. You're focused on the football team, e-commerce, and anything *but* the store."

"You can say that, but at least I'm willing to try with it! Dad wasn't. He was about to sell the damn thing!"

"What… is that true?" Cal asked, bewildered.

"He went back and forth over it. It's been bleeding money. The new president he hired had a lot of success—"

"In a value business," Cal sighed. "In discount stores for middle-class people. Delphine's has never been chasing that customer."

"Well, whenever I try—it's pointless!" Davey shook his head. He dropped to the floor with the rest of us. "I… I am holding onto all of it by a thread, Daphne. You sniping at me—"

"I'm not sniping. You gave me a position I'm not qualified for to placate me! You treat me like a child. I'm not, Davey! I'm good at business. I have ideas about how to fix it. I've poured over the financials. I have a proposal and the votes on the board to make it work… not that you care."

"I don't think you have enough. I don't even know what to do. I know you're smart and talented. I have spent my entire life trying to outperform you." His voice lowered. "I thought for once I had. I thought Dad finally saw it."

Instead of anger, I felt compassion. "And I thought he always loved you more."

"He didn't. I'm sorry if you felt that way, Daphne."

* * *

Cal

"Your father loved you all. Stop fighting!" Danna said, annoyed. "This is ridiculous. Davey, you must listen to Daphne and let her have a stake in the company. You're convinced you know best—blinded that you don't always know what is good. Your father was a brilliant man, but in the end—the last few years—his acumen failed him. I think he saw it. He resigned himself to it, hoping new blood would spark change. He felt he lost his biggest sounding board and reverted inward. Even before the cancer took over, he was like this."

"His biggest sounding board?" Daphne asked.

"Cal," Danna said. "Calvin, I know you were always there for him, but as you grew *your* business and built massive buildings, he realized his silly questions probably distracted you. Then you ran for mayor, and he gave up. He didn't have a clue how he fit in with you anymore. The apprentice became the master and felt ridiculous monopolizing your time."

Davey and Daphne appraised me as I fought tears. Daphne looked ready to comfort me, even as she sat in pain.

I felt terrible for everyone. I'd wounded Danna by sleeping with Daphne. I insulted Davey by existing. Davey's righteous anger hurt Daphne in more ways than one. Even David's memory seemed insulted.

Voice soft, I said, "I always thought he pulled back because he was sick, and that is a hard pill to swallow. I didn't ever think he was being silly. I owe him so much. I hate that he felt that way and never said it."

"You know how Dad was," Daphne said. "Sweet to a fault, but always wanting to carry the weight of the world on his shoulders."

"Now we must," Davey groaned.

"We—all of us," Daphne reminded. "Not you. Not Mum. All of us—together."

"Yeah, with Cal Markham to ride in and buy us out, right?" Davey's words cut deep.

"Why the fuck would I do that?" I chuckled.

"Because you could."

"I'm flattered you think I care so much. I don't make unwise business decisions for companies with bleeding balance sheets. There is still time to save it. I suspect Daphne's plans might make it worth the investment. However, as it stands today, I'd not buy it."

"Well, then fucking buy the retail ops and make Daphne President or whatever." His tone was more exhausted than dismissive.

Davey knew he was outhorsed but felt compelled to hold it together as the new patriarch. I knew how he felt. My mom was a single mother from the beginning until I started college. No one was there for me. But unlike Davey—still a boy in many ways—I grew into it and liked being that point person. Davey had never done this before. Daphne or David had been there to lift him when he tripped.

"Well, he'd be stupid to do that," Daphne said. "One,

because it's a massive conflict of interest, and I have to pull a bunch of permits if I get my way. Two, we're sleeping together, and the press would have a fucking field day."

Davey glared at her, then me. "Now, why the fuck would he do something as stupid as sleeping with you, Daphne?"

"Because I love her." I gently rubbed Daphne's shoulders. "Because I'm stupid—not stupid enough to buy your retail holdings, mind you."

Daphne snickered.

"I didn't realize… it was serious," Mum said. "Just like that—"

"Love is stupid, and I don't make the rules. For once, I'd like to admit I have no grand plans. The only roadmap I have is for the company. My life is… disastrous at times, but I am trying to choose happiness. Beyond Cal, it's just the business. And if I can throw myself into it, I know we can make it work. Davey, let's save it—together. Please!"

Davey softened. "You're right. We have to save it. Dad only contemplated selling it when he realized he'd leave me with this mess. And I guess he never thought I could manage it. Fuck! That's a kick in the teeth."

"I'm sorry," Daphne said. "You're doing a good job with almost anything else."

"Yeah, sure," Davey sighed. "I don't have a passion for a dying business."

"It doesn't have to be, though. Can you just let me try?"

"I need to fire someone," Davey sighed. "The board will have to approve—"

"We'll soon have enough votes," Daphne said. "This is how things began. Cal was… he helped connect me to some important people. I know the girls won't stand in our way. Derrick will do whatever we need him to."

"Cal was meddling to take me out?"

"That wasn't my goal," I said. "My goal was to help you all save the store."

"And get in Daphne's pants?"

"That didn't play into it," I said. "Not in the least."

"No, she's just a fringe benefit?"

"Stop talking about her like she isn't here!" Danna's sharp voice vibrated through the entry. "Your sister deserves respect. I am *not* pleased as punch about her and Cal running around behind our backs, but he is right about the business. And if he loves Daphne, who am I to judge?"

"They've been together for, like, what? A fucking month?"

"Your father and I fell in love in a matter of *days*. It was wild, too soon, and he proposed a month after we met. We just knew."

"You are crazy," Daphne giggled. "That's insane, Mum!"

"It was the best choice I ever made. I got the love of my life and six beautiful children. I wish we'd had more time. Your father wasn't perfect. And in the end, I think he made some bad choices out of fear. But who is perfect?"

"He was perfect for us," Daphne whimpered, now in tears. "Fuck. Grief sucks! Why can't he be here?"

"I know," I said. "I'm sorry. I miss him every day. I know it's nothing like the rest of you, but... he is missed."

* * *

Daphne

"Should we get you up and put you to bed?" Mum asked.

"I need to get off the floor for sure," I agreed.

"C'mon," Cal rose to his knees.

"Cal, I will break your back."

"You most certainly won't," Cal chuckled. "I had to carry

you around all day yesterday, with Chloe threatening to end me if I dropped you."

"What exactly happened?" Davey asked.

"She has some bruised ribs," Cal answered. "From Chloe's horse doing something known as teleportation."

"So, down I went. I'll heal," I assured.

Cal hoisted me with strong arms. I didn't think he'd drop me. I trusted he could manage it. I could walk, but I'd rather he babied me a bit. I'd never had a man dote over me. Cal was the first to wait on me hand and foot. Last night, watching him take care of Laurie and me, I felt better than I had in years. Physically, I was a wreck. Emotionally, I was home.

"Where am I headed?" Cal asked.

"Her room—same room as ever," Mum said.

"Apologies, but I have no idea where that is," Cal said.

"I can direct you," I said.

Cal climbed the stairs, not complaining that I was the most awkward sack of potatoes he ever carried. I pointed him around before we finally entered my childhood bedroom, where he tucked me into bed. Davey stayed downstairs, not getting involved. Mum hung around, annoying me. I wanted Cal to kiss me and tell me everything was alright. I didn't want him to do that before her.

Cal stood back, letting Mum dote.

"You sure you're alright? Has he fed you anything?"

"He's kept me fed and watered," I promised. "But I'd like to sleep a little."

"Okay, well, I will leave you. I'll check on you in a bit."

She gave me an embarrassing kiss on the forehead and departed. Cal took in the bedroom.

"It is weird being in here. Just say it," I said.

"It's very, very weird," Cal laughed, sitting on the bed.

"But I'm just glad you are okay. I am so sorry for the scuffle and everything—"

"I love you. I know you didn't do that to hurt me. Davey didn't either. Men are just stupid."

"True."

"I want you to stay out of the drama from here on out, okay?" I asked. "With family. Spare yourself."

"Baby, your drama is my drama."

I rolled my eyes. "I don't want that, though. Your life is neat and easy. I'd rather keep things separate than feel guilt for dragging you into my mess."

He squeezed my hand. "My ex dropped her baby at my house last night. That's drama. We all got shit. We're grown-ups with grown-up problems. There is no woman on earth I could date without baggage—at least not someone age-appropriate. Although, according to Lady Danna, that's debatable."

"They had a huge age gap, so she's full of shit," I snickered. "Ignore Mum."

"I will. I will stay out of the business. That's for you—and Chloe. She has it covered. She'll do well."

"Do you trust Davey?" I asked. "I don't know if I do."

"He's hurt, Daphne. What I saw there was a man full of pride—I'd know—who was in deep pain over the loss of his father. He has always felt like he played second fiddle. And while I cannot fault your father for it since I love you, you have always been his favorite. He'd deny it, but that is just facts, princess."

Cal brushed my cheek. "Try to trust him. But, for now, get some rest. Tomorrow we'll have plenty of fuckery to combat."

"Don't remind me," I said.

34. THE OLIVE BRANCH

Daphne

A UK GOVERNMENT NUMBER DISPLAYED ON MY PHONE AS I SAT cross-legged on a workbench in an airplane hangar watching Derrick. He was home for a quick bit of leave. I hadn't spent time with him since Dad's funeral. Not wanting to neglect my baby brother, I sat around while he worked on one of Dad's old planes.

I took a deep breath and nervously answered.

"Daphne, please do not hang up!" Chandler pled.

"Chandler, I am busy with family right now. Should you need anything, you can go through our attorneys—"

"She doesn't want to talk to you, fuckwad!" Derrick approached with a wrench.

I shooed him away. He wiped his brow and rolled his eyes.

"Let me at least plead my case—"

"Chandler, there is nothing to say."

"You are exploiting a man having a child," he choked up. "I know this hurts you in more ways than one. I knew it would when you found out. I tried to bury it, but my lawyer wanted to hold it over you. I didn't want to be cruel. If so, why would you be—"

"I don't believe a word you say, Chandler."

"I come in good faith. I'm standing at the doors of the office. I am prepared to sign—"

I bought none of that, betting he was legs up on his desk at Whitehall. "Good. Do it. We don't need to chat."

"Daphne, I don't believe you. Our child will be under scrutiny. My girlfriend—"

"Chandler, how much does this have to do with this poor woman versus your electoral possibilities. You need to rise in leadership. This is about that."

He stammered, "I know you hate me. I am sure you have all the rights in the world to. But, darling, if you ever loved me, you won't—"

"Chandler, let us end this and I promise it will go away."

"I sense you will leak it anyhow."

"I won't. Have you ever trusted me?" I asked, hurt. "Because I think I deserve better than that. I have *always* taken the high road here."

Chandler paused. "Fine. Let us end this. But if this leaks before the election, so help me—"

"Chandler, you have my word that it is not my intent to do anything as long as you set me free. And, in the process, set yourself free. You can live for *years* on what I've offered," I said, near tears. "Just please, let me go. Let yourself go."

"I have worked my entire life for this. The *party*—"

"The party may have buried this for now, Chandler, but it cannot keep it hidden forever. I am not going to say anything. It *will* come out, but hopefully it can stay under wraps until after the election. I'm not... I don't want to hurt you. I'm not a monster. However, I do want my life back."

He sounded contrite. "You're right. It's over. I'm... I will let it go."

"Thank you, Chandler," I hung up.

Concern covered Derrick's face.

"Stop it. You look like Dad when he was judging me!" I laughed.

"You just let that asshole win? After everything?"

"Derrick, when you get older and have a wife, you will understand that sometimes you make choices for you both that feel a little... sad. And you do it because it is right, not because it is a way to win."

"I like winning. I thought you did, too."

"I do," I said.

He wiped his brow with a shop rag. His face, by now, was covered in grease. I laughed.

"What?" Derrick asked.

"Nothing. It just reminds me of Dad. Here. This place." I looked around. "It even *smells* like him."

"It's why I came out here," Derrick said. "I honestly miss him every time I get behind the controls. He taught me all of this."

"I know. I don't understand planes—I don't care," I admitted, fighting tears. "But I loved how much *he* loved it."

Derrick read it without even looking at me, "Don't start crying, Daph!"

"I'm sorry. It's just hard to think about. He's not here. He'll never see your children."

"You assume I will have them," Derrick chuckled.

"I assume and know you will," I said.

"I think you still will," Derrick said. "Unless Cal is opposed."

I blushed.

"Daph, we all know. It's hard to deny because Mum talks about it like it's a real thing, which is how I *know* it is real."

"She loathes it."

"She pretends to. We all find it odd, okay? But you're

happy. It's been a really long time since I've seen you smile. You used to be much lighter. Then, a cloud came and took you away. A cloud named Chandler Walker."

My phone rang. It was my attorney.

"It's my lawyer," I announced, answering. "Yes?"

"Daphne, congratulations. He's signed the agreement. You're free."

A level of relief washed over me like I'd never experienced. As I hung up, free of my greatest burden, I rushed to my brother, not caring that he was covered in airplane grease.

"It's over," I said. "I won."

Derrick squeezed me tight. "I'm so relieved."

A car pulled up at the hangar. I peered out to see Davey climbing from his new Maserati.

"Hey!" He called, removing his sunglasses. "What the hell are you both doing here?"

"Daphne's divorce is done," Derrick said. "And we're fixing a plane. Want to help?"

Davey turned his nose up. "Not really, man. Knock yourself out. Daph, congrats!"

He gave me a quick hug.

"Thanks. I'm so relieved."

"Of course. Actually, it's good we can talk. I need to ask you a couple of things."

"Step into my office," I joked, climbing on the workbench table.

Davey joined me, laughing. "God, we used to do this when we were kids."

"I know. We were tiny back then."

Davey watched Derrick work and shook his head. "I don't know what I'm doing, Daphne. That's the honest to God truth."

"It's why you came here, too?"

"Mum said Derrick was here and… I just needed a mental break."

I rested my head on my brother's shoulder. "I know the feeling, but it will get better."

"I don't know. Look, I'm struggling. Bernie is attempting a coup."

I sat bolt upright. "Really?"

"He wants to sell to a VC firm. I need all of us on the same page. We need to stop this in its tracks and keep it out of the media. He's got cronies and you were right. He doesn't give a flying fuck about the company. Dad made a bad choice and I just couldn't believe that."

"You heard Cal, Davey, he wasn't all there. I don't believe he wanted it stripped for parts."

"The company?" Derrick called, walking over hands on his hips. "Fuck that shit!"

"I know," Davey agreed. "Well, so, we need to do some damage control. I'm going to sack him, Daphne, but I need you to step up. That plan you've worked on? I need you to present it."

"Okay, but Bernie won't tolerate—"

"I don't really care. I need you to quietly circulate it. Can you do that? Let's seed doubt and impress people with the vision we do have."

I shook my head. "Not so fast, brother. If I do this, I need a leadership stake. I did all the work—"

"And you will need my finesse and connections to make it a reality."

"We are a team, Davey, but only if you swear you won't bench me ever again."

"Daphne, I won't bench you. I have plans. You need to trust me."

"Not plans to dump me in HR?"

"Fuck no. Trust and you will see," Davey said.

* * *

Cal

"Clear my evening and make sure no one will bother me," I said to Jo.

"What now?" Jo asked. "I hope this doesn't have to do with your girlfriend's happy news."

I did a double-take, "You heard?"

"Oh, it's *all* over the news. 'Legendary Chicago Heiress Settles Divorce in Landmark Settlement'. Check out the *Trib's* front page right now."

"Well, it does," I said. "We are going out to dinner."

"Cal, this is still a bad idea—"

"Her divorce is signed. It will be finalized—"

"You shouldn't count your chickens yet. Look, I think you care about her. Something about her being David's favorite kid probably doesn't hurt, does it?"

"This doesn't have anything to do with David. It has everything to do with how I feel about her. I am allowed a personal life," I insisted. "She makes me so happy, Jo. She supports me."

"I am begging you to *please, please* hold off until after the DNC.. Anything that could distract from your keynote is a bad idea."

"All we are doing is going to dinner. I'm not confirming or denying anything, but in the past few months, I've never taken her to dinner. She has just fought a battle. I want to celebrate it."

Jo shook her head. "I've said my piece, but I stand by it, Cal. This is your choice, but also your sword to fall on."

35. AN EVENING OUT

Daphne

"WELL, YOU LOOK LOVELY."

I spotted Mum in the mirror by the front door. I'd waited until the last minute to put in my earrings.

"I have a date—a real date. A date out in the world!"

I couldn't hide my excitement. My divorce was signed. For now, I was an almost divorced woman, and Cal was willing to chance a public dinner. I'd gone all out on a new dress and shoes.

"Where are you going?"

"Bolgheri. It was my choice."

I finished, fluffing my hair.

"You didn't straighten it?" My mother grimaced.

"Cal likes it down, and so do I."

After twelve years of straightening my hair at least five times a week to please others, I was done. Cal didn't care. He loved me with wild hair. He loved me when I woke in the morning.

"I think it looks—"

"It's my hair, Mum," I said, annoyed. "Can you just for

once let me be happy? Cal wants to take me on a nice date. Do you know how long it has been since a man has taken me anywhere that wasn't a political gathering or charity event?"

Mum looked down. "I suppose I could be more supportive. I don't love you dating him, though."

"I am well aware."

I pushed my clutch bag under my arm and turned to the door.

"The dress is nice. I hope he is always so good to you."

"He will be. He always has been," I said. "Can you just… reserve judgement? The man loves me. And he shows me in every way how much he cares. I've never had someone fawn over me like this."

"I know he didn't at the end but Chandler was always—"

"Mum, that's what love bombing looks like. It's not healthy. Now, I have to go."

I opened the door, still shaking at my mother comparing Cal to Chandler. They had the same job, but they weren't anywhere near similar.

The restaurant was a few blocks away—a trendy spot between Cal's place and mine. He somehow managed to get a roof deck table. The hostess seated me as Cal wasn't yet there. Looking over Lake Michigan, I realized I'd be miserable back in London right about now. There were days I'd miss it like mad. I still planned to go back. However, for now, I was happy with things here. I never thought I'd say that. I spent my entire life trying to run far from my family's shadow. Now, I was glad to be home.

Cal eventually arrived, giving me a surprisingly long kiss before sitting.

"Should we really be doing that?" I shifted nervously.

"Do you not *want* to?" Cal asked. "It's been a couple of days and I missed you."

"I do," I said. "And I like it. But… if people—"

He kept his voice low. "If people see us, they'll think I'm the lucky man who was able to land a hot young girlfriend and let it go."

I blushed.

"You look gorgeous, by the way. It's going to be a shame when I toss that dress on the floor in a couple of hours."

"Cal!" I giggled. "Stop it!"

The waiter approached. "Do we have requests for wine? Any starters?"

I looked across the table at Cal. "I was thinking we could do a cocktail to start, get the charcuterie, and then decide on mains and order wine?"

"What she said," Cal sat his menu down.

"What would the lady like?" The server asked.

"This thing with the grapefruit," I said. "No clue how to pronounce that in Italian, I'm sorry."

The waiter nodded. "And you sir?"

"Sazerac. With whatever top shelf rye your bartender thinks is good."

"I will put in the order and bring your drinks." He left.

Cal said, "Thank you for *not* panicking."

"What?"

"I like a woman who just *orders*. Anything else is exhausting. After Kristy, I went on a series of bad dates in which women were afraid to speak up. They'd talk my ear off anytime they weren't being asked to select food and drink."

"We're judged," I said. "I'm just out of fucks right now."

Cal furrowed his brow. "What's wrong? I thought things were getting better."

"They are—well with the divorce. No. It's not that. It's Mum judging my hair and saying she wishes you were anyone else or pointing out that Chandler fawned over me. Which he did, but only after we'd had a massive fight and he was trying to keep me happy."

"She will get over it," Cal assured. "Your mother will come around."

"Just like yours?"

"That I cannot promise, but that has more to do with her sworn hatred of *your* mother. I have a better chance getting your mother to like me than mine to like me right now."

I laughed. "Well, you win some, you lose some."

He squeezed my hand. "I love you. It will work out. You don't have to worry."

I gave a small smile.

A man in a nice suit approached. "Cal! Is that you?"

Cal looked over at the man.

"Gary," Cal said, standing to shake the man's hand. "How are you?"

"I took the wife out to dinner, but all she can do is complain that it's all too *new*. She misses Heritage."

Heritage was a posh old standard on Ontario. My parents used to go. It was a place for old people.

"What did you think?" Cal asked.

"The food was excellent and the waitress was pretty." He elbowed Cal. "And who is your dining companion."

"Oh, shit. I'm on my worst behavior! Gary Pulaski, this is Daphne Delphine. Daphne, Gary is an old friend."

"Well, no wonder you seemed so familiar. You're David's daughter!"

"I am," I nodded.

Gary shot Cal a look, then chuckled, patting his back, "Well, enjoy it—all of it."

I wanted to roll my eyes.

Cal returned to his seat, whispering, "As I said."

"Who is he?"

"The head of the Illinois Democrats," Cal said. "So, sort of my boss. He's been up here constantly planning the DNC."

"Oh, that's right! That's happening here."

"I am speaking at the DNC," Cal said. "Two weeks. No stress. Just tons of public safety meetings while my entire police force wants to kill me. What could go wrong?"

"It will work out."

Cal nodded. "It *will* work out. Speaking of which, do you want to come with me to the afterparty?"

"Afterparty?"

"It's a party convention. There are *dozens* of parties. But this one is a big cocktail party. Come with me."

The hope in Cal's face made me want to say yes.

"Please."

Our drinks arrived and I tried to hide my disappointment. We were here at a beautiful restaurant on a perfect night. We had this chance to have a lovely evening—an evening just about us—but it always turned into something. I felt like an object.

Cal sensed my disappointment. "What did I say?"

"It's not you. It's just this. Cal, I've played the Good Wife most of my adult life. I don't know how I feel about debuting our relationship at a political gala."

"Oh," Cal understood. "You don't have to. I... I get it. That wasn't my motivation, though."

I'd hurt him.

I squeezed his hand. "I love you. I know that's not your intent. I just... I want more time before we entangle those two things."

Cal said. "Whatever you want, baby. In time, it will work."

* * *

Cal

As Daphne slept, I couldn't. We'd had a nice evening of drinks, dinner, and fabulous sex. All I could think about was her telling me no. It wasn't even a *no*. It was a "let's see", but it was enough that it hurt. This was a big moment for me. I wanted to share it with her. But, just like what happened with Kristy, she didn't want this. And if she didn't want this, what was the fucking point?

Daphne slept curled up on my chest, trusting and sweet. I rubbed her back, feeling her soft skin. I loved that she encroached. It proved she loved and trusted me. After all she'd been through, she trusted *me*. And here I was doubting her sincerity? That was cruel. She had her reasons. She needed time.

I couldn't fall asleep, extricating myself and tucking her in. She was peaceful and I couldn't wake her.

I pulled my phone from the charger and walked to the living room. The city was just beginning its evening sleep. The lake was calm. Why couldn't I be?

While we'd been in bed, Kristy texted.

KRISTY

Heard you were giving a big speech

ME

Cat is out of the bag.

I didn't expect her to text back. It was two in the morning. Then, the typing bubbles appeared.

KRISTY

So, why are you still up?

ME

Couldn't sleep.

Why are you still up

KRISTY

Sleep regression. Blame the kid.

ME

I cannot blame her. She's blameless.

Kristy's face flashed on my phone. I debated whether to answer, thinking about Daphne in the other room. But Daphne knew about Kristy. They'd been friendly several weeks ago when we'd volunteered to do childcare. So, I picked up.

"It's easier to talk than type," Kristy admitted. "Sorry."

"It's okay.

"How's Daphne?"

"Asleep," I answered.

"Oh, so she's basically living at yours now?"

Oh, how I wish!

"No. We had a date. She's over for the evening. We went out to dinner, but like a normal person, she fell asleep.

"She's not a normal person, Cal. She's basically a princess."

I snickered. "She's a normal person."

"So, is she joining you for the speech?"

My stomach dropped.

"She's still in the middle of divorce proceedings, so who knows," I said. "Hopefully. She might be in London, though."

"You always said you'd never trust someone who was divorced."

I set my jaw, "Kristy, that was a decade ago. Besides, she wasn't the reason her marriage failed. This isn't petty—"

"No, it's just wealthy people fighting over inheritances and real estate."

"That man hurt her," I said.

"I'm sure she'll be fine."

"Kristy, he hurt her," I raised my voice. "And I don't want anyone poking fun about it."

Kristy waited a minute. "Oh... okay. Sorry. I have hit a

nerve. I wasn't aware she had any problems with him apart from the cheating."

"The cheating was just the tip of the iceberg. She doesn't like talking about it."

"But it's going well?"

"I think so, yeah," I said.

"If you're happy that's good."

I love her.

"I think we're going to give it a go and have another baby… with science in the mix," Kristy said.

"You and your artist?" I asked. "Well, good for you both."

"I have a nanny. Don't worry. I'm not going to dump two babies on you at once. And he's moving here so we will have two sets of hands."

"Good for you both," I said. "But honestly, Daphne would take two kids and enjoy them."

"And so what? Is she willing to go through with it, marry you, and have kids?"

I wasn't sure how to answer that.

"It's really fresh, Kristy," I said. "We haven't discussed it."

"She wants kids, though?"

"Yes," I said. "And believe it or not, I still might, too. But that time may also have come to pass."

"And yet you're still with her?"

"I love her," I said. "That's the honest-to-God truth. I have to believe things will work out, but not at this second. In the future, I hope things will just fall into place."

"Rather than you waste years of your life without being honest?"

Ouch. Kristy swore I'd not been transparent with her from the start.

"I don't agree. I was honest with you. I always loved you—and cared about you—but it didn't work. I never lied and said—"

"You decided to run for office. That was—"

"I never promised I wouldn't just like you never told me you'd never, ever marry me."

"Well, now you have everything you want, I guess… once Daphne is divorced."

I paced, not wanting to toss my phone against the marble floor. "Kristy, did you call to argue with me?"

"No. I wanted to congratulate you." Her voice fell. "I don't want to argue with you. I value you as a friend, Cal. I also worry for that girl."

"Can everyone stop calling her a girl? She's a grown woman!"

"She's young, okay? Compared to us. And… if you aren't honest about what you want and she's not on your page, you might hurt her."

"I agree, but I have been," I said. "I don't want to go down this road again, okay? Thank you for your congrats. I appreciate it."

36. GIVE ME EVERYTHING

Daphne

One morning, several dates into *real* dating, I found Cal in the kitchen making a bagel and pouring coffee. It was the most normal morning. It felt *right*. I loved waking with him and being lazy before greeting the day. Cal was an early bird—the type to go out for a run at 5:30 just to wake up. I was *not*.

After a night where he wasn't in the mood for anything other than blowing off steam in bed, I woke to my phone buzzing.

Davey was in a panic. "Daphne, can you be in the office today to meet with the board?"

"I can. I have to get ready—"

"Okay. Great. Are you home—"

"I'm at Cal's."

"Okay. Well get here when you can. I have to fire Bernie today and will need you to wow them if you're going to be the replacement. This is on you. I cannot move these mountains for you."

My heart leapt. It was intimidating, but also the chance of a lifetime.

"I will be there," I promised. "With bells on."

"You've got this Daphne."

I rushed to the kitchen, hoping to catch Cal before he left. Normally, he'd find me in the kitchen after his shower, see me, smile, and kiss me with abandon. I always felt like he wanted me there. Today was different.

Cal's face pulled in a difficult, tight way. He barely acknowledged me beyond a "good morning". Something was wrong.

"We've got a mess on our hands," Cal said after a moment. "I have to get into the office and I cannot promise I'll see you tonight."

"Oh?"

"It's going to be a mess, Daphne."

"Why?"

"It just is. And us? It's already out there. I am not sure who leaked it."

"Oh. How do you… feel about that?" I asked nervously.

"I'm not upset about that, but I wanted you to know."

He never looked up. It was like something was festering. I didn't dare speak. When I spoke, I wanted him to blurt out how proud he was, not dismiss it.

"Cal, can you just tell me what this is?"

"It's labor disputes and exhaustion. I don't have time for this, Daph."

I felt tears welling at his cruel tone. I did nothing wrong. Cal reacted immediately, his face showing compassion.

"I'm sorry, I shouldn't have snapped at you."

"No, you shouldn't."

"I'm wrapped up in a lot, Daphne. I really am sorry." He approached, his hands cupping my face. "You're lovely and deserve better than my short temper this morning."

He kissed my forehead slowly and tenderly. I leaned forward, wrapping my arms around his waist and burying my face in his shirt.

"It's going to be okay," I murmured.

He rested his chin on my head. "Probably. It's got to do with the DNC and my stress level is through the roof."

"I love you. It will be okay."

"I love you, too. I just have to survive the day. But this will be a long one."

"Don't feel like you have to see me every night," I said, pulling back. "If you're busy, just tell me."

"But I *want* to see you every night, baby." Pain crossed his face as he shook his head. "I want you here every night to come home to and to wake up like this. I love this part of us."

Us. We were a *thing*.

"It's more complicated, though. And I should actually talk to you about that because my situation is—"

"I get it," I stopped him. "Today is not the day to have this talk about moving in or not, okay? Besides, I have my own agenda to worry about. Today, Davey will fire the asshole and if I don't completely fuck up, I'll be president soon."

"I want to be there for that," Cal whined. "That's amazing news! Why didn't you—"

"You've been busy. And Davey just called and told me to get my ass in gear."

He took my face in his hands, then pulled my chin towards him. "Look at me. I am not the only important person here. I want to share these things. I know I've been a bit of a raincloud. I'll work on it, but damn it, Daphne, I want to see you shine. I want to see you light up like a fucking Christmas tree at your own accomplishments."

"I... I don't know what to say."

"Don't turtle in on me," Cal said. "Be the woman I fell for —unapologetically."

"And who was she?" I winced.

"Confident, demanding, a little angry. She was also a bit of a disaster, but in the best way. I love you—and your chaos. I love you for all you bring. Please don't hide that, okay? If you can manage my fuckery, I can show up for you."

I wrapped my arms around his shoulder, breathing in the sweet scent of his cologne. I kissed him slowly, letting him know how much it meant. To hear him say he cared—that he wanted to be there—was everything I needed to want to jump over the edge head first.

"Okay, I have to go. I really am sorry. Keep me posted. Let's celebrate tomorrow—even if it kills me."

"Alright," I said.

He gave me one last kiss on the forehead and departed, not even touching his food or coffee. He had no time. I felt a little guilty, but decided to pick up where he left off. After polishing off the leftover bagel and having two cups of coffee, I packed to leave—pulling a clean set of clothes from the drawer I now owned. I was home here in Cal's world. Unfortunately, just as I felt happy and safe again, my world was rocked with bad news.

Meredith's number appeared on my phone.

I hopped off the elevator and waved at the desk attendant as I answered.

"Is it done already? That was too fast, right?"

"There is no status change on your filing. No court date yet, either."

"Okay," I said, confused.

"Are you in a place where you can watch a video? Near a computer?"

"No," I answered. "Why?"

"I need to send you something. It's about to come out and… it will be jarring."

My mind went a million places at once, assuming Chandler did something very stupid. But nothing met the reality of what I received. I'd made the mistake of assuming I could be happy, but as I sat on Mum's couch and watched my new reality unfold, I knew it would never work.

* * *

Cal

"Sir, Daphne Delphine called twice," Susan said as I passed her desk on the way back from my first meeting of the morning.

"I will call her after lunch," I said, unable to think about anything else.

My day couldn't have looked grimmer if I tried. I had zero guarantees of security coverage for a political convention. I had our DNC chairman barking at me. Angry administrators *texted* me. I turned my phone off around nine. It was a disaster and I didn't see a way out other than to pressure the police union with public shaming. So, I'd scheduled a press conference for later today. I'd either have good news or need to put them on blast. Either way, I had a deadline to do *something*.

"It's an emergency. She said to tell you she needed you to call her immediately. She sounded really upset."

"Has someone died?"

"I don't know, sir."

I looked at the clock, then shook my head. It probably had to do with the board vote. I assumed she was panicking ahead of it.

"I will call her late this afternoon. If she calls again, tell her I am in back-to-back meetings."

I hated to duck Daphne. I wanted to be there for her. However, if I did not put these fires out, there would be no me left to do anything. I was so embarrassed I could even look at her this morning. I worried I'd lashed out and ruined everything, but somehow, she clung to me for reassurance. I didn't want to ruin her moment. She had to understand.

Around two, still very hungry. I stood in a press room at a podium with a series of talking points. But immediately, all my best laid plans went out the window. I spoke for only two minutes explaining that by holding up negotiations, the union was putting the lives of their own officers at risk leading up to the DNC. It killed me to throw anyone under the bus, but I needed everyone to trust us. I needed to project strength.

Jeremy Mont, a reporter from the *Daily Tribune* raised his hand. "Sir, do you wish to comment on the allegations about Daphne Delphine?"

I rolled my eyes and leaned into the training Jo gave me earlier. "My personal life is irrelevant. Can we please get back to the very serious matter at hand?"

A *Times* reporter's hand shot up. "So, are you or are you not dating her?"

I shook my head. "What difference does that make?"

"Some people have doubts about her suitability given the video."

What video? I stammered, "I... I am allowed to take dinner with anyone I want to."

"Even if they are involved in... adult videos?" Another reporter asked.

"What video? Adult videos?" I scoffed.

John piped up. "We received this about twenty minutes ago from a UK paper."

"Well, are you going to elaborate or show me?" I demanded.

"Sir, the video is graphic. I don't really—"

"Either show me or stop talking about it," I was sharp and impatient.

My heart raced as John stepped forward. I'd known him for about twenty years. As long as I could remember, the old man was a reliable reporter—one who cared deeply about the city. I trusted him more than anyone else in the audience. He wasn't always easy on me, but he was honest. Right now, his pained face gave me pause. What could be on the tape?

John hit play and handed me his phone. It was thankfully on mute. Unfortunately, someone had gleefully captioned it —complete with onomatopoeia. The video showed Daphne in a bra and panties down on her knees—frightened. She looked up at someone—someone I assumed was Chandler. She was clearly being forced to give a blowjob on camera. Her face looked washed out and miserable. If the tape was real, it was a very bad night for her. If it was AI, it was just as insidious. Chandler fired back at her for the divorce, and he'd decided to take us all down with him.

I handed the phone back, fighting an emotional breakdown on cable.

"I don't know what to say other than Ms. Delphine would never in a million years release such a tape. Whether it's a deep fake or not, I couldn't tell you."

"Is that you in the video?" Someone called.

"Absolutely not!" I shouted.

The room quieted and I tempered my anger. "I am sorry, but this is not the press conference I expected. The point being is, I've known and worked with Daphne for more than ten years. She is a person of exceptional character and capability. That is all I will say."

The press erupted with more questions.

Someone shouted, "So do you know she was named President of Delphine Holdings in a shakeup this morning?"

"I was unaware," I lied. "Good for her."

"And you own shares in—"

"A company I own owns shares in Delphine Holdings. Its executor, however, manages all of those matters."

"But is it not true that you were seen out with Miss Delphine several times over the last week?"

"Again, what I do personally—"

"Do you think this is an attempt to discredit her?" Another person shouted.

"I have no idea what this is. I've not had time to speak to anyone about it. I am sure she is taking legal action. Thank you. I am done here."

I stepped back as Jo rushed the podium, shouting over the din. "He said he's done. There will be no further questions."

37.REACTION TIME

Daphne

THE DOOR KNOCK AT OUR CABIN UP NORTH STARTLED ME. I crept up the steps and into a guest room looking over the driveway. I stared at women wearing ball caps—Chloe and Lanie. It wasn't the press. Instead, my family found me in record time. I did not want to talk to them. So, I rolled up on the floor and prayed they didn't stick around.

"I see the light is on!" Lanie called, annoyed. "I know you're fucking in there.

"I can pick locks. It's one of my skills!" Chloe added. "And we have so many snacks we could wait out here for days. Hope you are prepared!"

Knowing my sister and Chloe, they'd stick around to smoke me out. I debated waiting an hour, but worried they'd only escalate and actually pick the lock. So, tail between my legs, I slunk down the stairs and opened the door.

"Thank God!" Lanie said. "I thought we'd have to wait you out."

She was more worried about time spent than my well-being, but I suppose it was good she didn't think I'd actually do something stupid.

"What are you doing here?" I asked.

"We're here to return you to Chicago."

"I'm not going back," I said. "I have enough in my bank account to survive a couple of weeks until my divorce is signed and my accounts are unfrozen."

"Why?" Lanie demanded. "I know this is rough and unfair. I know he did this to hurt you, but Daphne, you were just named President—"

"Davey is going to pull back."

"Did he tell you that?"

I shrugged.

"Last I heard," Chloe said, "he was trying to find a way to finesse it."

"He should. I'm toxic. He says we need to talk about it now. Talk about it means I'm already out."

Chloe said defiantly, "If my shares matter at all—and I think they do—I am not voting to remove you. You aren't, either. Nor are your sisters. I don't see how there are the votes to do it."

Lanie hugged me. I wanted to fight her, but I couldn't. It was the first hug I'd had since the morning before—just ahead of my world crumbling. I fought tears, finally breaking down.

"You aren't toxic." Lanie rubbed my back. "You are being abused by a man who doesn't deserve you. He's toxic. You're not."

"I don't understand how he got away with this," Chloe said. "Is the video real?"

"It is real," I said. "He took it one night ages and ages ago. I forgot about it and told him to delete it. He got me very drunk."

"That is rape," Lanie said.

"No, it's not."

"Yes, yes it is," Chloe said. "Either way, doesn't that break a law? You didn't consent to it? It's revenge porn."

"And who will prove it?" I asked. "The problem with the UK revenge porn statute is it is almost impossible to meet the burden of proof to even bring charges."

"There has to be a paper trail."

"To even get his internet records or anything is going to be complicated. We'd essentially need a warrant. And then Scotland Yard would need to agree to do forensics."

"You really think he was smart about it?" Lanie asked. "I refuse to believe you are helpless here. Delphines are *not* helpless."

"No, you're stubborn as mules," Chloe snickered. "C'mon. There has to be something. A guy like that is going to squawk to friends."

"I dunno. I filed a report. I doubt it matters. The public will not care."

"We do," Lanie said. "The *family* does."

"Cal does, too," Chloe said.

"Cal is fucking stupid if he thinks he should still pursue me. He should cut his losses."

"He hasn't," Chloe said. "Dumb or not, the man is trying to bring you home. Daphne, he loves you. He got blindsided by the video at a press conference."

"I called him dozens of times," I sobbed. "I tried. He ignored me!"

"He's been fighting with the DNC—"

"Trying to save himself and put a bit of distance between us, Chloe."

"Let me finish. Well before the video came out, he was dealing with the police union and the DNC. I don't think anyone even wants to discuss his speech right now—he doesn't. He does, however, want you home safe. He'd be here if he wasn't trying to do damage control—knowing it will help you. Daphne, this will pass. The cops will catch the obvious person at fault here. And you will get to call out his wrongdoing on your day in court."

"But if you don't go back, Mum will come up here and I suspect Cal will, too."

"She hates road trips. Derrick offered to fly her," Lanie said. "But we figured we wouldn't do that to you, sweetheart."

"How did you know I was here? And how did you manage to find me so *fast*?"

"Dora Elizabeth looked you up on Find my Friends. You have yours turned on, dumbass! We watched you traipse up 94 and then 131. Once you got north of Traverse City, I knew you weren't going to Sarah's. We kept following you."

"Shit!"

"Gen Z is out to get us," Chloe snickered. "Thankfully, Dora only uses her powers for good."

"I do not need Mum calling me an idiot. I'll probably never talk to her again." I sniffled and dropped to sit on the steps. "She can't even look at me."

"Mum is enraged—at Chandler and herself for ever defending him. She's brokenhearted and just wants to take care of you. She wants to fight like hell for you."

"That cannot be true."

"It is. She keeps spinning her wheels worrying about what could have been if she never intervened at Sarah's wedding."

"And it's not just her. We *all* want you back—that includes my dear brother. Even now, he's gotta be pacing waiting for me to text him and say I've laid eyes on you and you're okay."

"It's best if he never sees me again. I listened to his press conference while I was on my way out of the city. It was an ambushed disaster."

"Why would you do that?" Lanie gasped.

"Because I knew when the *Mail* was going to drop the story, and I couldn't help myself. I told myself it would tell me everything I needed to know. And… it did. He denied any connection to me like a very good boy. It's best if we never talk again."

My voice broke. I sobbed.

Chloe sat beside me on the stairs and rubbed my back. "You aren't destroying his life. In fact, if you write Cal off, you'll break his fucking heart, and I'll lose my shit."

I looked at her, tears running. "Chloe, this is complicated."

"Love is complicated!" Lanie declared. "Which is why I avoid it. You, though? You're different. You crave that sense of security. You've never really had it. You lied to yourself for years. Since you have been with Cal, Mum says that changed. She says things are better and you are happy. She *hates* that it's with Cal."

"That works out all around," Chloe added.

"But she loves that he treats you well. So, don't break his heart. Let him fucking love you at the time you need it most!"

Her voice boomed. I suspected Lanie wasn't wrong, but knew the reality would be worse than she anticipated. Of course, if I didn't go back, I'd never know what could have been. I'd regret it if I never took the chance more than if I did. I'd regret losing Cal.

"Okay," I relented. "But I need to talk to Davey before anyone else."

38. BACK HOME IN CHICAGO

Cal

Chloe texted Daphne was safe and accounted for. I breathed relief for the first time in months. She was safe. They found her where I suspected they would. After a bit of hustling, they drove her to Traverse City for the night. She refused to return directly, and Chloe would not drive eight more hours. Meanwhile, I made some progress with the police union. In a bizarre twist of fate, the thought of my girlfriend being the victim of revenge porn made female union organizers more sympathetic.

"Knock, knock!" Jo poked her head in. "How are you?"

"Still responding to emails," I sighed. "You?"

"If you did less on your own—"

"I'm a control freak, Jo. You know that is me in a nutshell."

She smiled and sat on the couch. "Will you actually sleep at home tonight?"

"No clue," I said.

"You should. Do yourself a favor. Your gym is not a replacement for your shower. Nor is this couch a real bed."

"I don't know how to relax. Chloe found Daphne. They made it to Traverse City."

"Good," Jo said. "So, what now?"

Her face revealed the thing she didn't want to say—the thing she'd avoided mentioning for fear of setting me off.

"I hope to speak with her when she returns. Jo, she was violated by this guy."

"I don't doubt that. I feel awful about it. I know David was a good man. I know he cared a lot about those kids and you do, too. However, right now, you're about to take the stage as a potential political superstar. We're talking you could go all the way up. When you think about standing there—yourself—someday, do you see yourself standing next to a woman who has been seen half naked… doing… that?"

"I could only be so lucky," I said. "What happened to her happens to too many people."

"Well, if you don't prevent it—"

"Jo, I don't need you to answer this, but think about it. Have you ever sent a nude? And if so, what if it ended up in the wrong hands? Should your husband write you off over it?"

"No. But I also never have."

"Never?" I asked in disbelief.

"I know you have. It's in your oppo," she sighed. "And it was one of our threat surface concerns. But, unlike your girl, Kristy is reliably private and not vindictive."

"I don't believe in holding this against Daphne."

"Look, I don't want to blame her for this. He violated her, but that's not what the public thinks. Good luck making it all the way to the top. What about that senate run you always talk about, Cal? What about that?"

"If it never happens, it never happens. But it also is unlikely to happen while I'm unattached. I'm not planning to spend the rest of my life celibate and lonely."

"There are women who—"

"They aren't Daphne." I was firm. "I love her. She's unlike anyone else I've ever known. She's addictive and comforting and literally everything I need."

Jo's mouth dropped, not expecting me to lay it out there more than I did.

"I'm sorry… I got emotional."

"You need to choose," Jo sighed. "Because you're right, you may be able to have both, but you also for sure put yourself at a disadvantage if you go there."

"I will keep it quiet," I said. "I will keep it low-profile for now."

"It's best for both of you to do that." Jo patted the sofa arm and stood. "Go home. Sleep. Think about what you want."

She left. My heart ached. Sparing myself by putting Daphne back in the closet felt ultimately wrong. At the same time, I entered politics to do good. I wanted to go above and beyond my current station. Loving Daphne might put that at risk—even if not of it was her fault.

* * *

Daphne

After 10 hours driving—mostly in road construction and subsequent traffic on I-94—we reached home. Mum nearly took me out at the knees, giving an unexpected hug and kiss. When she stepped back, I spotted Davey, Derrick, and Dora waiting to check on me. My older brother's face showed concern, not anger.

"I am okay. I mean, physically," I clarified. "I am sorry for frightening any of you, but I needed to feel safe. I needed to disappear for a bit. I still do. I'd appreciate it if no one said I'd returned."

"While I am glad that is the truth—that you're well," Davey said, "I cannot grant you that. Daphne, you're Delphine Retail Holdings's new president. The entire office needs you to show up."

"I think it's unwise—"

"Daphne Eugenia Delphine!" Mum was sharp. "Your father would want you to step up, not back down."

"Daddy would have been mortified—"

"I'd like to think his ghost will haunt Chandler all his life!" Dora said.

I stared in disbelief, surprised such harshness could exit her sweet mouth.

"I mean… if I believed in ghosts… which I don't. But fuck him!"

Derrick raised an eyebrow. "Maybe you need a hard reset, kiddo."

He pretended to look for a button on her back.

"Don't patronize me!" Dora slapped his hand, then stood stock still and obedient, realizing she'd sworn and Mum loathed women swearing.

"There, there. We'll work on your feminine rage over time, Dora Elizabeth," Lanie joked.

"Daddy would stand by you—as he always did," Mum said. "Because you all were the most precious parts of his life. He had no patience for others, but he had *endless* love and compassion for you kids. And when someone messed about like this, he wanted to have them strung up. What Chandler did was unforgivable. I know you are mortified, my love."

Mum took my face in her hands and looked into my eyes lovingly, "You, my love, will thrive. This will be a blip. He did this—not you. He betrayed and hurt you. All you did was play the role of a loving wife and he betrayed your trust. But now… now we all need you to focus on the good. I believe in you—Davey does, too."

Tears rolled as I looked at my big brother.

"Daphne, there is not a part of me which wishes for you to resign. We may need to do some damage control and to explain things to the board, but… I intend to keep you on as president."

"Why?"

"Because we should keep the business open. That's what we owe Dad," Davey insisted. "And you're the person to do it, Daphne. You are the one we need right now—regardless of what an angry politician tells us."

I sighed, annoyed.

"Besides, you're about to get your life back," Lanie said. "And in doing so, you're going to stick it to the bastard. Do you want him to own your own narrative, woman?"

I shook my head.

"Do the right thing. Stick with it," Davey said. "I will be behind you one hundred percent, but I need you to show up for work on Monday."

"Okay," I agreed. "I can do that. I know you're right."

It hurt. Everything felt wrong, but looking at their faces, I couldn't say no. The family needed me—and I needed them.

"I'm taking my life back," I said. "And all of you are coming with me."

39.PRIORITIES

Cal

"I DELIVERED HER BACK," CHLOE SAID.

I was on edge all day, waiting to hear about Daphne's safe return. Chloe, exhausted, collapsed on my office couch. Though I was relieved to see her, I knew the story wasn't over.

"Thank you for that, Chlo. I am so grateful," I said.

"Yeah, well, it's not over until the fat lady sings, right? You still need to get your girl. She wants to come around but she's afraid of hurting you."

I winced. "I want to say I don't care. And I really don't. But the DNC—"

"They're going to find evidence that her ex did this," Chloe said. "I know you aren't sure how to manage a scandal. And I am sure seeing her ex's cock wasn't like… a great experience, but—"

"Can we not say cock?" I grimaced.

"We're both grown-ups, Calvin. Look, I know what you want to do. You both want to run to her and also stay away for another week and a half, but you cannot do that. This woman is struggling without you."

"She wouldn't answer my calls—"

"And you wouldn't answer hers!" Chloe sat up, blonde ponytail flopping. "Look, you two need to talk about priorities, but you should know that he coerced her into that, got her very drunk, and then swore he deleted it. She's a victim several times over here—of multiple crimes. Don't add insult to injury because Jo told you running around with her was a bad idea."

"It's not forever. It's for both of us—"

"It's a fucking cop out. Do you love her?"

"I do."

"Do you want to have a future with her?"

"I do."

"Then fucking suck it up, grow a pair and get your priorities straight. Is the DNC going to take care of your old ass in your golden years? Is it going to give you babies?"

I snickered. "I fucking hope not."

"She will. That woman ran away because she wants to spare you, Cal. Spare *her*. Tell her. Do the right thing."

I contemplated my sister's wise words. They made sense. If I wanted a chance at forever with someone, it was with Daphne. There was no "cooling off period" for us. I couldn't treat our relationship as a priority only when it was politically advantageous.

"Where is she?"

"Her parents' place. The gilded mansion." Chloe rolled her eyes. "Every time I drive past that place, I cannot believe anyone lives like that."

"Says the poor little rich girl—"

"From the burbs. These people are American royalty, brother. But, she's also a wonderful person who cares too much about everyone around her. If you love her, it's worth it. I will laugh, however, when Mom falls head-over-heels for her grandchildren knowing full well, they are also Lady Danna Delphine's grandkids."

"Why are you so sure—"

"Because no man in his right mind babysits his ex's kid unless he himself wants them. You always have. You always loved me, brother, and took such good care of me. You deserve to have that for yourself. And Daphne wants the same. Don't let it pass before you get too old to actually enjoy it!"

She stood to leave. "Now, I am supposed to meet someone for a beer."

I wrapped her in a hug.

"You are so wise sometimes, kid. Where did you get it from?"

"Sometimes, I learn something from my elders," Chloe laughed. "I'm not always so wild."

I looked at the street below, then back to my laptop. Today had been about speech preparation, denial, and endlessly scrolling social media in hopes the tide would turn and they'd announce Chandler Walker had been arrested on revenge porn charges. Instead, slightly blurred, grainy photos of Daphne met my gaze on every page.

That *wasn't* Daphne. I longed to run to Daphne but feared Jo's retribution. Every press conference or appearance came back to Daphne—my "dirty little secret" in the worlds of the *Daily Tribune*. The press swarmed her doorstep. I settled for a phone call, unsure if she'd answer.

She did, sounding sleepy. "Hello?"

Relieved, I choked, "Hi, Daph."

"I'm okay, alright?"

"Okay," I agreed. "And… I'm sorry for anything—"

"You did nothing wrong, Cal. And I think… I don't even know."

I leaned back on the couch, feeling the need to tell her everything but unable to utter much.

"The words I said to the press aren't the truth. Daphne, I didn't want to add more fuel to the fire."

"That and you have a speech coming up—"

"I don't care about that."

"Lying isn't your thing. It's okay to want to give a keynote."

"Daphne, when the dust settles, I *will* have you," I said. "I will show you that I'm the one person who never leaves."

"Even if it kills all your chances for a second run?"

"I still think that's hyperbole. Chloe says the truth will come out. I must trust her. She's the media-savvy one. And I know this wasn't your doing. I know you don't deserve any of this, baby."

She wavered from tears, "I just wanted us to be happy. I'm so sorry."

"We will be. I promise you."

"Uh… I must go away for awhile. Don't be alarmed. Thank you for checking on me while giving me space. I… I have a plan, and it might be my last chance to clear my name, Cal."

"Okay, Daphne. What do you need from me?"

"Just your undying support and all the good vibes," she sniffled. "I will call you when I can."

40. THE SCHEME

Daphne

I DIDN'T SEE A SWIFT TRIP TO LONDON TO CONVINCE AN MP to roll on his buddy in my future, but it was my best hope. If stage one was rallying my family, reclaiming my family name was stage two. Todd Deyoung—the man desperate to serve as Home Secretary—was hungry for power and one of Chandler's best cronies. If anyone knew where the bodies were buried but longed to steal Chandler's sunshine, it was Todd.

The timeline was tight. I'd arrive Friday morning, meet with Chandler's frenemy, and return to the States within hours. While I'd be jet-lagged the day I made my save-my ass board presentation, this was the only way forward. Lanie rode with me, despite her frequent refrain that politics "bored her to tears".

I reached out to Todd Thursday and wrapped up the meeting details over the Atlantic as I rose. He met us at a private club Chandler was now banned at. I forced him out while keeping my membership active. It was just one more "fuck you" I lodged at him. Todd, recently divorced, was an easy mark. Given how Lanie dressed for the meeting, it was clear where we were headed here.

"You don't have to do this, Lanie," I said. "Not like that."

At the Savoy, we dipped into a room just to freshen up. Soon, we were on an elevator headed down to our meeting.

"Men are dumb. Politicians are *especially* dumb. No offense to your man, of course. Cal is smarter than the average bear. He also isn't a bigoted nutcase."

I snickered.

"I will be the most tempting helper in this scenario."

"I will settle for charming. Please do not sleep with him."

"The man voted to leave. I'd *never* sleep with a leaver."

"So did Chandler," I groaned.

While she claimed no political opinions, Lanie got into a screaming match with Chandler over his preference for leaving the EU when she was a teen.

It reminded me that for *years* I held my tongue on politics all because arguing with Chandler was exhausting and futile. Even a simple discussion spiraled into him ignoring me for days. I squeezed Lanie's hand.

"Never again," Lanie whispered. "We're going to end this."

"Beautiful Daphne," Todd saw us approach and gave me a polite cheek peck. "It has been too long, darling."

"It has," I lied.

If I went another year without speaking to Todd, it would be too short.

"And who is this beautiful young thing?"

"This is my sister, Lanie. She's in London with me."

"I begged to come with," Lanie said. "I was *so* bored."

Lanie's voice changed from its normal timbre to a flirtatious, higher pitch. She was acting—as any good actress would. Lanie could sell this. She might be my best move to play even if I'd doubted her. *Never doubt a Delphine, Daphne.*

"Well, I see you all managed to come out beautiful," Todd said.

We took a seat while a server approached. "May I get you all something?"

Chicago time, it was only ten, but it was four London time. I had a drink to get through this.

"I will have a good aged Balvenie," I answered. "Surprise me with whatever the bartender prefers."

"And I will have an espresso martini and add a cherry in for fun, thanks."

"A lady's drink," Todd nodded at Lanie.

"She knows what she wants," Lanie said in third person, her eye contact *smoldering*.

Bless her for trying so hard!

Lanie talked Todd's ear off, lulling him into security until our drinks appeared. Now, it was time to strike.

"We wanted to talk to you about the unfortunate matter that hit the press," I said. "I wanted to see if you knew anything. I heard a little birdie say that you might be my knight in shining armor who would illuminate things."

Todd coughed.

"He seems more prince than knight, Daph." Lanie laid it on. "Can you help us, Todd?"

He fell for her flattery.

"I could *try* to recall anything," Todd said.

"That would be great," I said. "I'd so appreciate it."

Lanie leaned in further, "This was incredibly painful for all of us, Todd. I mean... can you imagine?"

"I... I cannot. It is very sad. That is why I agreed to talk to you, Daphne."

I smiled. "So, there is a matter of how this got out. Might you know something about it?"

"I... I don't..."

He looked at Lanie as she recrossed her legs as slowly as possible, her skirt inching higher.

"Uh…" He stammered more. "I… uh…"

"Well, let's cut the shit," I said. "Because I've never been one for flowery language. I know Chandler did this. I have evidence of it from other sources but none of them tie back to his physical location in a way that give us enough to charge him. But, if you were to say… help me with that or provide additional information, Scotland Yard would investigate."

Todd snapped to me. "Daphne, with the election—"

"Wouldn't it be fab to see him do a perp walk and get out of your way?" Lanie asked, slowly removing the cherry from its skewer.

Todd considered. "So, with him out… it could… help?"

"You could prepare your future PM to denounce him," I said. "It's a bit of a hit job, but what isn't in this game?"

I waited for him to put it together. "I… I'd need to talk to John, of course."

"Of course." Lanie oozed sex, "you would want to run it by leadership. You're a clever man, Todd."

His lips curled into a slight smile as he stared at her tits.

"You're… you're right."

"You could be the hero, Todd. Daphne's hero, the party's, and *mine,* of course."

He was sold. I could have been offended by Lanie's success in getting Todd to do the right thing with nothing but her feminine wiles, but I couldn't be bothered with the why. If he got me my freedom and good name back, it was worth everything.

Todd cleared his throat, stood, and adjusted his trousers. "Let me call John."

He walked to the corner, turning back every other minute to look at my sister.

"He's going to have massive blue balls after this," Lanie said. "I *almost* feel bad about it."

"Nah, he's going to cream his pants once he realizes he's going to be Home Secretary and Chandler won't," I whispered.

"I'll give him my number, Daph, then block him."

"You'd do that for me?"

"Daph, I'd do whatever to stick it to that twat. Promise."

I smiled; happy she had my back.

After a few minutes, Todd returned.

"I will level with you," Todd said. "And this might hurt, Daphne. I'd never want to hurt a lady, but I will be honest."

"Yes?"

"He sent the video to a number of us—using his email."

"His government email?" Lanie said too loudly.

I shot her a look of admonishment.

"Sorry. It's just so stupid."

"We worried about Labour running with it. So, John asked us all to delete it and keep it quiet for fear it would hurt us in the election."

Because you're fucking cowards.

"But as you've illuminated—and if you are willing to go on record about how much this hurt you—we can run with it."

I extended my hand. "Todd, you have a deal."

I knew full well that this would backfire on them as soon as the inquest revealed they received the message and did nothing about it, but by that time, they'd be the party in government and have the moral high ground. As long as they were in office, the rest didn't matter. It was a brutal truth, but just the game of chess we played. If my name was cleared and Chandler served time, I'd live with the fact that these men ultimately betrayed me before timidly agreeing to help.

Mission accomplished.

* * *

Cal

DAPHNE

I did what I could do. I will call you when I
know more.

Daphne's text came in the late afternoon just before I met
with DNC officials for handshaking and a dinner with
community organizers. Somehow, I managed to skate by.
The party wasn't *happy* for my recent drama, but the younger
audience couldn't stop watching the trainwreck that they
assumed was my private life.

ME

Good. I am sure we will have better news
soon. When is your presentation.

DAPHNE

Tomorrow. I'm so nervous!

I was about to respond when Jo poked her head in. "Are
you ready to go?"

I shrugged. "Sure."

I followed Jo to the waiting car. She hammered me with
details. After ten minutes, I called for a ceasefire.

"Jo, look. I know you want me to be at the top of my
game. And I know that means remembering whoever's
nephew interned at whatever place, but… I need a break. I'm
really struggling today."

"You can't afford—"

"Jo, if I cannot afford to be fucking human, what good
does it do!?" I shouted, beyond help.

I expected Jo to shout back—she had every right—but she
called the driver, "Can we circle? The Mayor needs a minute."

She turned to me. "What is going on with you? What do you need?"

"Compassion. Time. I don't know."

She furrowed her brow. "I've never seen you like this."

"I have never loved anyone the way I love this woman, Jo. Daphne is fighting for her life and I'm here doing stupid shit I don't care about. I should. You've done so much, and I appreciate it immensely. I do. But…"

"Your mind is elsewhere?"

I nodded.

She took a long, deep breath, as if defeated.

"I wish you would leave her—not that I think she's a bad person. The timing is *terrible*—but I need you at the top of your game for this speech, Cal."

"I know. I am telling you that I cannot be—not until I can see her. We have another week of this. I have a week to get my head in the game. Unfortunately, until I clear some things up with her, I won't be able to do that."

Jo patted my knee. "Fine. Get done here. Do the best you can and go see her. If that is what you need to calm down, do it. I can't handle this right now—you, like this. Stop being a sad sack, Cal."

41. THE RETURN

Daphne

"Daphne, sweetheart, are you awake?"

I shifted, pushing myself to see my mother's concerned face, "I wasn't, no."

"Well, we've had dinner. Would you like any leftovers?"

"No," I answered. "I'm not hungry."

"Sweetheart, you must eat."

I remained too overwhelmed to eat—worried about Chandler's mess and my board presentation on Monday. I wanted comfort and quiet, but Mother forced me to eat three times since I came home.

"Well, you should go to bed upstairs."

"I know," I said. "But I just want to spend a little more time here."

"Alright," Mum sighed.

She left me on my father's office couch. I retreated here when I reached home. It was late. And yet, I couldn't leave. If my father was alive, I would have run to him. He would have hugged me tight and said it would be fine soon. But right now, he couldn't. So, I came to this place as it reminded me of him—down to the feel, smell, and look. This was where he did his best thinking. We climbed all over, crawled on the floor, and never bothered him. Because for Dad, there was no *way* we could. As Mum said, he had patience for us he lacked with others.

I rolled onto my side again, focused on Dad's Tiffany desk lamp. He always kept it on, which annoyed Mum to no end. I stood, turned it on, and returned to my spot on the couch. Shortly after, there was a knock. Dora peeked her head in.

"Dora, I just want to rest," I insisted.

"I brought you a brownie. I made them," Dora said, sweetly. "If you gotta eat, why not a brownie?"

"I'm good, thanks," I said.

She sat it on the side table. "Well, it's here. And you should eat."

I groaned. "You're sweet, but I'm fine."

Dora disappeared and I looked at the brownie longingly. That *did* sound good. And she frosted it. It was sweet of her to make my favorite dessert. *Fine, what the hell!*

I dug in, enjoying its chocolate chunks and delicious, fudgy texture. Dahlia was the chef, but Dora was a close second when it came to cooking.

There was another knock.

Mouth full of brownie, I shouted, "Dora, leave me alone! I'm eating your fucking brownie. Just leave me be!"

"Uh, Daph, it's me," Cal said.

I tried to choke my brownie down and pull myself together. *Why was he here?* He hadn't even texted first!

"Uh... go away?" I winced. "I am a disaster and... I don't know what to say."

"Daph, I doubt that is true. On your worst day, you're still wonderful," Cal said. "And you don't have to know what to say. I don't either except I am so sorry."

I sighed, took a deep breath, and set the brownie down.

"Come in, but you're about to regret ever bothering with me."

Cal entered the study slowly. "I sincerely doubt any of that is true, baby."

I wanted to believe him. He'd seen me bruised, battered, and covered in dirt, but I hadn't showered or brushed my hair. My face was puffy from tears. I was a disaster.

He pulled the door closed. "I'm so relieved you're alright."

"I am alive," I said. "I am not sure I'd say I was alright."

"Can I sit?" Cal asked.

I shrugged. He sat on the sofa—a safe distance from me. I worried the space signaled something sinister.

"I love you," Cal said. "And… you're beautiful… so please don't say you're a mess."

"I am a definite mess."

"Well, you're *my* beautiful, definite mess."

His.

I squeezed his hand and turned to his gaze, his big brown eyes melting me. "I am sorry you had to clean up my PR disaster, Cal. I feel awful."

"Oh, baby, please don't. What happened was awful. It was abuse. If they cannot see it, then I don't need to care about them."

"The DNC, though? What is the plan, Cal. You want to go above that?"

"I'd like to run for senate—"

"Cal, I don't want—"

He gripped my knee and cut me off. "Daphne, I don't care about that right now. I want you more. I asked myself what I'd regret most. I asked myself over and over and every time you won out. Because, as Chloe reminded me, I want everything with you, and I need to tell you. It's too soon. It's too fast and probably frightening for both of us, but I want to have a *life* with you."

I fell silent and tears rolled.

"Daphne, my place is so lonely without you. I missed you every day. And… I just want you near me. Always. Because you make me happy and because you deserve to be treated like a queen for once in your fucking life."

I swallowed hard, unsure what to say. I'd been here before, but maybe the movie ended differently this time?

* * *

Cal

Daphne stared—almost through me—speechless. I laid it all bare, telling her exactly what I wanted. I told her what I needed. I couldn't stop myself. Emotions ran over and I couldn't hold back. What I wanted with Daphne was a lifetime. I already missed too much, so if I could have her in my life, I wanted it more than anything.

"Cal, I… I couldn't…"

Her words drifted and I sank. I dropped her gaze, fighting my own tears.

"No, stop!" She scooted close.

I met her gaze. Her eyes were filled with soft tears, not sad. She wasn't saying no.

"I just meant you shouldn't give up on your dreams all because of me, Cal. If my past is too much, I wouldn't want to ask you to do that."

I wiped her tears, then held her face. "Daphne, I love you. You have waited decades to put yourself first. You've always played second fiddle because of the men who stood in your way. I've had a lifetime to reach this place. I'll take the heat so *you* can shine."

Tears ran her adorable cheeks. "But what if you resent me?"

"I won't. I couldn't. Baby, this is a blip. In ten years, we'll look back and shake our heads. We'll probably still be salty about it, but it won't matter. You'll have turned the company around and be riding high."

"And you? What will you do? Do you really plan to peak here?"

I cried and laughed all at once. "I'm the mayor of a world-class city, Daphne. I'll fucking survive. Unless that isn't good enough for you?"

"You are plenty good enough," Daphne took my face in her hands.

She leaned in, kissing me sweetly. I tasted her tears and breathed her in. Daphne was my everything. This was where I belonged.

She pulled away, staring a moment before asking, "You really think we will just shrug about this disaster in ten years?"

"I suspect we will be preoccupied with raising children, busy with work, and enjoying life to giving a flying fuck what Chandler did."

"You'd have children with someone like me?"

"Daphne, I could only be so lucky."

"After everything. You must have been horrified—"

"I was. But the way I learned the news... it was... jarring," I admitted.

"But you still want to love me? You aren't embarrassed—"

"The video disturbed me," I said.

Daphne looked away, tears falling on her arm.

"Daph, it wasn't because of what you did in an intimate moment with a partner who betrayed your trust. It was because you looked so out of it. He'd hurt you. Chloe said he coerced you. He—"

"Stop," Daphne cut me off. "Don't say it. I don't want to talk about it. But he did. And I'm ashamed—"

"Don't be. You did nothing wrong, baby. Nothing. You loved and trusted a man who promised before all of us—me included—that he would honor and protect you. He didn't. You have such love in you for your family that you'd give up on a dream and throw yourself under a bus. But if you do, I'll never forgive myself—or you—for it."

"I won't," she said. "Davey threatened to fire me if I'm not at work on Monday."

"Well, then I guess you should go?"

"Yeah, I should," Daphne agreed.

"So, are we… are we good?" I clarified.

"If you are willing to take the hit, yes."

"I will take any and all hits if it means I get to wake up next to you tomorrow."

"Cal, I… I don't know."

"I've been without you for days. And we ended on a bad note the day you got the news. Please? I need you, Daphne."

"And I need to be here for everyone else right now," Daphne said.

"Am I prohibited from staying the night?" I nuzzled my nose to hers, then kissed her slowly.

Daphne remained hesitant. "I… I don't know. You really want to commingle our ridiculous families?"

I chuckled. "Chloe was quick to point out that she couldn't wait to see Mom do the mental gymnastics of falling in love with grandchildren she had to share with Lady Danna Delphine. Honestly, it sounds like a great time."

Daphne snickered. "It will be a growth experience for them both."

"I think it would work out okay."

Daphne's gaze telegraphed enough. She slowly leaned in, pulling my shirt and kissing me. It started sweetly and calmly, then turned into a deep, sexy, hungry kiss. I needed to run my fingers through her hair, but it was tied back. I yanked her hair tie and undid her mass of hair, curls flowing into my palm.

While lacing fingers tighter, I gently pulled her roots. She moaned into my mouth and pulled herself closer. Before I knew what to think, Daphne straddled my lap. Pulling back, I stared deep into her green eyes. Her nostrils flared and her ragged breaths could be seen well beyond the neck of her tank top as her shoulders rose and fell. Feverishly, she kissed me again. I wanted more. I wanted to watch her ride me. I wanted no time to pass until that became reality. I had to pull back.

* * *

Daphne

"Let's stop," Cal pulled away from my kiss.

"What?" I panted. "Don't you... I thought this went along with the whole declaration of wanting everything with me."

"Daph, not here. Look around," Cal said. "I want to do this —to have all of you—but not here right now on this very couch.

I crashed back to the surface. He was right. I was on his lap in my father's study. Maybe dead men didn't matter. Maybe it wasn't a matter of superstition, but Cal and I had a wholesome, honest attachment to this place. He was right. We should take the party elsewhere.

"My room, then?" I winced. "It sounds awful."

Cal brushed my hair behind my ear. "Why?"

I pressed my forehead to his. "Because, baby, it's just *weird*."

"Not *this* weird."

"I need to buy a house. I swear I will the minute—"

"Shh," Cal whispered. "You'll move into my place, or *we'll* buy a house. Either way, we will figure it out."

"Can the mayor have a live-in girlfriend?"

"Is the mayor fighting every urge he has to behave himself at this very moment, Daphne? Yes."

I snickered. "Okay, to my room, then."

We climbed the former servant stairs and slipped into my bedroom. I locked the door to ensure some sort of safety. At least Mum wouldn't walk in, and it wouldn't scar her. Cal climbed on the bed as I tossed my clothes. By now, he'd already discarded his pants and shirt.

"I don't have any condoms, and I don't care," I admitted. "If you don't care."

"And if something goes wrong, will *you* care?"

"I dunno. Do you want our tawdry love child all over the front of the *Daily Tribune*?" I settled into bed.

"Our love child would be *anything* but tawdry, baby. It would be magnificent. Your eyes—"

"And your chin? I'd take it," I giggled.

Cal kissed me again, slowly lowering his hand to caress my breast. He kissed down my torso, sucking my other nipple. I moaned loudly, throwing my head against the pillow. My hips lifted towards him. As he continued to suck my nipple like it was his entire fucking job, he slid his right hand between my legs and slowly, delicately brushed his pointer finger over my pussy until I let out a glorious growl.

"More, please," I begged.

"More?" He slid two fingers inside, making my legs quake.

"I've… missed… this," I panted.

"Good girl. Are you going to cum for me?" Cal kissed my neck.

"My name isn't… good girl," I moaned louder. "Please."

"Okay, princess. Are you going to cum for me?"

"Yes… oh God… yes!"

His fingers picked up speed, sending me into overdrive. I felt myself head over the edge, into heaven.

"Don't fucking stop, Cal. Don't stop," I commanded.

Cal continued until I reached my climax. I tried *not* to scream, certain I frightened my mother and sister, but I couldn't help it. After days without him and with no assurance it would work, here he was. Cal Markham was *mine*. No matter what, he was with me. And right now, he wanted to be everything to me. It was the best feeling.

42. RESOLUTION

Daphne

I RAN MY INDEX FINGER DOWN DAPHNE'S SOFT ARM AS SHE LAY on her side, slowly stirring in the morning light. We'd been like this for ages now, but she was finally coming to. Waking next to her—even in the strange place that was her childhood bedroom—felt wonderful, but knowing she was all in was better.

"I love you like this," Daphne whispered. "With your hair a mess—as only I know you."

I kissed her. "I love this, too."

"I don't want to get up. I don't want to deal with anything. Meredith is going to call me to discuss what Scotland Yard has and how we can remedy this."

I stroked her face, watching her melt into my touch. I loved the slight smile on her lips. She trusted me immeasurably—even now.

"What are you waiting on?" I asked.

She kissed me slowly. "It went well. Lanie may have a new admirer who doesn't have a chance in hell, but we did what we needed to."

"And Scotland Yard?"

"Well, they pulled the emails directly from the government's server," Daphne said. "He's such a fucking dumbass."

"He sent it using his government email?" I scoffed. "What the fuck?"

"The guys covered for him until they realized it was better to fuck him over. Lanie and I made it clear. And she sold it—hard."

"She and Chloe are good wingwomen. They are ruthless."

"They are. Thank God for vindictive sisters."

"And when will the news break?"

"If they can find enough to charge him—and I suspect it will take about thirty seconds—they will do it tomorrow. It will break fast. Be prepared for the overflow."

"Great. It's not like I don't have to speak tomorrow about future plans. We locked up the police deal."

"I'm sorry to sidetrack you with my trashy life."

I pulled her chin towards me. "Daphne, you never have to apologize. I am glad to defend your honor if I'm prepared. And I will."

"About that," Daphne said. "What is the schedule for the DNC?"

I did a double-take. "I… I can have Sue send it over."

"Great. I will get you my assistant's info. You might even just send your daily schedule."

"Daphne, are we… are you?"

"I am all in, baby. The DNC is happening. I will be there."

I quickly kissed her, relieved and overwhelmed.

"You aren't afraid, Daphne?"

"Nah, baby. I couldn't be. The way you stood by me says it all. You put it all on the line to support me. You didn't worry about what would happen—other than losing me. I trust you. I want to love you in the light, and I refuse to hide anymore."

I pressed her back against the bed, her hair waterfalling

over the pillow. She stared up with love. Here we were—so in love we couldn't fight it. Daphne ran her fingers through my hair, pulling me into a kiss that shook me to my core.

I parted Daphne's legs with my body.

"Fuck me," she whimpered, going from sentimental to sexy in a hot minute.

I reached up the shirt she wore as a nightgown to pull her panties aside, finding that they were blissfully absent.

"Once more, Ms. Delphine, you have lost your panties."

"Maybe I'm a bad girl in need of punishment?" She raised an eyebrow and ran her finger down my chest.

I wanted to be inside her but waited. I'd get her good and wet first, then have my fun. Longing to hear her lose herself, I kissed down Daphne's torso, pushed the shirt up further, and kissed between her legs, soaking up her taste and smell. Her sweet, perfect pussy never tempted me more. Daphne twisted her hands tighter in my hand, bucking her hips against my face desperately.

"God, I love you," Daphne growled. "Your tongue is so good at this."

I hoped it was good enough to get her off this time. I pulled back to watch her face as I ran my fingers through her slick wetness, then thrust two inside. The look on her face as I did was sweet as could be.

She bit her lip and moaned my name, stretching the "a" out for a mile. "Oh, Cal!"

I got to work—licking and sucking her clit while my fingers thrusted. She vibrated as I got closer, writhing and growling. Daphne's unhinged reaction to me always through me over the edge. The woman was beautiful. She was perfect.

"Oh, Cal, I fucking…"

I knew she was cumming. I could feel it.

"Oh, fuck!"

She came, her pussy pulsing and chest rising. "God... I... I love you."

I tossed my boxers aside and pressed against her. My cock teased her entrance as I took in just how beautiful and delicate she was—even after the screaming and growling. Daphne was a sight to behold.

"I love you," Daphne moaned.

I kissed her, soaking up whatever energy she had left.

I pinned her hands behind her head. "I love you, too, Princess."

"Oh fuck. Don't start that," she moaned.

I thrust inside her forcefully. Daphne's eyes rolled back, and she panted. With every determinate thrust, I got another moan. It was rewarding and I couldn't help but savor the look on her face.

"I'm the only one who can do this," I said.

"You... you are. And you're..."

She didn't finish the sentence as she reached her second climax. She fought my grip above her head, but I pressed on, gaining speed.

"I'm what, Princess?"

"You're the... fucking... best," Daphne whimpered.

"I fucking love it when I do that to you," I said.

"Do what?"

"Make you cum until you cannot finish a sentence."

"You do it... so good," Daphne panted. "Oh, fuck."

"Yeah, you like that, princess?"

"I want you to cum. Cum inside me," Daphne pled.

"Oh fuck," I said.

The way she begged drove me closer until I couldn't fight it anymore.

I realized we came *together*. As I came, she threw her head back, unable to function as I slammed my hips against hers one last time. We hung there, suspended and breathing heavily.

"That was amazing," Daphne said.

"It was certainly memorable," I chuckled, unsure what to say.

"Hard to top."

"Tomorrow before you leave for work?"

"I won't stop you." Daphne curled into my arms. "I might need the boost to get through all of it—the business and the political chess."

I chuckled, then kissed her. "You're good at this politics thing, Daphne."

"Don't judge me."

I nudged her nose with mine. "Never. It's hot, Daph."

A knock shook us both out of our loving stupor.

"Daphne, Marta made breakfast. There are crepes. You might want to… get dressed… and come down here. And, if your… friend… would like to join us, that is fine, too."

We snickered.

"Sure, Mum! We'll be down."

"Fuck, that's awkward," I said.

"I told you. I warned you not to sleep here."

"I can handle it. I have seen some shit," I said.

43.FIRST DAYS

Daphne

"You're going to kill it," Cal said.

He gave me a long, sweet kiss.

"You will, too," I said. "Let's celebrate tonight."

"Always, baby," Cal said. "I need to head out. Will I see you when I get home?"

"I think so," I said. "I doubt I will be working around the clock tonight. I don't even have my office in order yet."

"Well, enjoy it. You've earned it."

Cal dipped out, leaving me to finish my much-needed coffee in peace. Somehow, everything felt *right*. Today was the start of forever. I would use my presentation to put everyone at ease and maintain my position. As I walked into the office, Davey found me.

"Daph, good. You're here."

"Yes. I was summoned."

He pulled me into my office and shut the door.

Davey put his hands on my shoulders, "Daphne you have the goods. This presentation will end all debate about whether you're right for the role. Don't look at it as a challenge, but an opportunity."

I choked up, "You sound like Dad."

"Delphines make lemonade. We don't settle."

I smiled, then gave him a big hug.

He wrapped his arms around me, "I just... I want to make it clear I'm with you. So much so that I have an article in *Chicago Business Weekly* celebrating my sister's return the family business."

I pulled away, mouth agape. "Davey, that is... bold."

"Today, you'll watch this fucker do his perp walk. Tomorrow, the whole city will understand our future. *That* is worth celebrating, okay? I believe in you. Let there be no doubt."

"Thank you, Davey. I really do want to save this place. How candid can I be?"

"Think about what Dad would do and do that," Davey urged.

So, very candid.

I collected myself, taking in the city and calm, now-warm Lake Michigan in the distance. Today, I regained my power. Tomorrow, we started to fix so many broken things. And I wouldn't be alone.

Rejuvenated, I entered the conference room and queued my presentation. Chloe shot an encouraging look, but had no idea what I was announcing. I hoped the speech would be *just* as exciting for her as for me. I ignored the annoyed faces of other c-suite execs and board members. I'd overcome their doubt and stay the course. My sisters filed in, ready to do battle. Once they settled, the meeting began.

Davey commanded the room. "So, as I've written in my statements, Daphne remains our President. All of you here have personally expressed doubt in this choice given Daphne's legal battles—"

"All but me!" Chloe declared.

"Yes, all but Miss Markham and the other family members. Uh… you see… while there are challenges, the family remains in charge of this business—"

"I would like to call for a vote of no confidence," our CFO said.

"And I would second it," Mr. Menedez said.

It hurt, but I let Davey speak.

"You do not have the votes, but we'll take a roll call," Davey said.

I hoped they would have held off and let me speak, but I'd take my lumps. Davey called the vote and settled when it failed.

"No majority. The motion fails." He straightened his suit. "So, I've made an executive decision on the matter of president. Daphne is more than qualified. Her work in acquisitions is unmatched and her plans for the business are exciting. Rather than wallow—and I'd like her to explain this in more detail—she has moved forward with some exciting marketing plans. I will let her get to that."

I brushed off the criticism and stood.

I lifted the clicker with shaky hands. "Uh, hello. To begin with, let me be abundantly clear, the video is more mortifying for me than anyone. I was coerced into it by my ex-husband. Scotland Yard has investigated the matter and my legal representatives in the UK assure me it will be handled today."

The room murmured.

The CFO said, "How so?"

"We believe there is a basis to charge him with a crime," I said. "The UK revenge porn law. I cannot get into specifics, nor will I deny there will be ongoing press coverage, but I will see this through so he cannot hurt anyone else. I would hope that all of you on this board would agree to support that cause. It is what my father would want."

My siblings all nodded. Davey looked around protectively.

"Now, with that out of the bag, let's discuss our new retail strategy. I want to bring on new brands. In the past few days, I've worked to build out an influencer strategy that should boost a few key demographics."

I pointed to a graph. "The fastest growing segments in luxury are people under forty and plus sized shoppers. As stated before, I want to expand our concierge experience, but I also plan to use influencers to signal that Delphines is *the* place for customer service, elite brands, and innovative beauty—a segment growing by leaps and bounds. I plan to bring in a variety of brands—one of which we've landed in the past few days."

I flipped to a slide. "Elise M's brand deal with Sephora has lapsed. The company, thanks to the help of Chloe Markham, has secured a preliminary brand deal that will hopefully wrap by the year's end. We will be the exclusive home of this brand outside their online presence."

Jaws dropped.

Menendez chuckled. "And did the mayor help?"

"No, Chloe did," I said. "Mayor Markham had *no* influence here. Elise Markham was generous enough to work through brand channels with me. Her attorneys have sent a brand partnership to *David, Jr*, not me."

I didn't mention that all this was done from our hotel room in Traverse City. Chloe reined in the details to make it happen. I owed her the world. Cal would be overjoyed but probably blindsided.

"It is a game-changer," Davey added.

"And as younger shoppers are less focused on price point and more on organic experience, we will bring in influencers to move this ball. That is why we will appoint our first Chief Social Media Officer—Chloe Markham."

Jaws dropped. People stared.

Chloe announced, "Ta-dah! I couldn't be *more* excited."

"It will be controversial," I said. "But she has done so much. Please trust me. Brand interest was up when Bernie left, and we dropped news of a luxury-first concept."

"I included a lot of research in your board packets," I continued. "That will give you an idea of why this new direction is our most viable step forward. And I know many of you will doubt me here. I don't blame you. However, I'd ask that you give me a chance. Please. Because this brand is in my soul."

Heads nodded. I didn't get a standing ovation, but dissent settled.

"My father always had an open-door policy," I said. "And that will remain with Davey and me. If you have concerns, come to us. We want honest feedback. The brand will only survive if we return to that brutal honesty and scrappy pursuit of new ideas."

* * *

Cal

"You have a bright future, young man." the DNC chairman, Colin Wu patted me on the back.

"Young man? You got the wrong guy." I chuckled.

"Ah, to me, everyone is young. Well done. That speech will go down in history. Just you wait."

I vibrated with excitement after any good stump speech but tonight felt different.

"Ah, the wife's after me!" Wu left.

Jo approached, "You did beautifully."

"And you doubted me."

She shrugged. "It's my job to hand-wring, Cal. But I also

know you well enough to know when I can trust you. I did. Once you got your shit together, you were fabulous."

"It's only up from here, right?"

She smiled. "Yeah. That and with the legal woes *sort of* figured out, I think there is a way forward. I won't say it will be easy."

"It won't," I said. "But you'd be bored if it was."

She pretended to wipe her brow. "Sometimes I'd take easy, Cal."

My eyes settled on Daphne, who arrived with her mother. Our gaze locked and I couldn't help but melt. She looked beautiful in a bright blue dress, her hair curled and falling onto her shoulders. I wanted to wrap her in a big kiss and spin her around triumphantly.

"Oh, there she is," Jo said. "Go on. Get the girl."

"I don't mind if I do."

I crossed the room with determination until standing before Daphne.

She searched my face. "What? Now you're out of words?"

I kissed her, unable to restrain myself.

She pulled back, confused. "Cal, we shouldn't—"

"I have plenty of time to apologize for loving you tomorrow, Daphne," I said. "But tonight, I want to celebrate everything."

She wrapped her arms around my neck, kissing me. "Well, after that speech to the nation, I couldn't love you more. You know you're really good at this, right?"

I smiled, brushing her chin with my thumb. "With you by my side, Daphne, I'm even better."

EPILOGUE

Daphne

"Delphine's is a huge part of my history. I'll never get over the joy of starting here as a lowly intern and feeling like I was part of something big," Cal said. "That, of course, was a million years ago."

The crowd chuckled.

"Now, it's a different world. The next generation of the family took up the challenge of modernizing the store and bringing it into the e-commerce and experiential marketing age—or so my sister's numerous discussions with the media would reflect."

Call searched the crowd for Chloe, standing to my right. She raised her glass, proudly nodding. Chloe earned it. The buzz with appointing her ruffled feathers—driving some old-timers out and giving a fresh face to the company. We were fucking shit up.

"But with those changes, some things remain—or even improve. That is why today, I am so glad to attend the tree-lighting event with you all. This tradition was a must-do every year for all the staff and volunteers that run the toy drive. And I am glad to see it is even bigger and brighter this year. The city is grateful for the continued efforts of the Delphine Family Foundation. And this year, we are even more grateful that the Dolphin Room's new Executive Chef, Dahlia Delphine, has agreed to donate her family's time and effort to feed more than 1000 holiday meals to needy families in the city. As a token of my own gratitude, I've also agreed to pitch in."

Dahlia moved back to reinvigorate our flagship restaurant. With her help, we managed to book our holiday reservations from November through January in a matter of two days. Dora's idea to donate two days of meal prep—Christmas and Christmas Eve—for needy family pickup meals hadn't fallen on deaf ears. Everyone pitched in, knowing Dad would have been full steam ahead. Cal rallied troops and connected us to community organizations in need.

"The toy drive they've hosted for the Chicago Firefighters Foundation has collected more than it has in years. To all of you, I say, thank you for your generosity. So many children and families will have a brighter Christmas this year. Having known David Delphine for so many years, I must say that this has been the sweetest way everyone could have honored his memory. His loss will be felt deeply this holiday season, but we'll keep his history of charity and giving alive."

I fought tears. The toy drive was a half-century tradition that Davey and I felt passionate about continuing so long as we could. Dad would be so proud of Dora's benevolence and Dahlia's idea to set aside two potentially profitable days to give back. Davey supported whatever the rest of us wanted. I was on the fence about spending Christmas doing *anything*. Grief sidelined me at Thanksgiving, but Mum felt that doing something impactful would make the day pass easier. So, I put aside my fears and agreed to help. And like with all things, if I did it, Cal was on board.

"So, with that said, I'd ask David Delphine, Jr., the CEO of Delphine Holdings, to step forward so we can light this tree."

Davey stepped forward. With the help of a lucky kid who'd won a contest to light the tree, the two helped set the tree lights aglow. The impressive real fir came to life in all its twinkling glory. I squeezed Mum's hand, looking over to see her tears. She rarely cried—not even when Dad died—so it hit me how big this was.

I wrapped my arm around her. "I know it's hard."

"Your father would be so proud of you kids. I just wish he was here to see it," Mum said. "This next chapter is all we wanted for you—and more. It's beautiful."

I hugged her tight. "He knows, Mum. I know he knows."

"I'm going to take a minute," she sniffled, departing.

"I've never seen her cry before," Chloe remarked. "Is she okay?"

"She's just emotional. Everything is hard without Dad."

"I get it," Chloe said. "I just hope she's okay."

"She will be," I assured.

Cal approached. "So, how did it go?"

"Great," I said.

"It was okay," Chloe said. "Okay, no notes. It was sappy and cute. It also made Lady Danna cry."

Cal's jaw dropped.

"The whole thing has her in tears," I confirmed.

"Well, I hope she's okay."

"She'll be fine." I squeezed his hand.

"Is there booze now?" Lanie said to Chloe.

"Is that *all* you care about?" Dora sighed.

"There are plenty of drinks at the bar on the ground floor," I said. "Go."

The girls fled to find harder stuff than the hot cocoa bar provided.

People milled, exploring the store for after-hours shopping. I followed Cal as we mingled, going upstairs to the ground floor after the girls. Parents who attended with children formed a somewhat disorderly, but excited queue to see Santa on the second floor. It could now be seen from the atrium.

"It feels strangely the same as it ever did," I remarked.

"And yet, altogether different," Cal offered. "Hey, come with me. I want to see something."

"Oh... okay? We aren't going to get up to anything too wild, I hope?"

"Nah. It's not like that. We're both on duty—our best behavior. I'll save that for later, baby."

I smiled, following him towards the gilded main elevators. Doors with the Delphine logo parted as we entered. He pressed the button for the sixth floor—one used mainly for stock and admin these days.

"What are we doing?" I asked.

"I want to take a good look at the tree. Trust me, Daph. It's the best view."

"Okay," I gave in.

Stepping off the elevator, we approached the floor's edge and leaned over the antique wrought-iron balcony wound with the official family motif. Below us, staff mingled, family chatted, and parents walked out with Santa photos, their children gleefully skipping. The tree and beautiful lit garland evoked the most cheerful feelings.

"I'm so proud of all of us," I murmured. "It came together so well."

"It was transformational. I came last year and it was a shell of what I remembered. The store looks amazing, Daphne. All the money you've put in—and all the time—

shows. Your Dad would have done the same at the end if he could have."

"Can you remember it so busy?" I asked.

"No, but you're doing great. Everyone is."

"Davey and I are transforming it. Of course, now he's got his own pet projects and mostly leaves me alone—"

"You'll be CEO once he figures out what is next for him. That's my projection."

I searched Cal to see if he joked.

"Baby, it's no joke. I believe that."

"You have so much faith in me!"

"I do."

"I'd like it to stay like this for a bit before it all changes. I mean, in a year, we've lost Dad, almost everyone has changed jobs, I got divorced, and then there's my idiot ex-husband's perp walk."

"And you fell in love with a man you never should have."

I smiled. "He was the best change, really."

He rubbed my back. "The most dubious, Daphne. That's what you meant. Change is the only constant we know."

"It's hard. I suspect it always will be," I said. "But I am grateful for the bright spots. I know this has been a hard time of year, but I love you and am so grateful for you."

"I love you, too. And I don't think anyone could have more gratitude than I do for you, Daphne Delphine."

He turned me towards him, pulling me into a long kiss. Lulled into the way I loved this man, I couldn't fight. Every day got better. We had one another. We chose *us* and didn't regret a minute. Standing here, I knew this was the only man for me. As he pulled back, he sweetly tucked a strand of hair behind my ear.

"Next year will be better," I said. "We'll focus on the good."

"We better," Cal dropped to one knee.

"Cal, what the hell are you doing?" I gasped as he fumbled through his jacket pocket.

"Well, I've been carrying this damn ring around for the perfect moment. I think this is a good one. Can you just let me do it?"

I laughed. "Okay, okay. Yes, go for it."

He pulled back a ring box to reveal a beautiful princess-cut diamond ring.

Cal asked the big question without hesitation. "Daphne, you make me feel everything—in the most impulsive way. Nothing about us is predictable, but I prefer it that way."

I giggled.

"You're everything I want and need. So, will you be my wife?"

I didn't skip a beat. "Yes, Cal. I will. Forever."

It wasn't my first proposal. It wasn't the *biggest* proposal, either. Instead, it was the only proposal I ever needed. As I kissed Cal, then slid the ring on my finger, I soaked up how good it felt to be not only adored but *needed*. I relished the way he loved me and always took care of me.

"I'm home," I said. "Thanks for seeing me even when I didn't see myself."

"You are right where you belong, Daphne. I'm not letting go," Cal whispered.

Loved it?

Grab a preview of Davey's story, *Power Move*, here.

ACKNOWLEDGMENTS

To my husband, thank you for supporting me as always. I am sorry for all the hanging clauses. Without you, this book would be about 20 pages longer than it needs to be.

To Becky, thank you for giving such honest feedback and believing in this story. There were several iterations of Cal and Daphne, but you stuck by them. I hope this final version feels like the best one yet!

To Helen, thanks for stanning these two in an unhinged way. You really are lovely.

To all my other beta and alpha readers and anyone who picked this up, thank you! It's been a labor of love.

ABOUT THE AUTHOR

Maude Winters is an author of open-door contemporary romance. She's a horse girl through and through. Though raised in Chicagoland, she lives in Michigan with her husband, a horse-obsessed child, and three dogs.

Maude loves to write strong female characters who challenge institutions and heroes who aren't afraid to let their ladies take the lead. Her readers expect the drama of a prime-time show with all the stakes and swoon they can handle.

instagram.com/maude_winters_fiction

ALSO BY MAUDE WINTERS

Find more titles by Maude Winters at palaspubishing.com

Can't wait for Davey's story? Preorder *Power Move* now.

If you love family scandal and royal intrigue, check out the Resplendent Royals Series.

www.ingramcontent.com/pod-product-compliance
Lightning Source LLC
Chambersburg PA
CBHW071358300726
48976CB00006B/1925